INTRODUCING
CHIP
HARRISON

LAWRENCE BLOCK

INTRODUCING CHIP HARRISON

including:
NO SCORE
and
CHIP HARRISON SCORES AGAIN

Afterword by Hilton Crofield

A FOUL PLAY PRESS BOOK
THE COUNTRYMAN PRESS, WOODSTOCK, VERMONT

PS
3552
L63
I55
1984

for
ROSE ADKINS

NO SCORE

CHAPTER ONE

"I SHOULDN'T EVEN BE HERE," SHE SAID.

"Oh, you should," I said. I looked at her, and I got this very sudden, very tight feeling in my throat, as though I had done a very ungood job of swallowing something large. I swallowed again, and the tight feeling moved downward through my chest and stomach and down to the very pit of my stomach, where it settled and put down roots and applied for citizenship papers.

Now, you really must be cool, I told myself. Because she's here and so are you, and if you just Stay Cool and Play Your Cards Right everything will work out.

But the trouble with telling yourself things, I've discovered, is that the part of you that's being told is always dimly aware that the other part, the part that's doing the telling, is trying to *con* you, for Pete's sake. I mean, it's like staging a wrestling match between your two hands or trying to commit suicide by holding your breath. (If you try that, you eventually pass out and start right in breathing again. So I understand. I experimented once when I was about thirteen, but I got to thinking that maybe this was just a big story and you really could kill yourself that way if you were very strong-willed. And I decided that I was a pretty strong-willed person and was thus running a real risk, so what I did was go into this fake swoon and collapse gracefully on my bedroom rug. I was in my bedroom at the time, and all alone, so you might wonder why I didn't just start breathing more or less naturally instead of putting on an act. That would be a tough one to answer actually, but anyway none of this has very much to do with what was going on between me and Francine.)

What was going on between me and Francine was that we were in my room, not the bedroom where I held my breath and swooned but the room I was renting now, which was in an attic upstairs over a barbershop. Francine thought she shouldn't even be here, and I thought she should.

And I had this lump, or tightness really, in the pit of my stomach. Or, not to mince words, in my, well, groin.

"I should go home now," she said.

"You just got here."

"As soon as I finish this cigarette."

She took a puff on her cigarette and just let the smoke find its own way out of her mouth. She sat there on my bed with one hand on her lap and the other behind her on the bed and she let the smoke trickle out from between her lips, which were parted just enough to let this happen. The general effect was as though something was burning inside her. I could believe this.

I was on the bed next to her. That sounds sexier than it was. Because we were both sitting side by side on the edge of the bed, and we might as well have been sitting side by side on a bench, watching a basketball game, for Pete's sake. All it really was was uncomfortable.

Come on, I told myself. (Remember what I said about telling yourself things, about all the good it does.) Come on, *do* something. At least *say* something. Be masculine. Take the initiative. Act.

"You're beautiful," I said.

"Oh, come on."

"No, I really mean it. You are."

"Oh, sure," she said, but there was something going on in her eyes and around her mouth. She fluffed her hair with one hand. Her hair was the soft reddish brown of oak leaves just before they fall off the tree. I reached to touch her hair and she shook her head and I took my hand away. I did touch her hair more or less in passing. It was as soft as it looked.

She drew on the cigarette and let the smoke find its way to the ceiling again.

"That's easy to say, Chip," she said.

"No, I mean it."

"I'm sure you tell every girl."

"No."

"Well, how do you mean it?"

"Huh?"

She turned a little toward me, crossed one leg over the other (or perhaps it was the other way around). "Why do you say I'm beautiful?" she demanded. "I mean, what about me is that way?"

"Oh, well—"

"Just for the sake of conversation."

I gave a quick nod then, a reflexive gesture indicating that I had Gotten The Message. I remember reading somewhere that beautiful women are inclined to be very narcissistic, meaning that they are in love with themselves, and that the best way to have success with them is to let them know that you think they're every bit as great as they think they are. I read this in a book that told how to succeed with women, and that even gave little poetic lines to say to them at tender moments, but I had never bothered to commit any of the lines to memory because they struck me as fairly corny. Besides, it seemed to me that if the author was really such an expert at making out with women he would be too busy doing just that to waste his time writing books. Like the books that tell you how to make money at the racetrack, or how to turn a shoestring into a million dollars. If anybody could do those things, why bother writing a book? Why not just go ahead and do it?

"Your eyes," I said. Another book had suggested that every woman thinks her eyes are beautiful. "Brown eyes flecked with green, and so large, and so deep."

"Deep?"

"You think about things, Francine. You have deep and profound thoughts."

"That's very true."

"And it shows in your eyes."

"Honestly?"

"Honestly."

"So you like my eyes," she said, prompting. And smiled a smile to let me know I was on the right track.

"And you have beautiful hands," I said.

"Do you think so?"

I reached out, trying not to let my own hand tremble, and I took hold of hers. She didn't draw away. This wasn't a pass, after all. It was part of the project of cataloguing Francine's charms. She made things easier by transferring her cigarette to her other hand, and I moved closer on the bed until I could feel the warmth of her body next to mine. We weren't exactly touching, but I could feel the warmth of her body.

I held her hand and told her how beautiful it was. As a matter of fact, it was a very fine hand, with just the right softness to it. The fingers were long and sensitive. There was just the finest tracing of soft downy hair on the back of the hand. And it had none of the faults that so many hands will have. It wasn't cold, it wasn't sweaty, it wasn't clammy. Of course, I didn't put things that way. I firmly believe in stressing the positive side of things. For the same reason I didn't mention the hand's one flaw, which was the nicotine stain between the first two fingers. I suppose I wouldn't have minded this if I smoked myself, but I didn't. I think it's a bad habit and I don't see any point in having bad habits. As a matter of fact, I do have one bad habit myself, but that stuff about it making you insane or blind is really a lot of nonsense, and anyway I've been doing my best to keep it to a rock-bottom minimum. And, of course, I intend to give it up as soon as I have a satisfactory substitute for it, which is what bringing Francine to my room was all about, actually, although from the way she had been acting you would have thought it was the furthest thing from her mind.

"And your hair," I said, reaching out to touch it. "And your tiny feminine feet, and your shapely legs—"

I went on like this. It was really pretty disgusting, when you come right down to it, but at the same time you have to realize that everything I said was the truth. Francine was so beautiful it could make your heart stop to look at her. A soft, beautiful, innocent face, and these gentle shoulders and slender arms, and her breasts—I still get weak in the knees just *thinking* about her breasts. You would think that breasts like those would be more at home on a heavier girl, but when your eyes moved down from those breasts (if in fact they did; mine often didn't, remaining there like two bees at two blossoms), you saw that the waist was very slim, and the hips just wide enough to be interesting, and the buttocks nicely rounded, and the legs as if they had stepped out of stocking ads. I could go on this way, but what's the point? Even if I pasted a photo of her right here, it wouldn't do it right, because all of us see things differently. So do this: Imagine an absolutely perfect girl (except for a nicotine stain between the first two fingers of the right hand, and a half-inch-long crescent-shaped scar on the inside of the left thigh) and you've imagined Francine.

I went on telling her this, leaving out those two flaws (only the first of which I knew about then) and wording my praise so that I came off more like an artist and less like a total sex maniac, and all the while I kept looking at her eyes, and the weirdest thing happened. She began to get hypnotized.

I don't know what else you could call it. She was nodding encouragingly in time to the rhythm of my words, and every now and then she would chime in with *Do you really think so?* or *Do you honestly mean it?* or just little *Yes* and *Uh-huh* and *Oh* sounds and grunts, and it was as if she was completely caught up in the sound of my voice telling her how perfect she was. I was pressing her hand as I talked and she was giving me little rhythmic squeezes in return.

You've got her, I thought. Now hurry, before the spell wears off.

But I guess I was afraid to blow it. Things were going so well, see, and I didn't want to jeopardize my position. Because it seemed as though I had been waiting forever for this to happen, and if it didn't happen soon I didn't know what I would do, except maybe go completely out of my head.

So I went on talking while the cigarette burned unattended between the fingers of her left hand—I was holding the right hand all the while. And very smoothly I went on talking and reached across and plucked the cigarette away and flipped it into the sink on the other side of the room. It was an easy shot because the other side of the room wasn't all that far away, the room being on the small side, but even so the whole maneuver was one of my smoother plays.

It encouraged me, and then, too, I realized that soon I was going to run out of parts of Francine to praise. So I got an arm around her and tipped up her face and kissed her.

At first it was like kissing—well, I was going to say a warm corpse, but that's really pretty revolting and it wasn't like that at all. Let's say it was like kissing someone who was asleep.

But then she started to wake up.

She kissed back, sort of tentatively, and I held her a little closer and kissed her a little more heavily, and she opened up like a flower. Her arms went around me and held me and her breasts pressed up against my chest and she sighed beautifully and her lips parted. There was a brief hissing sound as some drops from the leaky faucet put out her cigarette butt, and as the hissing died I let my tongue slip ever so gingerly past her lips and into the rich dark cave of her mouth.

She tasted of honey and tobacco and musk. She made the kiss a very urgent and hungry sort of experience, putting her own mouth into it and clutching my shoulders fiercely with her little hands.

First base, I thought.

I told myself to forget about the different bases, because that sort of thinking can be a trap. I had been to first base before, though not with Francine. I had been to second base a few times, and even to third base.

But, as you must have figured out by now, I had never been to home plate.

All right. Let's come right down and say it, let's put it down in black and white. I was a virgin.

What a stupid word.

I mean, it's a *girl's* word, right? Virgin, for Pete's sake. You really can't come up with a more feminine word than virgin. You hear a word like that and you picture a girl with flowers in her hair, wearing something with ruffles. But I don't know of any other word for it, so that one will have to do. I, Chip Harrison, was a seventeen-year-old virgin. I wasn't going to be seventeen forever. (Although there were times when it seemed that way.) And I wasn't going to be a virgin forever, either, if I could help it. (Although there were times, damn it, when it didn't seem as though I could help it.)

As a matter of fact, it sort of seemed to me that the two things, age and sex, were connected in some heavy way. That if I scored (which is to say got to home plate, which is to say stopped being a virgin) before I turned eighteen, then I won. Whereas if I didn't, I lost.

But the point of all this is that the business with the bases can be a snare and a delusion, or at least I have found this to be so, because they give you the feeling that you are making progress with the girl, in that each time you are with her you get a little closer to the goal line (wrong sport, sorry about that) and thus it seems to follow that sooner or later you will score. This is not necessarily true. And, in fact, it seems that the more you get into this kind of pattern with a girl, the better she gets at getting you to stop somewhere along the way. It isn't that you keep getting closer but that you keep not getting where you wanted to go, and all of this is not only frustrating (very) but it leaves her knowing that she can control you, and this is not a Good Thing in any sense.

Not that I am the World's Foremost Authority on all this. To be honest, some of this I got from the books on how to succeed with women, and some is just speculation on my part. But what it all boils down to is that the best way to do something is to do it, and the best way to Go All The Way with a girl is to just go ahead and do it. Not in stages but all at once.

Especially because, in this particular instance, I was not going to get another chance at Francine. Because she was two years older than I was, and practically engaged to some college jerk, and so it had been a case of wild luck that I had gotten her to my room at all. So the chances were very good that I would never see her again, which was too bad, but which was something I could live with If Only. If only I hit the first pitch completely out of the park and ran around the bases and crossed the plate before Francine realized what had happened.

So we held the kiss, and she clung to me as tightly as her sweater clung to her, and my tongue went spelunking in her mouth, and her tongue met it and got acquainted with it. We kissed for a long time. Then we came up for air and looked deep into each other's eyes, and when her eyes went slightly glassy I kissed her again, and it was the same, only better.

When we broke this time she said, "Oh, Chip—"

"Francine—"

"I must go."

"Francine—"

"Please, I can't—"

"You're so beautiful," I said, desperately.

"Oh, Chip."

"I love to kiss you."

"Oh."

"So beautiful. A goddess."

"Oh, my God—"

I drew her to me. She resisted, but not in any really meaningful way. She sort of stiffened, and I drew her close and got my mouth fastened to hers again, and then she got into the spirit of things again, as if the token show of resistance made it all right for her to surrender now. And in the course of drawing her close, somehow or other my hand managed to get on top of her breast.

Around first base and streaking for second.

Getting the sweater off was an absolute stone bitch. It really was. I guess because there is no entirely natural way to pull a tight yellow sweater over a girl's head. You can't just make believe it's happening by itself. It's possible to sort of slide into a kiss, or to let your hands accidentally settle on the more interesting parts of a girl, but sweater removal is just too damned obvious. Even if you're both all in favor of it, it's hard to pretend you don't know what's going on. Or coming off, I suppose.

I got the sweater out of the waistband of her skirt without too much trouble. But then I started to work one hand up under the front of the sweater, and she broke the kiss and put her hand on mine, and pushed.

"Please, Chip."

"Francine, you're so beautiful."

"Chip, I don't want you to do that."

"I think you have the most beautiful breasts in the world."

"I don't—you do?"

"Yes."

"You're just saying that. Chip—"

A kiss, but not a very successful one.

"You have a great line, Chip. My goodness, what a line you have."

"It's not a line."

"Oh, your hands just won't behave. Please don't do that."

"Francine, I want to look at you."

"Oh, come off it. I know what you want."

"I have to see you."

"Sure, you just have to *see* me."

"Your breasts are beautiful, Francine."

"You shouldn't talk like that. I hardly know you. I mean, after all—"

"Beautiful."

"Oh."

"Beautiful."

"If I thought I could trust you—"

"You can trust me, Francine."

"I mean if it wasn't so utterly physical—"

"You know it's more than that, Francine."

"I mean—"

"Francine—"

"Oh," she said, finally, and shrugged me away, and just as I was about to reach for her again and start the whole process over, she gave a little sigh and pulled the sweater up over her head. There was a moment when the yellow sweater covered her head completely while leaving her chest uncovered (except for the bra, of course) and that image imprinted itself on my memory. There was something really appropriate about it, the whole image of Francine with the best part of her right out in the open and her stupid mouth covered up. If I were an artist I would paint that scene. I think if it was painted right you could look at it and know everything you would ever need to know about Francine.

But she was only like this for a second, and then the sweater was off and the arms were extended and the lips parted and the eyes glazed, and it was at that very moment that I knew for certain that I could forget about bases and goal lines and all, that I could stop crawling around inside my own head and giving myself halftime pep talks, because it was all set and all arranged and all decided and it was all in the bag and Chip Harrison was going to stop being a virgin and start being a man.

I kissed her.

And we stretched out on the bed together.

Her skin was so soft. It's unbelievable how soft girls are. I got my hands around her and unhooked her bra, and although I am not the deftest person on earth it went well enough, and I eased it off over her shoulders and bared her breasts. And just as I was doing this our eyes caught, and I looked at her eyes and her mouth, the whole expression on her face, and she was pleased and amused and calm, and her eyes said that she knew what was happening and liked what was happening and that everything would work out just fine.

She was so beautiful.

I got completely involved in those breasts. I couldn't stop touching and kissing them. It wasn't a question of trying to do one thing and then another, of trying to get further and further with her, because it had already been established that we were going to do the whole thing and all that mattered now was to do it as well as possible. So instead of trying to put something over on her, I was trying to excite her as much as possible and to do things that I enjoyed, and it sure worked.

"Oh, Chip. That feels so nice—"

Her skin tasted of sugar and spice and secret girl smells. I liked her breasts like a little kid with an ice cream cone, wanting to take a big bite but wanting to make it last as long as I could. I nibbled and gobbled and she made these wonderful heavy breathing sounds and started squirming on the bed underneath me.

"Take off your shirt, Chip. I want to feel you against me."

When I take off my shirt, you don't get reminded at once of Greek sculpture. I'm not a ninety-seven-pound weakling, but I'm not exactly Charles Atlas either. I'm sort of bony and undernourished in appearance. But I took the shirt off, and when I glanced at Francine's eyes, she didn't seem that disappointed with what I was unveiling. As a matter of fact, she looked hungry.

"Oh, Chip—"

I kissed her, and our tongues renewed their old friendship, and our chests pressed together. Mine got the better of the deal. Her nipples were as hard as little rosebuds and I brushed my upper body back and forth over them and she moaned and wiggled in response.

After a long time of kissing and touching and feeling, after I had told her how beautiful her breasts were and how delicious her flesh tasted and felt, and after she had told me how wonderful I made her feel and how sweet I was and how much she cared for me, after all of that, she lay down and closed her eyes and raised her hips a little so that I could take her skirt off. It wasn't hard at all. I just opened the button and unzipped the zipper and pulled the skirt down and off—it was a green plaid skirt, for those of you who don't have color sets. And then it was off, and she was lying there in her panties, and I discovered the half-inch crescent-shaped scar on the inside of her thigh, and I didn't think of it as a fault at all. In fact, I didn't think that Francine had any faults. Only good points, and an abundance of them.

I ran my hands over her legs. Until that moment I don't think I ever realized just how important legs are. Girls' legs, I mean. How important it is that they be great-looking. I had always paid a lot of attention to faces and breasts and behinds, and I knew the difference between great-looking legs and lousy-looking legs, but I was never that excited about legs.

You live and you learn. Francine had great-looking legs, and all spread out like that, naked except for the panties, I was really able to see the whole girl. As an entity, I mean. And I realized the importance of the legs.

(I don't know if this is coming through very well. Call it an intuitive flash, a sudden burst of insight, which after all is how most great discoveries come about. The major breakthroughs never occur because someone sat down and thought things out. They come in flashes. Newton and the apple, for instance. Paul on the road to Damascus. Archimedes in the bathtub. Chip Harrison in bed with Francine.)

"Chip?"

Her eyes were closed, and if there was any expression on her face, I couldn't read it. She seemed very calm, completely relaxed, but I could see she was trembling inside.

"You can take them off."

I put my hands on her shoulders. I ran them very slowly down over her breasts and stomach and grazed her panties and went on all the way down those legs to her feet.

"My panties. You can take them off."

"Yes."

"You can ... do anything."

"Yes."

"Anything you want to."

Her voice was different than it had ever been before, older and younger, both at once. Softer, mostly. And as if for the first time, I was hearing Francine speak without any phoniness in the way.

I wanted to say something but I couldn't. My throat was blocked, knotted up.

I took off her pants. I took off her wispy nylon pants and squeezed them in a ball and held onto them with both hands. I wanted to nail them to the wall over the bed as a trophy. I wanted to sleep with them under my pillow. I wanted to chew them up and swallow them.

"Chip—"

I put the panties aside. I put my hands on her thighs and she opened them, parted her thighs, and I looked at her.

I could smell her.

I put out a hand, touched her. She was moist. I put my finger into her just a little ways and I felt her. She was all wet and hot and sticky.

And it came to me, all at once, that this was not just a dumb girl with a great body that I was going to ball. It came to me that she was far more than this. It came to me, as I crouched over her with my finger inside her, that I loved this girl. And that she was what I had been looking for, a beautiful passionate woman whom I could love and honor and cherish forever.

But first, by God, I was going to ball her.

I played with her with both hands. I played with her, absolutely delighted with the way she was built and the way she felt and the effect it was all having on her. And she lay there, hips rolling so nicely, so sweetly, so gracefully, and she kept her eyes closed and her hands at her sides, and the words flowed in a stream.

"Oh Chip, it's so good, it's so good, I like it, I love it, it's so good. I'm so hot, I like it, I love it, Chip, it's so good—"

I fingered her with one hand and attacked my own clothes with the other. To do this properly probably takes great skill and coordination, like rubbing your tummy while you pat your head. I tugged on my belt to unhook it and I pulled so hard I very nearly strangled myself at the waist. But I did get my pants down, and wriggled until they were off, and my shorts as well. I had kicked off my shoes some time ago. I never did get my socks off. I might have taken the trouble, but while I was getting the shorts off my other hand slipped a little, and without really planning it that way I discovered Francine's clitoris.

(I hadn't planned on mentioning that. After all, it's pretty clinical, and maybe not in the best of taste to come right out and talk about something like a clitoris. Not that there's anything wrong with a clitoris, for Pete's sake. But that there might be something wrong with mentioning it. But the thing of it is, I had known about this part of a girl from my reading, and knew of the great importance of it, but had somehow not gotten around to looking for it, being so preoccupied with other goodies. But now just by accident I had found it, and a good thing it was.)

"Oh, wow! Oh, God, yes! Oh, Jesus Christ, do it! Oh, do it forever!"

I got on top of her. I kept touching her, and I got on top of her, and I thought that this was it, this was really it. I was still seventeen and in a second I would stop being a virgin, which was a damned good thing, because if you were old enough to fight for your country you were certainly old enough to have sex, and with a sexual revolution going on the idea of an eighteen-year-old male virgin was pretty ridiculous, and here I was, getting ready not to be one anymore, and here Francine was, all wet and open and ready, and I loved her, by God, and I would love her forever, and wasn't I the lucky son of a gun?

I said, "I love you, Francine."

"Do it!"

"I love you."

"God, God, stick it in!"

And it occurred to me, albeit briefly, that this might be a kind of graphic thing for a girl to say, and maybe not in the best of taste, but then I decided that it was all to the good, that Francine was, after all, carried away in the throes of passion, and that it was a fine sign that a girl like Francine, so demure on the outside, could be so carried away by passion, and then I stopped thinking entirely, and readied myself for the move that would change my life once and forever, and stabbed blindly ahead, and missed, and took aim again, and—

And paused, because it seemed that a herd of elephants was stampeding up the staircase and down the hall, and voices were shouting, and Francine was roaring at me, begging me to do it, to stick it in, and I lay there, paralyzed, and the door to my room exploded inward, and a man the size of a mountain charged inside. He had a hand the size of a leg of lamb, and in that hand he had a gun the size of a cannon.

"You son of a bitch!" he bellowed.

And pointed the gun at me, and pulled the trigger.

CHAPTER TWO

I SUPPOSE YOU'RE WONDERING JUST WHO I AM, anyway, and how I got myself into this particular mess. At least I *hope* you're wondering something along those lines, because if you're not, it means that you aren't interested, which in turn would mean that I have failed to hook your interest and rivet your attention in the preceding pages. And if I fail to get high marks in hooking and riveting, I probably won't be able to sell this book when I'm done writing it, and then I don't know what I'll do. For the past two weeks I've been living in a room about the size of a midget's footlocker and eating Maine sardines and stale bread. The sardines are seventeen cents a can and the bread is free, but even if they were both free they would not be all that much of a bargain, because a sardine sandwich, even when you haven't had one in a while, is not exactly a dish to set before a king, and when the sardines are the cheapest ones available and the bread is stale and the menu never changes, well, I'm not fussy about food, but I can think of things I'd rather have.

I'm sorry. I'm getting completely off the track. The point is that the last chapter was supposed to hook and rivet you. And now that I've got your attention (if I haven't lost it already by wandering off the subject), I really ought to tell you who I am and how all this happened.

My name is Chip Harrison. It wasn't always, although I was always called Chip, as what you might call a nickname, because when I was a little tyke my first word was something that sounded like *Tsib*. (God only knows what I was trying to say. *Mama*, probably.) Anyway, *Tsib* wasn't anybody's idea of a teriffic name for a kid, but *Chip* was pretty good, as in *Chip Off The Old Block*. So I got called that a lot.

Then in late 1963 I started getting called that exclusively, and my actual name began not being entered on school records and things like that. Because my name, you see, was a combination of family names. Leigh, which was my mother's maiden name, and Harvey, which was my father's mother's maiden name. So that my name started out as Leigh Harvey Harrison, and ever since late 1963 people named Leigh Harvey Anything have been very willing to be called something else.

"The sheerest coincidence," my father told my mother. "The sheerest possible coincidence. But when there are enough people in the world, coincidences have to happen now and again. I went to school with a Jewish lad named Adolph Gittler. His parents named him this in all innocence, you know, never dreaming—well, the point is clear. The boy changed his name to Arnold Gidding. Didn't do him all that much good. The teachers called him Arnold, but we all called him Adolph. Or Der Fuehrer. Or Sieg Heil."

"Boys are so cruel," my mother said.

"Leigh Harvey," my father said. "A perfectly sound name turned frightful overnight. We'll change it to Chip. That's what everyone calls him anyway. Chances are no one really knows his full name. When he gets older, why, if he wants something more distinguished, he can select it himself."

If I ever do, I suppose I will.

I wasted all of yesterday writing out the story of my childhood, and where I was born and where we lived while I was growing up and the schools I went to and things like that, and I used up a whole lot of time and paper, and I just got through tearing it all up. Because in the first place I can't imagine anyone being very interested in all of that, since there was nothing the least bit unusual or attention-grabbing about it. And in the second place I'm not one of these people who can practically remember emerging from the womb. I have partial recall, and it's vague at best.

So why don't I just say that I came of rich but dishonest parents, and went to a couple of different private boarding schools, until that one jarring day when my father shot my mother in the back of the head and shot himself in the front of the head and made me, in the wink of an eye, an orphan.

I was playing basketball when I learned this. I'm fairly tall, which always leads people to think that I ought to be good at basketball, until they come to the realization that my lack of coordination offsets my height, since I'm not Gulliver or anything, just fairly tall for my age. This particular coach hadn't caught on yet, it being my first year at this particular prep school, so I was out there on the court missing lay-ups and muffing rebounds when some kid came down with a note asking me to report to the Head's office.

The Head—he was always called this, and while this is true of a lot of headmasters, it really fit in his case, because he had a head the approximate size of a basketball, perched on a skinny neck above an insignificant body, the head itself as hairy as a doorknob, with vague indentations and protrusions here and there to indicate eyes and nose and mouth and all that. Anyway, the Head did a lot of pacing around his office that day, and told me what had happened, more or less, and then went on to tell me more or less why my father had done this un-precedented thing.

What it amounted to, without the hemming and hawing which the Head put in, was that Chip Harrison's parents had spent their lives as con men (well, con man and con wife) and had made a good if shaky living for many years, working one swindle or another, and had been in the process recently of pulling off a remarkable stock swindle, until suddenly the roof had fallen in, leaving my unpoor but unhonest parents (a) stone broke and (b) jailable. Evidently my father decided that there was No Way Out, whereupon he did what he did.

I can't understand why. I mean, it seems to me that there must have been something he could have done. Gone to Brazil or joined the Foreign Legion or some-thing. But I guess he just had the feeling that all the walls and the ceiling were coming in on him, and it seemed simpler to go bang bang and end it.

"I never knew him," I said, dazed. "I was never around much, and then when I wasn't at some school or other, well, I was usually off at summer camp, or else I was with them and we were traveling. They always seemed to be moving to one place or another."

"One step ahead of the law," the Head said darkly.

"Uh, I suppose. I guess I never really knew what he did for a living. When kids would ask, I would say he was in investments. I thought he probably was, but I didn't have any clear idea of how."

"Rather shady investments," said the Head.

"I don't suppose I thought about it too much. I took it for granted, ever since I was old enough to think about it, because little kids don't think about the subject, or at least I didn't until recently—"

"Would you like a glass of water, Harrison?"

"I don't think so. What I mean is, I took it for granted we were rich. We always had everything, and then being at schools like this one, I just thought we were rich."

"Ah, yes, errmphhh," the Head said. "That does, errmphhh, bring up a painful subject, Harrison."

"It does?"

It did. The subject was money, and the pain lay in the fact that I didn't have any. I wasn't just an orphan. I was a penniless orphan, a seventeen-year-old Oliver Twist. If my parents had seemed to be rich, they had managed this illusion by spending every ill-gotten penny as soon as they ill-got their hands on it. And over the past months they had been spending a great deal of money that they didn't have yet, all of this snowballing up to the point when everything went blooey, so that not only did I have an inheritance of absolutely nothing coming to me, but I was in hock to the Upper Valley Preparatory Academy for a couple thousand dollars' worth of tuition and room and board.

"I'm sure you understand the problem, Harrison," the Head said. The light glinted off the shiny top of the Head's head. He picked up one object after another from his desk top—a pipe, a pipe cleaner, a pencil, an ashtray, a file folder, you name it. He played with each of these things, and he watched himself do this, and I watched him, and it went on like this for a while.

Then he told me I would have to make arrangements, find relatives who would take me in and help me carve out a fresh start in life for myself. Perhaps, he suggested, someone might come to my financial assistance. I told him that as far as I knew, I didn't have any relatives. He acknowledged that he had rather thought this might be the case.

"I really don't know what I'll do after graduation," I said. "I guess college is out, at least for the time being, not that any of them have been in what you might call a rush to accept me, but—"

I got a look at his face and it put me off-stride. I let the sentence die and waited.

"I'm afraid you don't entirely understand," he said. "I don't see how we could conscientiously let you remain here until graduation, Harrison. You see—"

"But it's February."

"Yes."

"Almost March."

"Errmphhh."

"I mean, this is my last semester before graduation. I would be graduating in June."

"Actually, you owe us tuition, room and board since September, Harrison."

"I'll pay sooner or later. I'd go to work after graduation and I could pay—"

He was shaking his head, which in his case called for more than the usual amount of effort. I watched him do this. I felt, oh, very strange. Weird. I mean, thinking about all of this now, in what you might call historical perspective, I get all sorts of vibrations that I didn't get then. Like what an utter shit, pardon the expression, the Head was. And like that.

But at the time, I was having my whole little world turned not only upside down but inside out, and I was like numb. I didn't know how I felt about any of this because I didn't *feel*. I couldn't. There was no time to react because everything was too busy going on.

The Head stopped shaking and spoke again. "No, no, no," it—*he*—said. "No, I think not. No, I'm afraid we'll simply have to write off the money, chalk it up to experience. If there were mitigating circumstances, but no, no, no, I don't think so. Your grades are not bad, but neither are they exceptionally good. Coach Lipscot tells me your performance on the basketball court is generally disappointing. And, of course, the social stigma, you must understand. Murder and suicide and confidence swindling, no, no, no, I think not, Harrison, I think not."

I was shaking when I left his office. I don't think I was ticked off or scared or any particular thing, but I was shaking. Everything happening at once. I went back to the dorm. My roommate was lying in his bunk, reading a sex magazine, and when I walked in he went through his little act of trying to pretend that (a) he was only interested from the standpoint of a future psychologist and (b) he had been holding the magazine in both hands. I don't suppose the guy beat off more than average. It was his attitude that bothered me. (As a matter of fact, an obnoxious attitude in this area isn't exactly rare. Either they're like Haskell, going to great lengths to pretend that they don't even have genitals, let alone touch them, or else they go to the other extreme and want to talk about it, or discuss methods, or do it right out in the open. Or worse. Either way I find it pretty disgusting. I think it should be a private thing, like religion or squeezing blackheads.)

Anyway, the sight of old Haskell draping the sex book to hide his erection was enough to turn me off to the idea of talking with him, which hadn't been that outstanding an idea to begin with, I don't guess. He started babbling about something or other, and I wondered what he would say if I told him everything, and I decided it wasn't worth finding out. I turned away from him and went over to my dresser and started pulling out drawers. I thought I was trying to decide what to take and what to leave, but I guess I was looking for something without knowing what it was, something that would make everything go together in some, oh, meaningful way. If anything like that existed, it certainly wasn't in my drawers or closet. As a matter of fact, the more I looked the more I realized that there was nothing around that I particularly wanted to see again. It was just too much trouble to decide which stuff to put in a suitcase and which stuff to leave behind. It was easier to leave everything.

It was especially easy to leave old Haskell. I didn't even say good-bye. I mean, why do it? I thought about borrowing a few bucks from him—he always had plenty of money, everybody at Upper Valley always had money. The Head would just shake himself and say that he had expected me to borrow money before I left, and like father like son, and all of that.

So I didn't. Not from Haskell and not from anybody else, and the crazy thing is that if I had just gone and told people what was happening, not even getting specific about it but just that I was broke and with nowhere to turn and all, I could have collected a bundle. Not by borrowing, but as outright gifts, or on a pay-me-when-you-can basis. Because while the guys at Upper Valley were something less than princes, they were not a bad bunch. And if I was not Mr. Popularity, I wasn't anybody they despised, either. They were okay, and I got along with everybody. And, more than anything else, see, these guys were all at Upper Valley for a reason. They were all there because (a) they had money and (b) there was something less than wonderful about them, or else they would have gone to a better school. Either they were slow learners or marginal alcoholics or their family background had a bad smell to it or something of the sort. They had plenty of money and they knew how important money was and just what the limits to it were, and all of this added up to a gentle and wry kind of sympathy and all.

So they might even have taken up a collection for me, and it might even have come to enough so that I could have stayed at that crappy school until I graduated from it. At least it would have been enough to let me leave the school on a bus or train or something.

But I was, well, proud. And in no mood to explain anything to anybody, or take anything from anybody. In fact I couldn't even talk to anybody, although I had this need. I actually spent close to two hours just walking around the campus, trying to think who I could talk to. I couldn't work up any enthusiasm for talking to any of the guys or any of the teachers. I would have little conversations with some of them in my own mind, and it helped me get some of my own thoughts straightened out, but each time I came to the decision that I would just as soon talk to these people in my mind and not in the flesh. And I certainly didn't want to talk to the basketball coach. I did have an imaginary conversation with him. It didn't get too far, but it featured him explaining to me how, if I only drove more fiercely on those lay-ups and worked harder for those rebounds, if I could only be counted on to drop a sufficient percentage of foul shots, then my academic career might still be promising. "You've got the height and the reach, Chip kid," he said, in the privacy of my mind. "Not enough to interest the college scouts. A year or two and the rest of them'll catch up with you. But on a prep school level—well, you had your chance, boy. This was the place for you and I gave you every opportunity, but you just didn't give me everything, boy, you just let me and the team down. A winner never quits, Chip kid, and a quitter never wins."

I sat under a tree and looked through my wallet. I had a snapshot of my folks, and another more formal picture of my mother. I looked at these for a little while. I also had seven one-dollar bills in the bill compartment of the wallet, and forty-six cents in the change compartment. In the secret compartment I had a folded twenty-dollar bill and a lubricated Trojan with a receptacle tip. The two were related; I had planned, at some unspecified future date, to hitchhike to a city fifty miles away where, it was said, prostitutes plied their hoary trade. The twenty-dollar bill was to hire one, and the Trojan was to make sure that any scars left by the experience would be psychological in type. And the secret compartment, by the way, was not all that much of a secret. I had been carrying that stupid rubber for so long that you could see its elliptical outline through the wallet.

(I guess it worked, though. Not the secret compartment. The Trojan. In all the time I had it there, I never once caught a disease.)

I got up from under the tree and put the wallet back in my pocket. I had $27.46 and an old rubber. I had no place to go to and no one to turn to and I couldn't even stay where I was.

I went back to my room. Haskell, thank God, was not there. I think he was probably having dinner. It was about that time, and I could have gone over and had something myself, but I didn't even consider it. I got under the shower and washed myself a few times, and I got dressed in all clean clothes, and I brushed my teeth and combed my hair and made polishing motions at my shoes. I put things like my comb and toothbrush and a bar of soap in my pockets. I thought about packing a change of socks and underwear, but I didn't. I wanted to have my hands free. The phrase *walking away empty-handed* came to me, and it seemed proper to do this, and in a literal sense.

On the highway, neatly groomed and clean cut, I stood with my thumb in the air. A few cars came and went, as cars will do, and then a big Lincoln slowed down, and I got that good expectant feeling, and I straightened up a little and put a fresh, boyish smile on my face.

The car slowed a little more, and the driver looked at me, and stepped down hard on the gas pedal and roared off into the distance.

All I could think of was a joke. You probably know it. I guess it's the oldest joke in the world.

There was this guy who joined the paratroops, and after all the training it was time for him to make his first actual jump from a plane. Not off one of the towers but out of an actual plane in flight. And the flight instructor or jump instructor or whatever they call it, the guy in charge, went through the procedure with him. "When you jump, you count to ten. Then you pull the ripcord to open the chute. In the event that the chute does not open, pull the emergency cord to open the parachute. The chute will open and you will coast gently down to the ground. There a truck will pick you up and take you back to the base."

So the guy jumped, and he pulled the ripcord, and nothing happened, and he pulled the other cord, and nothing happened. And he said to himself, "I'll bet that fucking truck won't be there either."

Oldest joke in the world.

And I just fell out. I broke up completely. I rolled around at the side of the road, laughing harder than I ever laughed in my life. "That fucking truck," I said, and roared with laughter. "That fucking truck."

I never did cry. I don't know why, but I never did. And if I didn't that day, I don't suppose I ever will.

The car that picked me up, long after the laughter was over and done with, was a big Pontiac convertible with deep vinyl seats and power everything. The driver was about forty or forty-five, very pale and indoors-looking. He said he was a salesman and that he sold industrial bathroom fixtures. My first reaction was to wonder what an industrial bathroom was, and after I figured it out without asking him, I got a mental picture of an endless row of urinals stretching as far as the eye could see, with an endless row of workers in denim overalls, stepping up to the urinals, setting down their lunchboxes, and urinating industriously.

And it struck me that I had done this myself maybe a million times, except for the lunchbox and the overalls, but in all those times it hadn't occurred to me that there were people who made a living going around selling urinals, or that other people made their living buying them. I had just never really given much thought to the ways people made their livings. But now, as an orphan with twenty-seven dollars and change, the whole subject of work seemed more significant.

I found about a thousand questions to ask him. About the different models of industrial bathroom fixtures, and the colors they came in, and how you got into that kind of business, and, oh, everything that came to me. Now and then I would see him giving me funny little looks, as if he maybe thought I was putting him on by pretending to be interested in such a ridiculous subject. But I guess it was easier for him to believe that I was interested than to accept the fact that his work was all that boring, so he told me a lot more about his field than anyone in or out of it would really care to know. And he got a kick out of it, I guess, maybe because no one else thought he was so interesting. His wife, he told me at one point, didn't give a whoop in hell about his life's work. In fact, he said, she seemed ashamed of it, as though there was something dirty about sinks and toilets and urinals, when, in point of fact, the world would be infinitely filthier without them.

I wasn't faking a thing. I was really interested at the time. Honestly.

He picked me up in western Pennsylvania, where the school was. We took the Pennsylvania Turnpike west. It turned into the Ohio Turnpike, and we went about half-way through Ohio before he had to turn off. He left me on the pike. I had said I was going to Chicago, and while I didn't have any great reason to go there, I was stuck with the story.

Before he left me off, he stopped for gas and bought me a meal at the restaurant. He went to the john, and when he got back to the table, he was all excited and took me back to the john to show me all the plumbing fixtures and explain various things about them. We got some very funny looks from the others, let me tell you.

Through Ohio and Indiana and Illinois I talked to a lot of different people and had a total of six more rides. The conversations were something like the one I'd had with the salesman. I won't bore you with what the various drivers did for a living or where they picked me up and dropped me off, or the makes of the cars and appearance of the drivers. To tell you the truth, I don't remember it all that clearly. They tend to run together in my mind. Anyway, none of it was that sensational.

I got to Chicago a little before noon. My last driver dropped me north of town near the lake, and I spent almost an hour trying to hitch a ride back toward the center of the city. I suppose it must have been a whole lot less than an hour. In that wind, though, it seemed like forever. Finally a cop car came along and a uniformed cop stuck his head out and said something about hitchhiking. I didn't catch the words, but it didn't take an IQ up around the genius level to get the message, which was that hitchhiking was frowned upon. If he hadn't told me this, I might still be there, frozen solid, with my thumb out.

Now, though, it occurred to me to take a bus, which cost me a quarter and which was the first expenditure I'd had since I left school.

Sitting on that bus, all I could think of was the damned quarter. I mean, after all, I had gone something like twelve hundred miles and eaten three times and all I was out so far was a quarter. You'd think I would be thrilled, for Pete's sake. But I kept thinking that my $27.46 was now down to $27.21. And that I could afford to take the bus a hundred and eight more times, and then I'd have twenty-one cents left, which would buy me two cups of coffee and a gumball. The point being that I had no money coming in, so *any* going out was something to worry about.

I kept planning to ask the driver to let me out when

we got to the center of town, but I couldn't think of a way to do this without sounding like a hopeless hick, and for some stupid reason I didn't want to. So I just kept looking around and waiting. I had been to Chicago before with my parents but couldn't remember much about it. Except that we went shopping at Marshall Field's and stayed, I think, at the Palmer House—though when I went to take a look at it, I didn't notice anything familiar about it. I guess I must have been eight or ten at the time.

Anyway, I recognized the Loop when we first hit it, and when we got to State Street, I remembered that it was the main drag, or else I just recognized it from the song. The street signs have *State Street* and under it *That Great Street*. When I noticed this I was tremendously pleased. A point of recognition, as if the street sign was some old school buddy or something. Later, after I had walked all over the damned street, I began to realize how incredibly simple it was of them to put something like that on the dippy street signs. If everybody who goes to Chicago could just see one of those signs once, that would be fine. But to just have them there always, so that even the people who live there have to look at them—

I got off the bus at State Street and started walking around. I mostly stayed right there on That Great Street because it was a nice familiar name and if I left it I was afraid I might never find it again. I walked up and down and looked in store windows at things I didn't need and couldn't buy anyway. I kept seeing things that for no reason at all I suddenly wanted. A combination nail clipper and pocket knife, for example, which I needed like the Venus de Milo needs gloves. And although a guy had bought me breakfast just a couple of hours before, I kept getting these dumb yens for food. I couldn't pass any place that sold anything edible without starting to drool. I stood in front of a restaurant where the cheapest dish on the menu was over four dollars, and I actually stood there reading the whole menu as if I could go in there and dive into a steak. I mean, even if I was fool enough to waste the money, I wasn't dressed for the place.

Eventually I got annoyed and bought a candy bar just

to kill my appetite. They had the nerve to charge six cents
for a stinking nickel candy bar.

$27.15.

Two hours later I was stretched out on a bed in a room
in the Eagle Hotel (*$3.50 a night*), reading the want-ad
section of the Chicago *Tribune* (*free, out of a trash can*). I
used a yellow chewed-up pencil stub (*found at the curb*)
to mark the ads that looked promising.

There were jobs all over the place. Just looking at those
listings, you wouldn't believe there was anyone in the
country who wasn't working. The only problem was that
none of the advertisers wanted to hire a seventeen-year-
old kid with three and a half years of high school, no
experience whatsoever, and not an awful lot of ability,
either.

Not that they seemed to care too much about ability.
The main thing seemed to be experience. I would say that
ninety-eight ads out of a hundred wanted to hire people
with experience, and what they were really hot to hire was
someone who was already doing a much more important
job at higher pay in the same field. I didn't blame them,
but how could anybody get experience if you had to have
it to get a job?

Another thing you had to have was an education. Judging by the ads, if the job was one where you might come
up once a week against a two-syllable word, they wouldn't
touch you unless you had a college degree, and they
wouldn't be happy about it unless you had a master's. For
less intellectual jobs, like picking ticks off horses, they
were willing to settle for you if you had a high school
diploma.

It was very goddamned discouraging, let me tell you. I
folded the paper and put it down and sat up on the
bed—$3.50 a night doesn't buy you much of a bed,
incidentally—and said, aloud, "I'll bet that fucking truck
won't be there either."

This time it didn't break me up in the slightest. I went
back to the paper and kept finding the two percent of the
ads that I almost qualified for. Things like passing out

handbills on the street, sweeping the floor in a grocery store, jobs that were either temporary or part-time and that didn't pay all that well anyway.

When I was done, I stretched out on the bed and closed my eyes. The hotel must have been made out of second-hand egg cartons. You could hear absolutely everything. Whenever a toilet flushed anywhere in the building, it was like being next to Niagara Falls. Sometimes I could hear conversations, either two people talking together just low enough so that I could make out every fifth word, or else some drunk shouting at the top of his lungs. I don't know which was worse.

But lying there I realized what I was going to do.

I was going to Succeed.

Of course you can't just succeed. You have to succeed *at* something, and I wasn't quite sure what that something might be yet. But the impression I got from the men I hitchhiked with was that one job wasn't all that different from any other. Once you got past the slave level and actually got somewhere in business, the idea was to take something and sell it to someone else. And it didn't really make very much difference whether the thing you were selling was advertising space or snake oil or industrial bathroom fixtures. The object, whatever it was, was to wind up with more money than you started out with.

I sat up in bed. I thought of my father and mother, and the life they had led, and where it in turn had led them. I would arrange my life differently. I would be honest and hard-working and stable. I would take as my own personal day-to-day objective the same goal that made all those hitchhikers the same—to finish each day with more money than I'd started the day with. If I had to pass out handbills or sweep floors or pick ticks off horses, I would do it for the time being, and I would make damn well sure that each day's work brought me at least as much as I needed for my meals and rent.

And meanwhile I would find some job that had some kind of real Opportunity For Advancement. That was a phrase that appeared in a great many ads, and they couldn't all be playing games. I'd find a job with an

Opportunity For Advancement, and I would work long hours and apply myself and go to night school to get that high school diploma and then go on to take night courses at college and put myself through college, and work my way up the corporate ladder in the good old American way, using hard work and pluck and luck and good old common sense and elbow grease to make my way to the top.

And there would be women every step of the way.

My brain spun at the thought. Of course there would be women, I realized. The cheap-but-vital women in whose rough arms I would learn the rudiments of love. The secretaries and career girls with whom I would share idle moments of brief but intense pleasure. And, when I found her, the Right Girl who would share my hopes and dreams, and with whom I would climb the long ladder rung by rung and hand in hand, until together we would enjoy the fruits of success crowned by True Love.

I thought of the joys of True Love, and glowed at the thought. And then I thought of the Untrue Love that would come first, with the career girls and secretaries and cheap-but-vital women, and I began to be moved by these thoughts. The thoughts became quite vivid, as a matter of fact, and quite moving.

But then someone in a room down the hall was seized by a coughing and spitting fit, and that ruined the mood completely.

I burrowed under the covers. A cockroach scuttled out from beneath the radiator, which had begun clanking. It seemed to be giving off a whole lot more noise than heat. The radiator, that is. Not the cockroach. Well, maybe the cockroach too, for all I knew. Or cared.

I settled my head on the pillow, such as it was. If there were more than thirty-five feathers in that pillow, they must have been very small ones. The man with tuberculosis (my diagnosis) did his number again.

I fell asleep. Which should give you an idea how tired I was.

CHAPTER THREE

THE MAN WAS MOSTLY SHOULDERS. HE WASN'T really big, I was taller than he was, but he had these wide shoulders and no neck at all, and he was wearing a sinister short-brimmed hat and a black suit, and he looked like a Chicago gangster. Maybe he was nothing more desperate than a Chicago mutual funds salesman, but I don't really think so. I think he was a Chicago gangster. If not, he's in the wrong line of work.

In which case I know exactly how he feels.

He came toward me, and I picked up the rhythm of his walk and got my timing into gear. When he was just the right distance away, I took the pasteboard slip from the top of the stack and thrust it at him. If it had been a knife, and a couple of inches longer, it would have pierced his left lung.

But it was just a piece of paper and it never touched him. And amazingly enough he never touched it, either. He just kept right on walking and went past me as if I were invisible. I turned to look after him.

"Stay awake, Chip!"

I spun around. Gregor clicked the shutter, and I opened
my hand and let the piece of pasteboard float to the
ground. My gangster friend had missed his golden opportunity, all spelled out in smudged black letters on a yellow
card, and saying:

HELLO THERE!

Your candid photo has just been taken
by Gregor the Pavement Photographer!
Your picture will be ready within twenty-four hours! Bring or mail this card
with the some of one ($1.00) dollar to
Gregor the Pavement Photographer,
1104 Halstead! Find out what you look
like to others! See yourself as the world
sees you!

It was a pretty tacky little slinger, no question about it.
And even if you dropped the excess exclamation points
and spelled *sum* right and printed the message in un-
smudged ink on a less gaudy stock, it would still be nothing that most people would want to carry with them
forever. That few of them were so moved was readily seen
by a glance at the pavement to my rear, where any
number of the yellow cards presently reposed.

In plain English, there were little yellow slingers all
over the place, some of them crumpled, others just plain
dropped. Most people dropped them without even finding
out what they were, but almost all of them did take the
cards when I shoved them at them. The gangster was rare.
The average person has trouble not taking anything you
hand him. It's a reflex, I suppose. I don't know whether
the gangster had lousy reflexes or tremendous cool, or
whether he was so tied up in his own little world that he
hadn't even seen me. Nor did I have time to worry about
this, because I had to pass the next card to the next person, who would in due course add it to Chicago's littering
problem.

The gangster came by around a quarter after four, and

there wasn't another memorable person for the rest of the day. This was my sixth day working for Gregor, and by now a person had to be pretty remarkable in order for me to take any real notice of him. Every day I would see tens of thousands of people, and I would poke yellow slips at thousands of them. At first it was such a constant parade of new faces and bodies that I started getting a headache from it. But then it straightened out and smoothed out and the pedestrians lost their individuality. They were just part of the crowd, and I found myself tuning them out the way you tune out anything that's always there. I no longer really noticed the traffic noises, and I no longer smelled the smell of State Street, and in the same kind of way I no longer noticed the swarm of people. Every once in a while one of them would manage to be more than just another shadow in the crowd. The gangster type, and an occasional cripple, and particularly attractive girls, for example.

A few minutes after six, Gregor said, "Oh, the hell with it, keed, let's call it a day." He folded up his tripod and put his camera in the case. We walked to 1104 Halstead Street, where Co-op Photography was located. Co-op Photography was a name to put on the door, actually. Inside the door there was a large room jammed with desks and three smaller rooms, two of them darkrooms and one of them a slapdash studio with lights and a couple of backdrops. For ten dollars a month Gregor got the use of a desk, two hours a day of darkroom time, and use of the studio by arrangement. There was also a switchboard and a girl who functioned as a sort of collective receptionist, but it cost an extra five dollars a month to receive calls there, and Gregor figured it wasn't worth it. So we walked past the girl without asking if anyone had called, and Gregor put some things in the desk and took some other things out of it, one of them being a bottle of peach-flavored brandy.

"Jesus sonofabitching Christ," he said, reflectively. Gregor was a short dark mixture of various Balkan strains that didn't go together all that well. His eyes were sunken and his cheeks hollow. He had the heaviest beard of anyone I ever met. When he swore I always had the feeling I was hearing wrong, because he never sounded mad or aggravated or anything. He would say various obscene things in the tone of voice you would use to say, "I'm going down to the store for a new tube of toothpaste" or "I wonder how the White Sox did today." It took a whole lot of getting used to.

He uncapped the bottle and took a drink and asked me if I wanted one. I said it sounded like a good idea. He gave me the bottle and I took a drink. The first time he had done this I wanted to wipe the neck of the bottle or something, but then I decided that anybody who stood out in the middle of State Street all day the way I had done was already exposed to every germ known to modern man, and besides there was something vaguely insulting about insinuating that Gregor was diseased or something.

I don't know what good peach-flavored brandy tastes like, or even if there is any such thing, for Pete's sake. This was very cheap stuff. If you've never had it, you've got the right idea. I think you could duplicate the taste by mixing equal parts of the sweet syrup from canned peaches and Zippo lighter fluid, but if you mixed it that way it would probably cost you more than Gregor paid for it.

He took another drink himself and put the cap on the bottle and the bottle in the drawer. Another photographer, an old man who wore suspenders all the time, believe it or not, came over and asked how it had gone.

"How should it go?" Gregor demanded. "You take the pictures and you see what happens." He pawed through a handful of letters on the desk top, held one of them to the light, and squinted suspiciously at it. "So either there's a dollar in it or there isn't," he said thoughtfully. "And what difference does it make?"

You may have gathered that he didn't have the greatest money-making operation in the world. Good gathering. Gregor, from what I had seen, was a pretty fair photographer, but one look around that office told you that pretty fair photographers were in less demand than, say, pretty fair aerospace engineers. (Whatever they are: I don't understand the term, but the *Tribune*'s classified pages are filled with people who want to hire them.)

Gregor's business was straightforward enough. He stood there on State Street, taking pictures of people walking by, and as they passed I gave them a numbered slip, and theoretically they sent in the slip with a dollar, and theoretically the number on the slip enabled Gregor to find the right negative and print it and send the print to the customer.

"I don't always get the right picture to the right person," he had confided once. "Especially before I started using a kid. I would do the shooting and the card-passing all myself, and I would get the numbers a little off-synch, and then I'd get some jerk writing in from Denver to tell me that he got the wrong picture, and I should either send him the right one or send his dollar back. So how am I supposed to straighten it out? Some of the jerks write back three, four times for a lousy dollar. Think how many times I must make a mistake and they don't write at all. Sometimes I wonder if anybody ever gets the right picture. But what do they want it for in the first place, huh, keed? Answer me that. I have this way of making a buck and I am damned if I can tell you why anybody at all ever sends for the Jesus sonofabitching Christ photographs."

Tonight his mood was less reflective. He seemed annoyed at the volume of late mail, and he cursed pleasantly as he slit the flaps of the envelopes and shook out the dollar bills. There were a couple of checks, and one clown had sent a dollar in stamps, and another hadn't enclosed any payment at all.

He put away the orders he would fill tomorrow and added the money to his wallet. "The one with the stamps," he said, "should sit on a hot stove waiting for his picture to come, the son of a bitch. Let's see, keed, eleven-thirty to five-thirty is six hours at a buck and a half is what? Nine bucks?"

"Eleven to six. Seven hours."

"Ten bucks?"

"Ten-fifty."

He counted out ten singles. He didn't have any change,

he said. I had change, I said. So he discovered two quarters in his pocket and gave them to me.

"You're the only one making any money," he told me. "Don't spend it all on the same girl, huh?"

I laughed politely and counted the bills again, and counted the money in my wallet. "Hey, that's great," I said.

"You're in Rockefeller's class now?"

"Not quite, but at least I can pay my rent by the week this week."

"Whattaya been doing?"

"Paying a day at a time. It's three-fifty a day, but the weekly rate is only twenty-one bucks, so I'll be getting one day a week free."

"Jesus. You're paying twenty-one bucks a week for a place to sleep?"

"That's right."

"Keed, that's *wrong*. Where you staying, the Ritz?"

"As a matter of fact it's a real dump. But at the price—"

"You're paying way too much, Chip."

"It's the cheapest hotel in Chicago. Or at least in the downtown area. I looked all over."

"Hotels!" He waved a great sigh and shook his head. "Hotels are for a night, two nights, a weekend maybe. Hotels aren't to live. Who the hell can afford it? Twenty-one bucks a week and you don't even get any meals or anything, is that right? Son of a bitch, you know what I pay? Eighty-five a month, and that's two rooms and a kitchen and a bathroom. You got a private bath in that hotel of yours?"

"No."

"I pay the same as you for Aileen and myself, an apartment instead of a room. That's what it costs you to live in that hotel of yours." He scratched his head. "Tell you the truth, I don't see how you can live. What did I pay you today, eleven dollars?"

"Ten and a half."

"Whatever it was. So three and a half from that for the room leaves seven, and figure a buck and a half each for breakfast and lunch is three from seven leaves four, and a decent dinner if you eat it out has to cost you two and a half bucks at the bottom, leaves you what? A dollar and a half? You can just about go to the movies." He shook his head again. "On top of which there's no work when it rains and no work when I got a big darkroom schedule. I don't know what I've paid you altogether over the past couple of weeks, but it can't come to all that much."

It didn't. I had worked six days out of the past nine, and my total earnings were $57.75. But then my expenses weren't as high as he had figured them. My breakfast was seventy cents and my dinner ranged from a dollar to a dollar-eighty. My lunch was generally a candy bar, and I had found a place where they only charged a nickel for a nickel bar. And sometimes I had a cup of coffee next door to the hotel before I went to sleep.

So actually I was saving money. I had hit Chicago two weeks before with $27.46 in my pocket, and I had earned $57.75 from Gregor and another twenty dollars and change on other jobs I had picked up a day at a time, and my current balance stood at just over $36.

At this rate, though, it was going to take me an awfully long time to become what you would call wealthy. Also I was due for some capital expenditures, if you want to call it that. Like washing my underwear and socks at night meant I had to put it on slightly damp in the mornings, which wasn't all that much fun. And it might be nice having another pair of pants and another shirt, not to mention the fact that the State Street sidewalks were having a bad effect on my shoes.

"Chip keed, I got an idea."

I looked at him.

"Suppose you could pay the same twenty-one bucks a week, or for the sake of convenience call it twenty, meaning you're saving a dollar right off the top, and you get a place to sleep and it's a clean place and all, and you share a bathroom with two people instead of three hundred, and on top of everything else, you get home-cooked breakfasts and dinners included. How's that sound?"

"Where is this place? Madrid?"

"Right here in beautiful Chicago. Just three blocks from here." One of the sunken eyes closed very slowly in what I had grown to recognize as a wink. "C'mon, keed, let's get our asses in gear. I gotta tell Aileen she's running a boardinghouse."

I was a little uncertain about this. I mean, it sounded great, and if anything it sounded too great. The only question was whether I wanted to get that tied up with Gregor. My job was doing menial labor for a failure, and that didn't quite fit in with my goal of a position with Opportunity For Advancement. Not that I figured Gregor would want to evict me if I went to work for somebody else. I was bright enough to realize that my room and board would just about pay the rent on his place, and I'm sure I wasn't the first of us to come to this realization. But I didn't know whether I wanted to be around him off the job as well as on it, and I didn't know if I wanted to be what amounted to a part of his family, sharing two rooms and a bath with him and Aileen.

Then I met Aileen.

I moved in that night. There wasn't all that much involved in moving in, since I didn't even have to go back to the hotel. The nice thing about not owning anything is that you don't have to go back for it. So when I say that I moved in, all it really amounts to is that I went to Gregor's apartment and met Aileen and had dinner and stayed the night.

It was a million miles away from the Eagle Hotel, believe me. Dinner was spaghetti and meatballs, and while it didn't fit the homemade label Gregor had hung on it— the spaghetti was out of a box and the sauce out of a can— it was still far better than the blue-plate special in a diner on Madison. And afterward we sat around in the living room and watched television and talked a little, and before they turned in Aileen made some more coffee (instant coffee) and brought out some A & P brand jelly doughnuts, and afterward she gave me a sheet and a pillow and a pillowcase and they went to their room and left me the couch.

I wasted a lot of time and mental energy trying to figure out how to turn that couch into a bed. It wasn't designed to make the switch. It was just a couch, and by the time I figured this out for myself I was tired enough to sleep standing up in a closet. I spread the sheet on the couch and got undressed and rolled up in the sheet. I wondered if I ought to buy a pair of pajamas or something. Then I wondered about Aileen, and if maybe she would come out and kiss me good-night or something.

She was pretty spectacular. Longish light blond hair and oval cat's eyes and high Slavic cheekbones and a full wet red mouth. She had the most goddamned suggestive mouth I have ever seen in my life. Her body reinforced the Lustful Peasant image in a big way. Large heavy pointed breasts, a hint of a belly, wide hips, large rounded bottom, big well-muscled thighs. The dress she wore that first night was a bright canary yellow in what was supposed to be a shapeless style. Only when she wore it, it took on a shape. It was really something amazing to watch her walk around in that thing, with all that flesh making interesting movements against the cloth of the dress.

I kept thinking about her, and imagining things. She was about the most sexual person I had ever met in my life. She just exuded this constant aura. It wasn't that she put out feelers or gave the impression that she was hot for me or anything, but even if she decked herself out in a nun's habit and cut her hair in a crew cut it would still be hard to spend ten seconds with her without imagining what she was like in bed.

I imagined she was fantastic. I imagined that she would make love like crazy, and that she would take a man and screw him absolutely blind (I now knew why Gregor's eyes seemed to be falling back into his head) and then, when she was done with you and you were deliciously half dead, she would wrap you up in her arms and legs and breasts and keep you warm as toast all through the night.

I kept on with this imagining, and you know how it is, what with one thing leading to another, well. There was a point when I realized that no one was going to break the mood by doing something creative with the plumbing, and I also realized that she was going to change my sheet in the morning, and maybe you can think of more embarrassing things to have happen, and maybe I can now, but I certainly couldn't then, and didn't even want to try.

The next afternoon I bought myself a second pair of socks.

"Now was I right or was I right?" Gregor said every now and then. "Here you're saving all kinds of money and living like a human being. Was I right?"

He was right, all right. Each morning I got up bright and early and had a glass of unfrozen orange juice and a cup of instant coffee and a bowl of cornflakes or rice toasties or something like that. There was one of those undairy creamers to put on the cereal. The list of ingredients sounded like the secret formula for the hydrogen bomb, for Pete's sake. Well, there's nothing like home cooking.

Then, about five days out of eight, I would go to work for Gregor, putting in an average of six hours work. When he had some developing and printing to do, I generally kept him company in the darkroom. He wanted to charge me for photography lessons. I got out of that one by offering to help him in the darkroom for a dollar an hour instead of a dollar and a half. We compromised; he didn't charge me, and he didn't pay me. It was fairly interesting, and I learned what the different chemicals were and what they did. I also learned that one place I didn't want to spend the rest of my life was in a darkroom.

On my days off, I sometimes picked up day work handing out passes for television shows or going door to door in some place like Oak Park, taking sample bars of a combination soap and cleansing cream (*Neither soap nor cleansing cream, but new improved Urglegurgleblech*) and rubberbanding them to people's doorknobs. It's against the law to put anything that's not mail into a mailbox, and they wouldn't fit under the door the way handbills do, so you had to loop them on the doorknob, which was very time consuming.

I took a few home for Aileen. You were expected to—what the hell, a sample was so people could sample it, no? But I didn't do what I really wanted to do, which was to stuff the whole batch of them down a sewer and go to the movies. For one thing, I had come to see that a man gets ahead in this world by doing his job to the best of his ability and playing fair with his employers. For another thing, a kid from Missouri dumped his soap and the crew chief caught him and beat the living shit out of him.

The rest of the time, when I wasn't working or helping in the darkroom, I divided between the apartment and the rest of Chicago. I would go out at night with no particular goal in mind, maybe stopping at the library for a while and then roaming around the city. The idea of meeting a girl of some sort or other was always in my mind, but then it always had been, and it had never done me any particular good before, and it didn't now, either. Most of the time, as a matter of fact, I never even saw a girl, or if I did she was with somebody.

There are supposed to be slightly more women than men in the country, but if you ever wandered around a big city after dark you couldn't help becoming convinced that there are maybe twenty or thirty men on the open market for every woman. I don't know where the girls go at night, or what they do, but they aren't where the men are.

Once, in a sort of middleclass hippie place on Rush Street, I seemed to be doing pretty well with this girl with long hair and sunglasses. She was from some college. I told her I was a dropout, which wasn't all a lie. We were getting along fairly well, but then her date came back and that was the end of that. And another time a woman got interested in me at a diner. I was having coffee to keep warm and she was having coffee to sober up, I suppose, but it wasn't working. She had a puffy look, as if someone had taken a bicycle pump and put a little air in all the cells of her body. At first I thought she was about thirty-five, and the closer I looked the older she got. It was like watching the aging process through the modern miracle of time-lapse photography, as they say in the commercials.

We went and sat together in a booth in the back, and she kept breathing on me and dropping little single entendres. She put her hand on my leg. Then she put her hand a little higher and gave me a friendly squeeze. By this time she looked about a hundred and eight and I got this all-embracing wave of nausea. I said I had to go to the toilet. I was half afraid she would follow me. I wouldn't really put it past her. I went to the john, and then I went to the back entrance and slipped out, leaving her to pay for my coffee and find some other boy to molest. I went out of my way to avoid that particular diner ever after.

And you know something, by the time I was a couple of blocks away from that woman, I called myself every name I could think of. I mean I really felt stupid. Obviously she was nothing spectacular, but the thing of it was that she was *there*, for Pete's sake, and she was *willing*. And it wasn't exactly as though I had to beat women off with a club. I was, let's face it, a very horny kid with a desperate desire to stop being a there's-that-dumb-word-again virgin. She could at least have served that purpose. I didn't have to love her to ball her. I didn't even have to like her.

That was as close as I came to scoring in the streets of Chicago, that and a couple of offers and come-hither glances from faggots, with one of them going so far as to make a tentative grab for me while I was making use of an industrial bathroom fixture. I told them all no, and they all took no for an answer. I guess nobody found me exactly irresistible.

You might think, after all that, that I would have spent all my time around the apartment. I did spend a lot of it there, as a matter of fact, but what drove me out of there from time to time was the fact that Aileen was driving me right out of my head.

It wasn't just what she looked like, which I told you about. It wasn't just that their bedroom door was not very substantial, and that I could hear them whenever they made love, which they did almost every night. (If they hadn't, I would have worried about Gregor. Really.) And it wasn't just that she was so sane and healthy about her physical self that she was completely casual about walking around half-naked in front of me, giving me groin-grabbing glimpses of one part of her after another until I literally ached.

It was that, on top of all of this, I was really digging her and Gregor as human beings. And it was a strange relationship, see, because I really didn't know what sort of relationship it was supposed to be. They were both a lot older than me. I think Gregor was in his forties, and I suppose she must have been close to thirty. So some of the time they were something like replacement parents, and since they had come into my life so shortly after my own parents left it, this did seem a logical role for them to play.

But I had never felt about my own mother as I felt constantly about Aileen. (Or if I did, I wasn't aware of it, and I'd just as soon not find out about it now, either, Dr. F.) If Aileen was my mother, then I was King Whatsisname with the broken ankles. And proud of it.

They were also like an older brother and older sister, and they were also like my boss and his wife, and they were also like my landlady and her husband, and, oh, it was too involved to keep straight. So the outcome was that I felt very comfortable and secure hanging around the apartment, reading a book or watching television or playing knock rummy with Gregor or helping Aileen with the dishes. I felt very comfortable almost all the time, and then all at once, I would just have to get out of there before I started running around on all fours and chewing at the carpet.

I mean linoleum.

It was on a Friday night when Gregor got a phone call and said he had to go out. The first time this sort of thing had happened I got very ginchy about being left alone with Aileen, very hopeful and very anxious both at once, but nothing happened then, and after that I got accustomed to it and thought nothing of it. If anything, I found it very relaxing to be alone with her. I could talk to her when there were just the two of us in a way I couldn't with Gregor around. About my folks, for instance, and what I wanted out of life, and various heavy things it would have embarrassed me to talk about in front of Gregor. Aileen hardly ever said much, but she had a way of listening that went down very smoothly.

Gregor went out around eight-thirty, and Aileen and I talked and watched television for about an hour and a half. Then he came back looking happy.

"We're in business," he told her. "Mark can use as much as five hundred or a thou's worth of the right stuff." He turned to me. "A photography assignment, keed. You thought I made the whole nut snapping dummies in the street, didn't you? But sometimes something good comes up." To Aileen he said, "I've got the studio from now until four in the morning if I want it."

"You want to go there?"

"Right. And use the darkroom right there, and deliver the goods in the morning. And have the money in my pocket before that kike changes his sonofabitching mind. You want to get ready, keed?"

"Me?"

"He means me," Aileen said.

"My prize model."

I said, "No kidding? You do the modeling?"

"That's how I found her, keed. My best and sweetest model. You ever look at the fashion magazines? *Vogue, Harper's Bazaar*—"

"Greg, put a sock in it, damn it."

He smiled at her. "Sure, they're all dying to give her a spread, aren't they, keed? And she'd give them a spread in return."

"Greg, in one minute you can go take pictures of soup cans."

"Just kidding."

"I mean with photographic artistry like yours, Greg, the subject's not really important, is it? You could go take artsy-craftsy shots of sewer gratings and the museums would stand in line for them."

"Baby, all I said—"

"I mean let's keep track of just who we all are, why don't we?"

This went on awhile. I had the feeling that I'd walked in on the last reel of a movie that only made sense if you'd seen the first part. I was still thinking it over while Gregor packed his gear and Aileen went off to change her clothes and make herself up. When they were ready, Greg started picking up his equipment, and I offered to help him carry it.

He said, "Well, sure, I suppose—" and she cut in to suggest that I come along and watch a photographic session.

"You futz around in the darkroom all the time, you might as well get acquainted with all the sides of the photography business. Isn't that right, Greg?"

"You really think so?"

"Why not?"

"Well, it's fine with me, keed."

"It's certainly fine with me."

"If you say so."

"Because this would be a dumb time for modesty, I certainly think."

"If you say so."

"And Chip's practically one of the family, aren't you, honey?"

I listened to all of this without saying anything. I suppose you figured it out a long time ago, but then you're sitting down somewhere reading it all at once, while I was living it a little at a time. I knew there was a lot going on that I wasn't getting, but that was as far as I could go with it. I was lost, and waiting for someone to find me.

So we walked the couple of blocks to the office suite. It was empty except for a little guy at one of the desks who was catching up on his bookkeeping. He looked up when we came in and then looked down again. We ignored him and went into the studio. Gregor locked the door.

He set up his equipment and arranged various lights and things, explaining it all to me as he did it. I didn't catch much of what he was saying because I was too busy trying to figure out what I was missing.

Then he was ready, and Aileen gave an odd little smile and got up on top of this dark green velvet couch. She gave a tug and lifted her dress up over her head and tossed it across the room out of camera range.

There was nothing under it but Aileen.

Oh, I thought. Nude pictures. Cheesecake, so to speak. Now I understood.

But not entirely.

"It's a mutual thing we've got going," Aileen said, spreading her legs. "It's actually a beautiful relationship, Chip. See, Greg takes my picture, and in return I take his."

I looked at Greg. He was buried under the black cloth and looked as though he was part of the camera apparatus. I looked at Aileen again. She had her hands between her legs, one on each side of what I was looking at.

"Only I have a built-in camera," she was saying, "and I don't have to futz around with floodlights or exposure settings. I just take aim and snap away. Say cheese, Greg."

Greg didn't say anything. I suppose he was still under the hood.

I wasn't looking at him, actually.

My mouth was as dry as a sand sandwich and I had this weird chilly sweat all over my hands and feet and under my arms. And I couldn't quite catch my breath, and I couldn't stop shaking all over, and I couldn't take my eyes off the most fantastic thing I had ever seen in my life.

The shutter worked.

"Click!" Aileen said.

CHAPTER FOUR

FOR A LITTLE OVER AN HOUR I STOOD THERE with my eyes falling out of my head while Gregor took filthy pictures of his wife. After her opening round of flashy repartee, Aileen didn't have anything to say. Gregor stayed under the black cloth, and stayed quiet. And believe me, I didn't say word one. A lot of things came to mind, I'll admit, but I kept them to myself.

One idea that I couldn't get out of my head was that this was all a dream, and if that was so, I had to be very careful not to do anything to wake myself up before the dream turned wet. Because dream or no, I was in what you might term a state of advanced physical excitement.

It was really fantastic.

I don't know if I can clue you in as to just what it was like in that little room. (Which is probably a pretty dumb thing for me to say, for Pete's sake, because I'm supposed to be writing this, and if I can't handle it, that means I'm wasting both our time, and that it's going to be a long siege of Maine sardines and day-old bread.) Seriously, I could try to put down all the poses Aileen struck and to say which ones made me the horniest and all, and if I did this, well, you might begin to get your own idea of what it was like in there, but I'm not all that certain it would add up to anything.

Well, just as an idea of the whole approach the two of them had, this was how Gregor used up one particular roll of film. He did several rolls of individual series work, which came to an even dozen pictures, which would eventually get wrapped up and sold together, and which would tell some vague sort of a story.

This particular one was the banana series, and it started off with a muffled voice from under the black cloth saying, "The banana, keed." At which point Aileen got off the couch, went to Gregor's bag of tricks, found a pair of ripe bananas, and got back on the couch.

I remember seeing those pictures, the banana set, after they were developed and printed. And if you hit them in order and were in the frame of mind to believe them, it really looked as though old Aileen was getting her cookies that way. It was pretty realistic.

Only an hour or so had passed when Gregor came up for air. His forehead was dripping with sweat. I guess it was pretty hot under the black cloth. It wasn't all that cool anywhere else in the room, either.

"Wraps it up," he said. He dug his cigarettes out of his shirt pocket, lit one for himself, and offered the pack to me. I shook my head. Some people are just physically incapable of believing that some other people don't smoke. He tossed the pack and the matches to Aileen and she lit up and tossed them back. It was all very casual, almost athletic, with all of this underhand lobbing of cigarette packs and matchbooks. You could almost forget that Aileen was stark naked, and that she had spent the past hour holding her labia open and sucking on her own nipples and sticking bananas up herself. (I don't know if I ought to be quite that graphic about it, but that was what she was doing, and I think it would be worse to try being coy about it, for Pete's sake. I mean, if you're going to come right out and say that a woman posed for a batch of dirty pictures while you stood there watching, you might as well call a spade a spade, right?)

Aileen blew out a cloud of smoke. She said, "Is that all you want to shoot?"

"I think so, yeah."

"I thought you were going to take some pornographic ones."

I didn't do an enormous double take on that line. I just thought I was hearing wrong.

But he said, "Hard-core? No, the sonofabitching timer is on the fritz. I don't know what's the matter with it. Less than two years old and it just went. Nothing works any more and nobody gives a damn. The whole civilization is coming apart at the seams."

I must have looked puzzled. Aileen said, "It's a timer on the shutter. He sets up the shot and then he has fifteen seconds to get in the picture with me."

"Twelve seconds," Gregor said.

She ignored the correction. "That way we can do the more interesting things, Chip. What you could call hard-core pornography."

I nodded.

"What we shot now tonight is called soft-core."

"What's the difference?"

"Redeeming social importance," Gregor said.

"Huh?"

"That's what the Supreme Court calls it. You know, that you can argue it's a work of art and not a hundred percent obscene. If you actually show people fucking, then it's considered a hundred percent obscene."

"In hard-core pornography," Aileen said, "the man's core is hard."

"That's an old gag," Gregor said.

"Professional humor," she said.

"But the point is that the timer is on the bum." He sucked on his cigarette and clucked his tongue pensively. "I'll tell you something, you wouldn't believe what a short time twelve seconds is until you tried to set up a shot and then get in it yourself. You know the worst part?"

"What?" I managed to ask.

"Staying up. You know, erect." His eyes dropped to his trouser front, and mine fought the impulse to follow. "When you set up with the camera and all, you know, your whole concentration is on technical matters. You don't even think sex. You might have trouble believing this, but when I'm taking these pictures, there's no difference in my mind whether I'm taking a picture of Aileen playing with herself or of the Chicago skyline. It's all the same as far as I'm concerned."

He was right. I had trouble believing this. I had seen the Chicago skyline, and I had seen Aileen playing with herself, and there was no chance I would ever get the two of them mixed up in my mind.

"So I set up a shot," he went on, "and then I have to turn on the excitement so that I'll get erect, and then rush rush rush to get into the right position before the sonofabitching shutter goes bang. It's the most nerve-racking thing going. And the thing is, the way I like to work, you know, is to shoot as much film as fast as I can, just one picture after the other. Just keep watching through the viewer and click them off whenever the pose is right. And the same way, Aileen likes to get into the spirit of a sequence and let it build the right way."

"To a climax," she said, with a wink.

"Yeah, to a climax," he said winklessly. "It's the same as whatchamacallit, method acting. Living the part. Look, you don't know the business, but I can tell you that if you looked at a set of the keed's photos and a set of the average model, there would be all the difference in the world." I had no trouble believing this. "The average girl, she'll put on this sonofabitching mechanical smile that looks painted on her face, or maybe she'll pout a little, and there's nothing the least bit natural about it. Aileen, she's something else. Sometimes I think she has, you know, a climax. Just going through the poses."

"Sometimes," she said, "she does."

"But without the timer," he said, and then he dropped his jaw a few inches and actually snapped his fingers. "Hey," he said, as an imaginary lightbulb formed over his head. "Now why the hell didn't I think of that before?"

"Of what?"

He pointed at me. "You," he said. "You could take the pictures. You want to be a photographer, you got to start sooner or later."

While I was busy not saying anything, Aileen said, "I've got a better idea. Chip's a smart kid, but he doesn't know anything about photography. You can't expect him to have your touch with a camera."

"Well, that's true," Gregor said.

"And anyway, I think the world's getting tired of the same old pictures of you and me, honey. But suppose you take the pictures and Chip and I star in them?"

They had done this before, Aileen assured me. Twice, as a matter of fact, with a fellow who neither of them really knew very well, as another matter of fact. And it was really perfectly legitimate as far as she was concerned, because after all it wasn't really sexual. Which was to say that they really didn't do anything. They would just set up a shot and Gregor would shoot it and then they would swing into another position.

The other fellow never actually got inside of her, Gregor explained. And that, he said, was an absolute requirement as far as he was concerned. Because while he and Aileen might have a more liberal attitude in certain respects than the average married couple, in other respects they were what you might call old fashioned, and one of the respects in which they were old fashioned was that neither of them believed in having sex outside of marriage. He was absolutely faithful to Aileen, and she in turn was a hundred percent faithful to him, and that was the way it had to be.

The two of them took turns explaining these things and filling me in on the fine points of pornographic photography, and let me tell you, it was the weirdest conversation ever. I wasn't tongue-tied all the way through it, but I think I might as well have been. I would ask various dumb questions and they would chime in with the answers. Wouldn't Gregor be upset just seeing me in these various poses with Aileen?

"No, keed, because I know it doesn't mean anything and nothing's really happening."

Wouldn't Aileen be embarrassed by doing that sort of thing in front of her husband?

"Embarrassed, Chip? I've got a huge streak of exhibitionism in me. You must have figured that out for yourself. If anything, I got a kind of a kick out of you watching just now, during the soft-core shots. And you know, honey, I like you, and Greg likes you, and if anything I think it would be kind of, you know, fun."

Fun.

"We got time," Gregor said. "We got all night here and in one of the darkrooms, and we can probably use both darkrooms if it comes to that because I don't think the other one is booked at this hour. There would be a lot more dough if I had hard stuff for Mark. If you wanted to do it, well, I suppose I could pay you, and I don't mean any of that buck-and-a-half-an-hour crap. I could afford, oh, what the hell, let's say twenty bucks."

"Greg, honey, how on earth can you be so damn cheap?" She turned to me and grinned conspiratorially. "He'll pay you fifty dollars, Chip. How does that sound?"

After a few seconds passed, I realized we were all waiting for me to come up with an answer. "It sounds fine," I squeaked. If my voice had been any higher they would have thought I wasn't old enough for the job.

"Well, that's fine," Gregor said. "Fifty dollars—well, sure, I suppose so. The only question, and I guess nobody but you knows the answer, keed, if you know it yourself, is whether or not you'll be able to perform. Most of the time you can fake it, you know, but some of the shots have to show you—"

"With a hard core," Aileen put in. She rolled her eyes in exasperation. "Gawd," she said. "Of all the stupid questions to ask him. He's had the hardest core in America for the past hour and a half, haven't you, honey? So I don't think he's going to have troubles now."

We got things off to a sensational start by having Aileen put on her dress and shoes. And oddly enough the sight of her with clothes on really got to me. I'm not being sarcastic. I had just about gotten to the point where I was used to her being naked, and now that she had the dress on again I was taking it back off again mentally and remembering what she looked like without it and getting hornier than ever at the memory.

She sat down and patted the couch next to her, and I sat, and she looked at me and gave me a grin as big as O'Hare Airport. I don't know if I can explain it, but when she grinned that way I knew that things were going to be all right, that this was my mother-sister-friend-landlady-sweetheart Aileen, and that we were going to have a little innocent fun together without anybody getting messed up. You may have trouble figuring out how she packed all that into a three-second grin, but it was all there and I read it loud and clear.

"Now the whole thing is to get into the part," she said. "You tell yourself that you and I are crazy about each other and that I'm very desirable and we're alone together and we're going to make love. Don't even think about the camera for now. It's just a little clicking noise, it's nothing to think about. And don't worry about striking poses, or what angles Greg's shooting from. Just get into the spirit of the thing and we'll wind up with some decent shots."

I thought, *Decent*? And then she puckered up invitingly, and I leaned forward, not too sure what came first, and we actually kissed.

That's an understatement. We went right off the bat into a deep soul kiss, and not because it was my idea. I was too dumb to think of it, but before I could think of anything at all, her tongue was halfway down my throat and her breasts were pressing against me.

Click!

We held the kiss, and she shifted a little and took my hand and put it on the front of her dress, over her breast. I gave a gentle squeeze and felt the nipple stiffen.

Click!

She wriggled her hips invitingly. I put my hand under her dress and touched the inside of her thigh. She felt like—I was going to say silk, but it was more like warm

glass, except even smoother somehow. I felt the play of
muscles in her leg. Her kissing got greedier. She was
sucking on my tongue as if she wanted to swallow it.

Click!

If this was method acting, I know why they use it.
Maybe she liked to think we were just going through the
motions, and maybe Gregor liked to think it, but if they
really believed it they were both fruity as a nutcake
because Aileen was hot enough to burn. I let my hand
move higher, and my mind filled up with what I had seen
earlier, those pink thighs and that puff of curly blond hair
and all, and I touched her and she was all warm and wet,
and—

Click!

Jesus Christ.

Click!

I let her take the lead. It seemed only natural, since she
was the experienced one in every sense. Besides, I never
wanted to move out of one pose in order to get into
another. But she gave a reluctant sigh and steered us to
the next bend in the river, which consisted of her opening
the dress to the waist and letting me amuse myself with
her breasts.

Click!

By handling them.

Click!

And kissing them.

Click!

And so on.

Click!

I'm putting all the clicks in to give you an idea of what
Gregor was doing, but don't get the impression that I was
always aware of the camera. Some of the time it was as
though it wasn't there at all and the whole sex thing
between me and Aileen was entirely real. Then that sensation would fade, and I would be so completely aware of
the camera that I almost couldn't stand it. Then the clicks
would seem loud enough to break glass, and I would start
feeling like a machine making love to another machine.

But this never lasted long enough to let me cool down, and each time I got into the mood completely again I would just be that much hotter than I was before.

It didn't take long for both of us to get out of our clothes. Aileen had already been giving my groin some gentle feels now and then, so exposing myself was no big deal to me, and as for Gregor, I wasn't very keenly aware of him just then.

Click!

I did have a second or so of concern after I got out of my shorts when I saw that she was looking at me. I guess every man who ever lived must have done a certain amount of worrying about his equipment at one time or another. And while I don't think I was more hung up on the subject than most, there were times when I wondered whether it was too small, or funny looking, or ugly, or I don't know what. Since I had no way of knowing how you could tell a pretty one from an ugly one, or how much was enough, there was no real way to avoid these worries completely.

So I had that flash of anxiety. But the next second Aileen's eyes went from the area in question to my eyes, and she gave that grin again, the same as before, and her lips parted just wide enough to admit her tongue, and she ran her tongue hungrily around her lips, and got the most beautifully lustful look in her eyes—

Click!

I hadn't felt so proud since I got my first quarter from the tooth fairy.

She touched me a little, and I'm sure the shutter went on clicking, but I didn't hear it. Then she got up on the couch and stretched out on her back with her knees bent. She motioned me on top, and we touched bodies from chest to groin, and my thing proved it had a mind of its own by going straight for her thing. I no sooner touched her than she gave a quick twitch of her hips and got out of the way.

"Easy," she murmured. "Remember the rules, Chip. The sign on the door says *Private,* remember? *Admission Restricted To Authorized Personnel.*"

I wanted to cry with disappointment. I had begun to think, somewhere along the line, that all of that business about not going all the way had been, well, something we would conveniently forget when the time came. I had put it in the same bag with her statement that none of this was really sexual.

I thought about just going ahead and doing it. I could always pretend it was an accident, I thought. Just put it where it belonged and keep it there long enough to finish, and even if she thought it was rape, she wouldn't be likely to go running through the streets shouting for a cop. And if she and Gregor got mad, well, the hell with them. Whatever happened, I would at least have done the one thing on earth I really wanted to do.

Lots of luck. I gave a well-intentioned thrust, and the shutter clicked behind me, and Aileen got out of the way with no trouble at all.

"*Naughty*," she whispered. "*Bad boy*."

I guess I could never make it as a rapist.

At this point it really did become pretty artificial and mechanical and phony. We stopped pretending and just went through the motions as quickly and effortlessly as possible, and it made for a lot less nervousness for both of us (and maybe for all three of us, because I don't think Gregor was happy seeing his faithful wife an inch away from technical infidelity). So what we did was just get quickly into a position, take shots of it from two different angles, and then get into another position. I had done a lot of extracurricular reading over the years—I suppose that's pretty obvious, for Pete's sake—but even with all the times I went through the *Kama Sutra* and the *Ananga Ranga* and *Eros and Capricorn* and *The Perverted Village* I had never quite realized how many different positions there are to not quite have sexual intercourse in.

Click!

Click!

Clickety clickety click!

By the time Gregor suggested we all stop for a cigarette break, I had reached a stage where I was just as glad to relax for awhile. Not that I was relaxed in any meaning-ful sense of the word. I mean, face it, this wasn't a relaxing way to spend the evening. It just plain wasn't.

"Got some great shots," he said through a cloud of blue-gray smoke. "You want to know something, keed, you're a natural born actor. And how about the wife, huh? One great little actress."

He turned the key in the lock, peeked out. "Nobody home," he said. "Hang on a minute."

While he was gone I whispered to Aileen that I was going out of my mind.

"Poor baby," she said.

"I mean I don't think I can walk."

"You forgot the rules for a minute there, Chip. I've never done it with anyone but Greg. Not since I met him, and it's been almost six years now. You have to under-stand."

"I suppose so."

"You know, you're very nice-looking."

"Oh, come off it."

"You mean you don't know it yourself? You're a good-looking guy, and you've got a dreamy body."

"Cut it out. My bones stick out, for Pete's sake."

"I like the way you look."

"I mean—"

"I think we'll look good together."

She was beginning to get to me all over again. I started to say something, God knows what, but then Gregor came back in with his bottle of shitty peach-flavored brandy. I had the most unbelievable urge to take the bottle and shove it up his ass. I had the feeling that if I could just get him out of the picture, him and his goddamned camera, I could spend the rest of my life balling Aileen, and I couldn't think of any way I'd rather spend it.

He was saying that he thought we were all entitled to a drink. He tended to think of alcohol as a reward. I didn't know if I could hack the taste of that crud just then.

Aileen said, "Honey, I think just a short one, unless you're out of film."

"There's plenty," he said. "Why?"

"I thought like one more roll, that's all. I didn't do anything oral."

"I didn't know you were going to do that," he said warily. "I didn't even think of it."

"Well, it would be a case of faking it, really."

"I suppose," he said. "Son of a bitch, if they don't go for that stuff. You sure you want to?"

"Oh, I don't mind."

I went over and sat on the couch while he took a quick pull on the brandy bottle and then disappeared beneath the black cloth and went to work loading the camera with a fresh roll. Aileen finished her cigarette and came over and sat down next to me.

I reached for her.

"Not just yet," Gregor called out cheerfully. "I'll be set in a sec, keed."

"Aileen," I whispered, "you'll drive me up the walls."

"Poor baby."

"Look, I—"

She ran her tongue over her lips. This was a little trick of hers that didn't exactly leave me cold when she did it first thing in the morning over instant coffee and cold cornflakes. Now it was absolutely criminal.

"You'll like this," she said.

"Ready to roll," Gregor said.

"God in Heaven," I said.

"Lie down, baby." Her mouth inches from my ear, blowing into it as she whispered. "Poor baby has had a mean night, huh? Mama will fix." Her hand moved over my chest and belly. My stomach contracted violently. "Ticklish," she murmured, blowing into my ear some more. The hand went on its merry way and grabbed. "Got small again," she said. "But Mama's gonna fix that, too."

Click!

I really felt like a baby, too. I lay there like a lump and felt so small and weak and helpless and so goddamned young I wanted to curl up and die. She kissed me on the mouth, and then on the throat, and then her mouth moved downward so that her long blond hair brushed over my face and chest and stomach.

Click!

I had my eyes closed, and my body was sort of stretched out the way you do when you float on your back in a swimming pool. I had that same kind of buoyant feeling, too.

She kissed it, and her hands did things, and the camera made stupid clicking noises, and the hard core was harder than ever. I could feel the blood in my head and I thought I was going to have a brain hemorrhage and die.

She did a million teasing things with her mouth. But there wasn't any contact to speak of.

Just her warm breath.

Click!

Breathing in and out, in and out.

Moistly.

Oh God, I thought, oh God, don't stop, for Christ's sake don't stop, whatever you do, don't stop, just another minute, just another second, God, don't stop—

Click!

And she stopped.

Since then I must have tried a thousand times to figure out why she bothered getting started if she wasn't going to finish it. I mean, face it, it's not as though she was some drippy virgin who didn't realize that a man had to finish what he started or get horribly frustrated. Everybody knows this, anybody old enough to read Ann Landers' column can figure it out. And Aileen was a long ways from a virgin. She may not have slept with anybody but Gregor since they were married, but I'm sure she must have had a few hundred men before he came around.

So she obviously knew what she was doing, but then why do it? She wasn't a cruel person. She was nice, really, and she seemed to like me.

I mean, I could understand why she felt compelled to perform the act without any actual contact. That is, I could understand it about as well as I could understand why it was all right for us to pet like crazy but not all right for me to get into her. Which is to say that I didn't understand and it didn't make any sense but at least I knew the basic rules of the game.

But if she was going to leave me high and dry, why start anything in the first place? What was the point? Gregor had been ready to pack up and go. So had I. And she hadn't wanted to have anything done to her. I was just supposed to lie there and leave everything to her, and I did, and it hadn't ended quite the way I had hoped.

I lay there like a overwound watch, going pingpingping inside and staying drawn hellishly tight. I couldn't talk or think or breathe or see. I didn't know where she was, but I knew where she belonged. In Hell, with a hot poker rammed up her behind.

And then I heard her voice, talking, not to me, but beyond me, to Gregor:

"Honey, baby, I have to give him some relief. He's a kid, you know, and I guess it was all too much for him. The excitement. Being with me, and in front of the camera and all, and going through the motions, and the different positions, and then this last thing. I think it stopped being just an act for him, and he got very excited, and if you look at him now, you can see how tense he is."

"So?"

"I have to do something."

"Well, I don't—"

"I wouldn't be unfaithful."

"Because I wouldn't like that, keed."

"And I wouldn't do it."

"I should hope not. I should just sonofabitching hope you wouldn't."

Her hand on my leg.

"But this would be just like a massage. I knew a girl who was a nurse in a hospital—"

"That's the best place to be a nurse."

"—and she told me how they used to give the patients rubdowns all the time, and if they got excited they would give that a rubdown, too, and that isn't wrong, do you think?"

"I suppose not."

Her hand gripped me.

"Of course it isn't," she said, her voice softer than ever now, and now she was talking less to him than to me, and her words moved in a jerky rhythm as her soft sure hand moved up and down, up and down, pumping up and down.

"Of course . . . it isn't . . . wrong . . . baby . . . baby . . . it's all right . . . all right . . ."

Not like this, I thought. Not with your hand, and not in the middle of the air, not like this.

"It's all *right* . . . it's all *right* . . . it's all *right* . . . it's all *right* . . ."

Oh, yeah, I thought. Okay. Sure, sure, oh.

"It's all *RIGHT*!"

It was all right, all right.

CHAPTER FIVE

THE NEXT DAY GREGOR DIDN'T BOTHER DOING his sidewalk photographer number. He went off to see Mark Somebody to turn a suitcase full of dirty pictures into as much money as possible.

"Soon as I get back, keed," he said, "you get your twenty-five smackers."

"Fifty," I reminded him.

"Oh, sure. My mistake."

"Sure."

As soon as he was out the door, I went into the kitchen and cornered Aileen. She asked me how come I wasn't working that morning. I said that a photographer's assistant didn't have much to do when the photographer wasn't on the job. There wasn't much point in me handing out the little yellow cards if there was nobody on hand to take the pictures.

"I meant one of your other jobs," she said.

"Well, I didn't think I'd bother today. I earned fifty bucks last night."

"You make sure Greg gives you the whole fifty, Chip. Sometimes he tries to chisel people."

"He already tried."

"Well, you get the whole fifty. You worked for it."

"Yeah."

I wanted to reach for her but I didn't quite know how to go about it. You can't imagine how goddamned awkward the whole thing was. I mean, here we had gotten in this wild tangle the night before, with results that I told you about in probably too much detail already, so we won't go into that all over again, and now here it was morning and she was in the kitchen, wearing an apron and rinsing out coffee cups, and her whole attitude left me feeling that last night had never happened, that it was another dream of mine and when I woke up I would have a damp sticky sock in the bed with me. I mean, I knew it wasn't a dream, but it might as well have been.

"Chip?"

"What?"

"Are you angry with me?"

I looked at her. "Why should I be?"

"Because I teased you last night."

"Well, I knew what I was getting into."

"What you weren't getting into, you mean."

"Well."

"You're not angry?"

"No."

"I'm glad." She grinned quickly. "Because I like you a lot, Chip."

This time I did reach for her, and she moved her head aside, and I missed. I suppose practically any woman can make practically any man feel like an idiot, but it seemed to me that either she was particularly good at it or that I was particularly inept.

She said, "Last night was business, Chip."

"Yeah, sure."

"I'm not going to say I didn't enjoy it."

"You enjoyed it, huh?"

"Why, of course I did. I don't think there's anything wrong with enjoying your work, do you?"

"I guess not."

"I should certainly hope not." She put the dish towel on the drainboard and walked past me to the living room. There wasn't an abundance of room in the kitchen, and she managed to brush against me pretty good on the way, giving me the full treatment with that round rear end of hers. She got to me, all right. I suppose I'm pretty easy to get to, generally speaking, but old Aileen had a real knack for it as far as I was concerned.

I followed her into the living room. She went around straightening things up and emptying ashtrays, talking as she went. "There's nothing wrong with enjoying any kind of work," she went on. "I wouldn't pose for those pictures if I didn't get a certain amount of kick out of it. I like to think of all those people looking at pictures of me and getting excited. Sometimes I stop and think that there are men all over the country looking at naked pictures of me and playing with themselves. Having sex with me in their minds. And couples looking at different pictures of me, either alone or with someone, and getting so hot and bothered that they want to make love. When I think about that sort of thing I get a very strange feeling."

"Sure," I said.

She put an ashtray back on a tabletop and turned to look at me. "Just think of all the people who will look at those pictures of the two of us," she said.

"Yeah."

"Do you like the idea?"

"I don't know. I got bothered by that before. I mean, I thought somebody might recognize me, but than I thought that I didn't have anybody to care one way or the other. If some jerk I went to some school with saw it, well, what do I care? You know, let him envy me, let him eat his heart out. If I had any family it might be different, I guess."

"Poor baby. All alone in the world."

"Don't call me that."

"I called you that last night."

"I know."

She crossed to the television set, switched it on, collapsed neatly on the couch. My couch. She patted the cushion next to her, and I remembered how she had given the same invitational pat to the green couch in the studio last night. I felt lightheaded and shaky.

I pretended not to notice the invitation. "I think I'll have another cup of coffee," I told her. "You want one?"

"I'll make them."

"No, stay there," I said. "I, uh, I need the exercise."

She was still sitting in the same spot when I brought back the two cups of coffee. She said, "You know, Chip, that was fun last night."

"Here's your coffee."

"For you, too." She put the cup down on the coffee table next to mine. "We could have a lot of fun, you know. There are lots of times like this morning when Gregor is out and I'm home all alone. If you didn't try to force things, we could have a real good time."

"What kind of a real good time?"

"Like last night. Except without anybody watching or snapping pictures."

"And without finishing what we started."

She raised her eyebrows. "You finished, didn't you? I spent half an hour wiping the floor. If that wasn't what you would call finishing—"

"You know what I mean."

She put her hand on my cheek. "Didn't you get your kicks last night, baby?"

"I wanted to do it the right way."

"There's no right way, honey. Sex may be a game but there's no yo-yo keeping score. Whatever turns you on, that's the right way."

"I never got laid in my life, Aileen."

I turned away as I said this. I felt excited and happy and miserable all at the same time, and all tied in knots. She had my hand in both of hers and was petting it.

"I know that, Chip."

"It's pretty obvious, huh?"

"Well, reading between the lines of what you said. It's a big thing for you, huh? Being all hung up about being a virgin."

I nodded.

"Being a virgin, you know, it's something everybody is and something everybody gets over sooner or later. Even I was a virgin once. You may find that hard to believe—"

"Cut it out, will you?"

"Hey." I turned and looked at her. She gave me the wise grin, and some of the tension went out of me. "Now listen a minute, baby," she said. "We can have a little fun, if you want, or we can just let it stay nice and loose between us, if you'd rather have it that way, but one thing not to do is be so serious about everything, because that's nothing but a big bringdown."

I nodded again. "But why can't we—"

"Because we can't. Because that's where I draw the line. That's for Greg and nobody else. Look, if all you want to do is stick it in, you can go out and find a pro. You're getting fifty dollars from Greg. You're a rich man. If you want to just get on top of some syphilitic pig and get rid of your precious cherry, all you have to do—"

"You know what I want."

"Uh-huh, baby, but I also know what *I* want. And that's some nice tender sweetness from my baby, and you don't have to worry, I won't tease, I won't leave you frustrated. You'll come, honey, and so will I, and it'll be very nice, just leave everything to me."

"I don't know what to say."

"What's to say?" She laughed deep in her throat. "Come here," she said. "Do something brilliant, like kissing me."

Do you have any idea how many ways there are to do it without really doing it?

Neither did I.

There's just no end to the possibilities. There were just three rules to the game—or one rule, actually, that closed three doors to me. What it boiled down to, really, was that I couldn't enter her. (With what she still liked to call my hard core, that is. Other things, yes.) I guess there's precedent for this. In the legal definitions of rape and sodomy and other nice things like that, the dividing line is that same line Aileen used. Penetration. If you don't get in, the argument goes, then you haven't really Done Anything Wrong.

We didn't Do Anything Wrong.

But we did just about everything else.

You know something? I've thought about it, and I've come to the conclusion that if only I hadn't been a virgin at the time, I would have been the happiest man on earth. Because from a physical standpoint there was nothing frustrating about the relationship we had. I was getting there, and not in the therapeutic massage way I had made it in the photo studio, either. We weren't playing that little game at all. It had been strictly for Gregor's benefit, and now that we were on our own, we didn't try to hide the fact that the name of the game was Getting Kicks.

Sometimes we spent five or six hours in a row on that couch, and by the time we stopped I had made it so many times that I didn't have the strength to lift a finger, let alone my unhard core. So in simple terms of the amount of sex I was getting I was in the class of a man on a honeymoon with a nymphomaniac, for Pete's sake.

So in that sense it was really great. The more I got the more I wanted, and the more I wanted the more I got, and it looked as though it could just go on that way forever and it would keep getting better all the time.

Here's a comparison that you might want to pass up if you're very heavy on religion. Not to offend anybody, but I think it fits. It was like being Adam and Eve in the Garden of Eden, with Paradise there, just everything you could want all spread out for you, except for these two trees that you couldn't go near. You could eat anything else in the world but the fruit of the Tree of Life and the Tree of Knowledge, so naturally what did you want? Right the first time. Well, so did I. The fruit was a cherry instead of an apple, and I wanted to get rid of it, not take a bite out of it, but otherwise it added up to about the same thing.

(Incidentally, suppose Adam and Eve ate from the Tree of Life instead of the Tree of Knowledge. Or from both of them. They'd still be alive, and the earth would be up to its neck in people. That doesn't have anything to do with anything else, but it's been bothering me ever since I was a little kid so I thought I would put it in. I'm supposed to be writing this straightforward, keeping to the subject and everything, but I was also told that the book ought to let the reader know how I feel about things and the kind of person I am, and frankly I think if I have to just tell everything absolutely cold and straight without putting down other things that come into my head while I'm sitting here, then the book might as well have been written by a machine. When I read a book I like to have the feeling that a real human being actually sat down and wrote it, and that reading it will let me know something about him. Some books give you the feeling that the sheets of paper came out of the paper mill with the words already on them, for Pete's sake. Untouched by human hands, like the plastic food in turnpike restaurants.)

Well, to get back to what I was saying, if you're still with me, I sort of wish I could have rearranged my schedule so that I could have met Aileen five years later in life. That would have been perfect, I think. By then I would be twenty-two and years past being a virgin, but still young enough so that she would be the older woman showing me new ways to be the happiest kid on the block.

As it was, maybe I should have gone out and spent my fifty dollars (Gregor paid off in full, although he did make a halfhearted effort to make me settle for forty) on some professional prostitute. If I just could have crossed that barrier I would have stopped brooding about it. Or maybe I wouldn't. I guess not, really. I guess it would be impossible for anyone in his right or wrong mind not to want to ball that woman in every way there was.

I got to Chicago in late February, I was at the Eagle Hotel for about two weeks, I moved in with Gregor and Aileen about three weeks before we had the picture-taking session, and it was Memorial Day weekend when I got out of there. I just worked it all out with paper and pencil to save you the trouble, assuming you're interested, and the way I figure it there was a stretch of about six weeks between the night we took the pictures and the morning I left Chicago.

When I think back on it, sometimes it seems as though it couldn't possibly have been that long, and other times it seems as though it must have been closer to six months. They were six fantastic weeks no matter how you look at it. In all that time we never once crossed any of the cruddy lines she had drawn, and Gregor never got any idea of what was going on, and I don't think we once went as much as thirty hours in a row without having a shot at it. It wasn't always a five-hour stretch on the couch (although that happened plenty of the time) and sometimes it was just a fast fingering at the kitchen sink or a quick hand job at the breakfast table. But it was as steady as a pension from the Federal Government.

I remember one night when she slipped out of the bedroom after Gregor had zonked out. She did this quite a few times, and since she and Gregor generally knocked one off before going to sleep, the goods I was getting wasn't exactly untouched by human hands. Sloppy seconds, I think they call it. (Not really sloppy, because she would wash up first, but even so it used to bother me. At first, that is. You might be amazed the way a person can get used to things, and can stop being bothered by things that used to bother him.)

This one particular night a couple of winks and hand signals during the late movie had given me the message that I could expect company. So I was waiting for her from the minute she and Gregor closed their bedroom door, and the sound of their bedsprings was background music while I thought of all the things I wanted to do to Aileen. I was developing a pretty wicked imagination along those lines.

Then the door finally opened, and she tiptoed across to the bathroom, and I heard water running. And then she tiptoed some more, from the bathroom across the floor to the couch.

I pretended to be sleeping. We both knew it was a pretty transparent act, but she liked to find ways to wake me up. She kept finding ways, and they always worked.

I'll bet she could do the Indian rope trick just by touching the rope with those hands of hers.

Well, not to go off on tangents, I woke up, and she got on the couch with me, and we did things. Between her thighs, or under her arm, or in her hands, or between her breasts, or in the cleft of her buttocks, or—well, you name it. We made it, and I stretched out, and she curled up in my arms, and I felt like the King of the World.

"Oh, baby," she said. "You're so good for me."

I said, "Purr." Or something along those lines.

"You know what? I feel like a girl."

"You sure do."

"I'm serious."

I ran a hand over her. "You feel like a girl, all right. I'm glad, too, you know. I don't think I'd get as much of a kick out of all of this if you felt like a boy. I like these, see, and this, and—"

And a little later, when we came up for a breath of fresh air:

"Hey, I meant it before, clown. You make me feel like a girl again."

"You're not so old."

"Thanks a bunch."

"You're not that much older than I am, for Pete's sake. You do this mother bit all the time, but you're not exactly in the category of an antique."

"Keep saying it, baby."

"How old are you, anyway?"

"A hundred and ten."

"Shit."

"You know why you make me feel so young? Hey, that's a song. No, it's because of what we do. Necking and petting and fooling around like a couple of kids. It takes me back to when I was, you know, younger. And a virgin."

"I didn't know you ever were."

"Don't be a sharp-tongued son of a bitch, Chip. Your boyish charm is your biggest asset. Don't piss it away."

"I'll bear that in mind."

"Please do." She put her hand between my legs and gave me a reassuring pat. "Yeah, I was a virgin once upon a time. Isn't that remarkable? And when I'm with you I'm a virgin all over again, and the whole sex business is, I don't know, cleaner and hungrier and hornier and everything rolled into one. It takes me back, it really does."

"Being in bed with me."

"Uh-huh."

"Sort of like hearing an old song on the radio that was popular when you were a kid. An oldie but goodie."

I couldn't see her face in the dark, but I guess she raised her eyebrows at that one. She had that tone in her voice, saying, "You making fun of me, Chip?"

"No."

"I think you were, a least a little, maybe. Yeah, like hearing an old song, in a kind of way. The way a song or anything like that makes you feel the way you used to. Sometimes I'll walk outside during the late summer when there's a wet wind blowing off the lake, on like a really warm lazy night, and I'll walk around the block or something and the air will be the way it is in Florida. Just the right temperature and humidity, I suppose. What's the word? Sultry? But before this can even go through my mind, I'll get this feeling of being seventeen years old again, because I spent a summer in Florida when I was seventeen."

"You were in Florida? I thought you were always in Chicago."

"Oh, I would travel from time to time."

"What were you doing in Florida?"

"Fucking."

"That was a straight question."

"Well, it was a straight answer, honey bunch."

"At seventeen? I guess I'm retarded."

"Worry about it, why don't you?"

"I do, I do. When did you start?"

"Huh?"

"When did you start making love?"

"What are you, Mr. District Attorney? I never started. I'm a virgin, baby doll. Handle me with care." And, huskily, "If we keep on talking we'll wake Greg, and he might take a dim view of this. So let's not talk any more.

Why don't I just lie here and you can lick different parts of me and see whether or not I like it? Sort of what you might call a scientific experiment."

(I was just thinking, looking at the last part, that I'll bet it's word for word the way that conversation actually went. Obviously, since I'm putting all of this on paper after it happened, I'm just getting the dialogue as close as possible to the way it happened. I didn't wander through life with a tape recorder hanging around my neck, and I'm not the total recall type. I'm not absolutely convinced *anybody* is, and there are times when I think people who pretend to be are full of crap. But this one conversation stuck in my mind very vividly. I can hear her speaking the words even now, as if I were playing myself a record of the conversation.

(I guess that's because I thought about it so many times since then. And it struck me, and strikes me now, that it was a strange combination of games that Aileen was playing. First there was the bit about feeling like a girl, a virgin. And at the same time she kept coming on with the older-but-wiser routine and a heavy dose of the mother image. I couldn't understand how she could be a virgin and a mother at the same time. As far as I know, that only happened once.)

During the six weeks of trading orgasms with Aileen, her genius of a husband never suspected a thing. I'm just about a hundred percent certain of that. I went on working with him, and I saw him at meals and during the evening, and neither of us acted any differently toward one another than we did before. I had thought for a while that I would be eaten up with guilt over what I was doing with Aileen. No such thing. It may be that I'm just not the type for guilt, that I'm of such low moral character that I can live under a man's roof and take his money and share his bread and not feel bad about taking his beloved wife to bed. I think, though, that there's more to it than that.

After all, I wasn't doing a thing to Aileen behind his back that I hadn't done to her right in front of him, with his approval. (Well, that's pushing it, I guess; we did enlarge our bag of tricks, after all, and we went at them with a hell of a lot more enthusiasm. But you get the idea.) And she was still being faithful to him as far as their joint idea of fidelity was concerned. And, more than anything else, I knew damned well that I wasn't taking anything away from Gregor. Just by listening to the creak of his bedsprings I could tell he was getting all the use he wanted out of Aileen.

I was like a conscientious kid with the family car. I never used it when the old man wanted it, and I always brought it home in as good condition as I took it out, with gas in the tank and air in the tires.

I suppose it must go without saying that I stopped picking up odd jobs on the days when Gregor didn't need me. When it came to a choice between slipping cents-off coupons under doors or slipping fingers into Aileen, it was the world's easiest decision for me to make.

I also stopped helping out in the darkroom. I think Gregor was surprised, but I let him get the impression that I was losing interest in photography as a lifetime career. Since he didn't pay me for help, he couldn't really bitch about it very strenuously.

I had never gotten around to finding out about getting my diploma by going to night school, and of course I couldn't really do anything about it at that time of the year, it being the middle of the term, but I had planned to find out what I had to find out and write away to Upper Valley for transcripts of my record so that I could start taking courses during the summer session. I didn't bother doing any of this, and when I thought about night school at all, I more or less thought in terms of starting in the fall instead of rushing things.

And I stopped going to the library as often as I had, and I stopped wandering around Chicago looking for women, and what it came down to, really, is that if I wasn't working or sleeping or sitting around with Gregor and Aileen, then I was in bed with her. Those were just about the only four choices during that period of time.

I spent some money on clothes, and I bought things like

new shoelaces and a nail file and like that, but even without working the other jobs I was saving money. I would earn between forty and fifty a week helping Gregor, and my room and board cost me twenty, and I still didn't eat lunch, and it wasn't at all hard to save fifteen or twenty dollars out of each week's earnings, especially because I never left the house unless I had to. There was really no way for me to spend money, so I saved it.

This meant that by the end of May I had almost two hundred dollars, including the fifty for the modeling session. And because the money was accumulating with no strain at all I had the feeling that I was really getting somewhere and really making the kind of progress I had sworn I would make that first night at the Eagle Hotel.

When I think back on it now I wonder if maybe all of that sex was rotting my brain, because if there was one thing I wasn't doing, it was getting ahead in the world. Not in any way at all. I mean, a good long look at the pattern my life had taken would make Horatio Alger throw up.

Instead of a job with a future, I was, let's face it, working as sidekick to the world's most pathetic photographer. That's what he was, really. Taking candid pictures of morons on State Street and every few months making a big score by selling dirty pictures of his wife. And the dumbest part of it was that he worked harder for less money than if he'd been swinging a pick on a road gang, for Pete's sake. He took risks and put in long hours on his feet and just took nickels and dimes out of the street photography business. The dirty pictures made his real income, and he would have to space out the cash over a period of several months until Mark called him up and asked for more.

Now and then I wondered why he didn't go into the dirty picture business in a bigger way, hiring a variety of models and finding a way to distribute the pictures and making some real money. Not that I think being a pornographer is the best way to sail through life, but if you're going to be one anyway, why not be a successful one? It seems to me that if a girl is going to be a whore, she might as well be an expensive one. Right? So if Gregor had been the Kingpin of Filth in Chicago, or if he at least *tried* to be the Kingpin, I would have respected him. Or if he was a complete bum who just tried to coast along on the least possible amount of work, that would have at least made sense. But he wasn't lazy and he wasn't ambitious either, and this was the guy I was working for, this was the man teaching me his trade.

I mean, how stupid can you be?

I had wanted to save money, and I was saving it, but I was making, say, fifty dollars a week and saving twenty, and at the rate I was going, in twenty years I would still be making fifty a week and still saving twenty, and if you save twenty dollars a week, it will take you approximately a thousand years of steady work to save a million dollars.

(This is figured without what the savings-bank ads call The Miracle Of Compound Interest. According to them, if you put your money in a savings account you can't help winding up rich. I remember seeing a billboard telling what Washington's silver dollar would be worth today if he had put it in the bank. The figure was something ridiculously high, so I got a book from the library on coin collecting to find out what the same dollar would have been worth if Washington had *kept* it, and it turned out he would have been better off. But for all the good it did Washington he was even better off throwing it across the river. Or in it. So much for The Miracle Of Compound Interest.)

The thing is, I wasn't making real progress, and I wasn't looking for a real opportunity. And it was the same with my sex life, if you stopped to think about it, which most of the time I didn't. Because while I was having all this pleasure I was still as much a virgin as ever, and I wasn't coming any closer to not being a virgin. In fact I was actually locking myself out of any chance of losing my virginity, the same way I was keeping myself from any chance of getting a job with a future. See, I was getting satisfied with what I had with Aileen, and in the same way I was getting satisfied with that stupid job and everything else.

That was one thing about the kids in the Horatio Alger books. They were never satisfied. No matter how well things started shaping up, they had the decency to go on wanting more and more and more. So they kept pushing, and whenever opportunity knocked they ran to the door and answered it. If opportunity knocked on my door I never would have heard it because I would have been too busy putting blurry yellow cards in people's hands or putting my own blurry little hands on Aileen.

Not that I had these thoughts all the time. That was the worst of it—that I didn't. That I was content with the way things were going. Take a man who is content with what he does and the way he lives and what have you got?

A happy man, obviously.

But that's not exactly right, either, because I wasn't really contented, because I didn't have what I wanted. I was settling for less, that's what I was doing. I was having little off-in-left-field climaxes with Aileen when what I really wanted to do was slide into home plate. I was getting by in a dumb job when I really wanted to get ahead. And no matter how comfortable that couch was when Aileen was on it with me, and no matter how often that happened, sooner or later I would have to be bothered by the way things were going.

On Memorial Day, a veteran sold me a poppy. He stuck that poppy into my hand just as neatly as I had learned to stick the yellow cards into the jerks' hands, and I took it like any other jerk, only I couldn't just drop it on the ground and keep walking. Or maybe I could have done this, but then he would have been within his rights if he brained me with his crutch. I gave him a quarter and he said something about the Last Of The Big Spenders. I stuck the stupid poppy in my buttonhole. That way at least I didn't have to buy another one.

But when I walked another block, it hit me that I was more a cripple than the guy who sold me the poppy. I don't know how I made the connection. It came in one quick flash and once I had it I couldn't let go of it. I kept seeing myself with a leg missing, lurching through life like that.

And I couldn't stick around with an image like that in my mind.

I waited until the weekend was over. The Sunday paper was filled with want ads, and I bought it and sat in a diner and went through it, and I found what I wanted. It wasn't a job with a future, either, but it was one that would take me out of Chicago, and I had enough sense to know that I couldn't stay in Chicago if I wanted to get out of the tender trap I was in. I had to travel, and then I could concentrate on Getting Ahead and all the rest of it.

Monday was a work day, but I took a long lunch hour, and during that lunch hour I went over and applied for the job. And got it. (No big deal—you had to have two heads or something for them to turn you down. They were easier to get into than the Army. More later.)

And Monday night, after old Gregor went night-night, I did everything possible to score with Aileen. I tried to break those silly rules of hers and get something straight between us once and for all, and as usual it didn't work. I had more or less fixed up a game in my mind, making a bargain with myself that if I laid her I would stay in Chicago but if I didn't I would go. I gave it the old Upper Valley try and when it didn't work I took Aileen's motherly advice to behave myself and be a good boy and make sweet love with her. I got on top of her and rubbed the two of us together in a way we had both grown to enjoy no end. I made sweet love all over her stomach and she danced off to wash away the sweet love I had made, and she pecked my cheek and told me I was her sweet baby and to sleep tight, and she went into her bedroom and got back in bed with the State Street Shutterbug.

I got dressed in the dark and put my extra clothes and stuff in a paper bag. I thought about leaving a note, but I couldn't think of anything that wasn't either hopelessly corny or slightly nasty, and I didn't want to be either. I told myself I would write her a letter someday. You can tell yourself things like that as often as you want and it doesn't cost you a thing.

I sat up all night in different crummy diners, drinking so much coffee that I kept shaking and peeing and shaking and peeing. I was downtown in plenty of time to catch my ride in the morning, and when our car left the city limits of Chicago it wasn't even noon yet.

So that was three months, and my $27.46 had turned into $191.80, which is better than it could have done through The Miracle Of Compound Interest. And I had spent more time on third base than Ron Santo.

That toddling town.

CHAPTER SIX

WHEN I RANG THE DOORBELL, THE CHIMES played the first two bars of a hymn. I couldn't tell you which one. I stood there patiently, wanting to ring it again but holding off, and eventually I heard the pitter-patter of little old feet. I timed myself so that I was whipping off my little blue-visored cap just as she was opening the door.

She wasn't the girl of my dreams. When you are young enough and horny enough (like I, Chip Harrison, for instance) you can't even open a Coke bottle without hoping there will be a beautiful girl in it. And on this job I kept waiting for the time one of the doors would be opened by a Neglected Young Housewife, or a Wanton Suburban College Girl Home From School, or an Off-Duty Whore. And instead the doors kept being opened by women who stopped thinking about sex the day Hayes beat Tilden.

This one must have gone to school with Tilden's grandmother, from the looks of her. She was a tiny wrinkled little lady with bright eyes the color of frostbitten lips. Her face cracked into a smile.

She looked up at me and said, "Yes, young man? You've come for the bake sale donation, haven't you?"

I said I was afraid I hadn't, and I went into a little explanation of who I was and why I had turned up on her doorstep. While I talked I held my cap in both hands and squeezed it in and out of shape. I didn't do this because I was nervous. That's just the way it was supposed to look, because according to old Flickinger the more nervous and earnest you seemed the more trustworthy you were, at least as far as old ladies were concerned.

It was hard to look nervous without doing the little bit of business with the cap, because I actually delivered my set piece without even paying attention to what I was saying. I might as well have been a record player. While my mouth got all the words out, my mind thought about how little this woman had in common with the girl of my dreams, and that I might have guessed as much, because nymphomaniacs don't go out of their way to have chimes that play hymns—at least most of them don't—and while I didn't recognize that tune, it certainly wasn't "Roll Me Over in the Clover."

"—free inspection with no obligation whatsoever," I finished up, and gave my cap a final twist, and hung my head just the littlest bit, because you couldn't go overboard and look too pathetic or you got tons of warm milk and cookies shoved down your throat.

"*Rowrbazzle*," she said.

That seemed like a funny thing for anybody to say, let alone Tilden's grandmother here, but then of course I saw that she wasn't the one who said it. It was her cat. He was standing next to her, and he was as big for a cat as she was small for an old lady. He was built like a Siamese, with a blackish-brown coat and horrible yellow eyes. I always liked cats, but then they had always said sensible things like *Meow*. This was the first one that had ever said anything like *Rowrbazzle* within my hearing and I wasn't sure just how I felt about it. It put me off stride a little, if you really want to know.

"Now just one moment, young man," she said. The woman this time. "You wait right here, and I won't be a minute. You wait now."

I waited. So did the cat. Now would have been a good time for me to step inside and let the screen door close behind me, which was the recommended procedure at this stage of the game. Whoever had worked up the recommended procedure had never met a cat that said *Rowrbazzle*. I stayed where I was, and old Rowrbazzle stayed where he was, and the screen door was the Demilitarized Zone.

Then the old lady came back, and I slapped my smile back in place and whipped off my cap again, and then I noticed what she had in both her little liver-spotted hands.

What she had was an old dueling pistol that was almost as big as her dippy old cat. Her hands were shaking, and the pistol was bobbing up and down like a red red robin, and it was pointing at me, and it looked as though it might go off at any moment.

I said, "Hey! Hey, hang on a minute!"

"This weapon is loaded and primed, young man."

"I believe it."

"And let me assure you that it works perfectly well. It is old, but age is not always detrimental. This pistol is in full possession of its faculties."

I was sure it was. I was perfectly willing to believe that it was still every bit as good as it was the day Aaron Burr shot Alexander Hamilton with it.

"You don't understand," I said.

"You will leave this block of houses at once, young man. You will leave directly. The people on this block are all good Christians."

"You don't under—"

"Except for the young woman in Number One-twenty-one," she said her voice quavering. "She is a Methodist, and I believe her husband is a wine drinker or worse. You may stop there if you wish. I would not advise it. Last September a boy a bit older than you examined that young woman's furnace and took it all apart and refused to repair it unless he was paid. I doubt she'd let you into her house after an experience of that sort, but you may try if you wish. I've enough on my mind without protecting Methodists, and them wine drinkers in the bargain. Not that I know for a fact that she drinks with him, but they flock together, you know. And I thought you had come about the bake sale. You have an innocent face in sheep's clothing. Read the Book of Ezekiel."

"*Rowrbazzle.*"

"Calvin dislikes you, young man. Our animals can sense things which we can only discover through reasoning. I am going to count ten, and if you are not off my property by the time I reach ten, I will shoot you. I do not hold with violence, but the Lord protects those who look to their own protection. Read the third chapter of the Second Samuel. One. Two. Three. Four—"

I scrambled down the porch steps and between two rows of private hedge to the street, expecting a musket ball to come tearing into me at any moment. The only reason it didn't was that I was well out of the way before her tinny old voice got to ten. Otherwise she would have shot me. No question about it, she would have blown my god-damned head off without thinking twice about it. If Calvin said *Rowrbazzle* to you, you just didn't stand a chance around there.

I passed up all the houses on that block. Even the lady in Number 121, the Methodist. I didn't care if she was a Sun Worshipper. I wasn't taking any chances.

Around the corner I almost collided with Jimmy Joe. He started to tell me he had just written out an order, but I cut in and told him about Calvin and *Rowrbazzle* and Grandma Tilden. "Oh, that's nothing," he said airily. "I've had more guns pointed at me than fingers. They never shoot."

"This one would have."

"Ninty-nine times out of a hundred the guns aren't even loaded. These people keep unloaded guns around just to put guys like you and me uptight. And the average person, especially a lady, they couldn't hit a barn from inside of it."

"This gun was loaded, and she would have shot, and she wouldn't have missed."

"Yeah, sure. Prove it."

"Okay," I said. I was still having trouble catching my breath. "Okay, smart ass. You go up on the porch and give her a pitch and see if she shoots you or not. I'll bet you ten bucks you get shot."

"It's a sucker bet for you. If she shoots me, how do you collect?"

"I'll take my chances."

He laughed. When he did this, it always reminded me of a big old boxer who belonged to one of the masters at a school I went to in Connecticut. That dog barked just about like that. "Forget it," Jimmy Joe said. "The important question is did she call the cops."

"I don't think she would. Never even threatened to. She's the vigilante type."

"That's all to the good."

"But I'm not supposed to go on that block because of all the God-fearing Christians. And one Methodist."

"Methodists are Christians."

"You want to go tell her? If Flick wants me I'll be working the next block over."

"They're all new houses."

"How's the one after that?"

"Better."

"Then that's where I'll be. Luck."

"Up yours," he agreed. "And watch out for the Christians."

"Right, and you watch out for the Lions."

I didn't meet any more old ladies with dueling pistols that afternoon, or any cats named Calvin with weird vocabularies. I did meet a whole lot of people who had no trouble closing the door in the middle of my pitch.

I had always thought that was about the most aggravating thing that could happen to someone working door to door, getting a door slammed in your face. It can be sort of jarring the first couple dozen times it happens, but I'll tell you something, once you get used to it you learn to welcome it. Not that you set out looking to get doors closed on you, but if you're going to strike out anyway, which is going to happen ninety-nine times out of a hundred to the greatest salesman who ever lived, you might as well strike out as soon as possible. The less time you waste on the stiffs, the more calls you can make in a given period of time. And the more calls you make, the more sales you make, and that's gospel. Old Flickinger says he'd rather have a chimpanzee who makes a hundred calls a day than a genius who makes fifty. Good old Flick.

"I been on the road for thirty years and more, kid, and if I learned one thing it's you don't lose money by ringing doorbells. And if there's one word of advice I can give you it's never get into any woman's pants without she signs on the dotted line. Once you got the order written it's another story. With the sale made you can afford half an hour in the kip, even an hour if you like the broad's style. But without you get the order there's no percentage. You just waste time you can't afford, and then all she wants to do is get you out of there without she buys anything, or else she keeps you around and gives you coffee and dangles it in front of you that maybe she'll buy, and you wind up going another round in the kip, and you waste the whole fucking afternoon without you get any order at all. Now maybe you'll give her a kiss or a feel to set up a sale, on the lines of what you might call a free sample, but that's all. If there's one word of advice I can give you that's it."

Good old Flick. The first time I heard that little speech I saw myself giving in gracefully to one woman after the next, and doing so well in bed with them that I got order after order, and— Well, there's no big suspense to keep up, since Francine wasn't in the picture yet and you know I was still as pure as Ivory Soap when I met her, so let's just say that it wasn't like that at all in the door-to-door game, at least not for me, and while Flick's advice might have been sound I wasn't getting a chance to put it into practice.

As I said, I got doors closed in my face, and I also got the usual percentage of dimwits who felt sorry enough for me to let me give them the whole speech, but who didn't feel sorry enough for me to let me sell them anything. And then just before it was time to quit I hooked a gray-haired lady who lived all alone in a Victorian house that must have had a hundred rooms in it. She had a cat, but it said what any normal cat says. She said its name was Featherfoot, and that it was a boy but she had had it fixed. She said it so daintily that I almost asked what had been wrong with it. She also had had it declawed so it wouldn't ruin the furniture. She might have gone all the way and had it stuffed so that it wouldn't go to the bathroom and to cut down on the cost of feeding it. If I ever have a cat, which I probably won't, since it's hard enough to keep myself in sardines, let alone two of us, I would let it keep its claws and its balls intact. I mean, if you don't want the complete animal, I don't think you should have any of it. I mean, how would you like it if you were a cat and they did *that* to you?

That's getting off the subject, but so did this old lady. She went on and on about one thing or another. She had lost her husband a year ago, she told me. I was sort of listening to every third word out of her mouth, so I thought at first that she must have lost him in one of the hundred rooms in that old barn. But of course she meant he was dead. I hate people who don't like to say certain words, so they say that the cat is fixed when they mean castrated, or that their husband is lost when they mean he's dead as a doornail.

She kept on talking, and I went around the house on a tour of inspection, and she droned on about how much trouble there was in keeping up a house when you were a woman all alone in the world. I knew I had her then. I worked my way around the back of the house until I found a spot where there were traces of sawdust on the concrete, and I whipped out my magnifying glass and made clucking noises.

"Oh, dear," she said. "Oh, land's sake."

I pointed to the sawdust. "See that?" I said.

She saw it and started apologizing for never having noticed it before. I developed a sudden thirst and asked

her if she thought I might be able to have a glass of water.
When she came back with the water, I showed her a test
tube half full of the little rascals. She almost spilled the
water.

"Oh, dear. And you captured all of them while I was in
the house?"

"That's right. There are some of the ones I missed. See,
there they go."

She looked, *tsstssing* unhappily as the little devils scurried madly over the clapboard siding. That was always the
real convincer. Even the most gullible person could look
at the ones in the test tube and still figure his house was
safe. There was always the hope in their minds that I had
picked up the last of them. And the suspicious ones might
point out that I could have brought the test tube along
with me. But when they saw those termites actually burrowing into their own house it got them where they lived.
No joke, it really did.

We went in the house and I filled out the service
agreement and got her to sign it. She didn't even ask what
the job was going to cost until after I had the agreement
folded and tucked away. I said that the price would
depend upon the extent of infestation, and that our costs
were nominal, and that all our work was guaranteed. This
didn't answer her question but she didn't ask again, so I
guess she thought she was satisfied.

Before I could get out of there she asked to see the
termites again. I gave her the tube. "Nasty nasty vicious
things," she said, with all the hate in the world in her
voice. And wouldn't you know that she insisted on taking
the tube outside and spilling the devils out onto the sidewalk and then divebombing the living shit out of them
with a can of spray insect killer. "Die die die," she said,
and the poor little critters curled up and did just that.

It was a nuisance, but no real harm done. Flickinger
had a five-gallon pickle jug swarming with the little
bastards, and it wasn't that much trouble to get a tubeful
of them. A pain in the neck, that's all.

That night I sat around the motel after I refilled the test

tube. Jimmy Joe and Keegan were at a movie I hadn't wanted to see. Lester went off without saying where, probably to look for queers at the bus station. He liked girls and his suitcase was half full of pictures of naked women, but queers were always easier to find, even in the fifth largest city in Indiana, which is where we happened to be just then. You could jump off the top of the tallest building in the fifth largest city in Indiana without doing much more than spraining your ankle, but for our crew this was considered a pretty big city. We worked towns you honestly wouldn't believe. We went all through Illinois and Indiana, and sometimes the towns were so small that Lester had to find himself the one queer in the town, or what you might call the town's faggot in residence. But he always seemed to connect.

The reason I could tolerate old Lester was that he had a reasonable attitude about what he did. He didn't run on and on about it and he didn't bug you with a lot of details you'd be a lot happier not knowing, but at the same time he wasn't one of those nerds who did it on the sly, like my old roommate Haskell who tried to pretend his cock and his hand had never even been introduced to one another, for Pete's sake. If you asked him a question he'd answer it, but if you left it alone he'd keep quiet. This made him relatively easy to take.

As far as Lester was concerned there was nothing revolting about going with a queer. The only thing shameful about it was that it would be a lot better and more satisfying with a girl. But he didn't figure it made him queer to be with a queer. Not that Lester is the first person on earth to ever come up with this line of thought. But it seems to me, if you happen to care, that when two men had sex together they were both queer and it didn't make a hell of a difference which one was down on his knees. It wasn't as though Lester was just phoning in his part of the deal. But whether you wanted to consider him queer or not (and if you did it wasn't a good idea to tell him about it), I got along fine with him.

See, that's one of the fringe benefits of selling termite

extermination service door to door. You become very tolerant of people.

Anyhow, I was less interested in accompanying Lester to the bus station than in seeing the movie with Keegan and Jimmy Joe. There was one other member of the crew, a recently divorced ex-Marine named Solly, who was inclined to have much better luck with women than the rest of us. He was having some of that luck right now in his motel room. And Flickinger, the crew leader, was doing what he always did after sunset. What he did involved a bottle and a glass. He never minded company, but if you were going to sit with him he expected you to drink with him, and even without trying to match him shot for shot I was in big trouble, because if I took a short drink for every three long ones of his I would still be drunk in an hour and sick for the next day and a half. One drink of Gregor's lousy brandy was all right, but I wasn't ready to handle anything like a whole night of serious drinking.

Besides, as I discovered the second of the two times I had kept Flick company, he never remembered in the morning just what he had said the night before. He never said anything particularly weird either of the times I was with him, and he behaved the same as he did when he was cold sober—he never took a drink before the sun went down, or passed one up after it did—but the thing of it was that he wouldn't know one night that he had told you certain stories on an earlier night, and anecdotes that are fairly lively the first time around get a little stale the second time.

And if you tried to tell Flick that you'd heard such and such a story before he argued with you.

So I didn't go to Flick's room, and of course I didn't go to Solly's room, and the other three guys were out somewhere, and I didn't have anything to read, and Flick owned the only car and had let Jimmy Joe and Keegan borrow it, which didn't really enter into it since I couldn't drive anyway. Well, I mean I know how, but they get agitated if they catch you driving without a license, and I never got one.

So there was nothing to do and no place to go, and that gave this particular evening a whole lot in common with most of the evenings I'd spent since I left Chicago.

Unless you happened to work on one of those traveling sales crews, you probably don't know what they're like. I didn't have the faintest idea myself until I was actually hired and on the job. The arrangement was simple enough. The crew consisted of five guys anywhere from eighteen on up (well, I lied) and a crew leader. You would be assigned a certain territory, which in our case was eastern Illinois and western Indiana, and within that territory you would go wherever the crew boss decided and stay as long as it was worthwhile. The crew leader took care of all your regular expenses—hotel, meals, car expenses, and so on—and got reimbursed by the company.

For every sale you made, the salesman got twenty-five dollars and the crew leader got fifteen. The crew leader did his own selling too and got to keep the whole forty bucks on his own sales. (Flick's percentage was officially a secret, but it was one of the first things he told you when he sat drinking with you.)

The point is that if you made a sale you wound up with twenty-five bucks free and clear, since you didn't have any living expenses at all. If you sold one lousy exterminating job a day, you could salt away better than five hundred dollars a month. And on the other hand if you had a terrible day or a terrible week or even a terrible month, you never had to worry about missing meals or being locked out of your room because your basic expenses were always taken care of.

I just read through that last paragraph, and it sounds as good now as it did when I first heard it. Because I haven't mentioned the one thing they didn't stress, either.

Which is that you go out as a crew for a three-month tour, and you don't collect nickel number one until you finish the tour. It wasn't hard to figure out why they did it this way. See, the system was based on the idea of five men and a crew boss, which was the best size group from an economic standpoint. And if two or three of those men decided to call it quits while the crew was working off in

East Crayfish or Fort Dingbat, the whole crew stopped being a profitable deal for the company. But if a guy had to go back at the end of the hitch to collect his money, that tended to discourage him from quitting.

Of course you would still be entitled to your pay whether you quit or not. But being entitled didn't mean anybody was going to hand the money to you.

Or, in Flick's words, "Any of youse quits without the three months are up, you just kissed your dough goodbye. And if I ever catches youse again, you can kiss your ass good-bye, too, because I'll kick it clear to Wausau County for you."

I don't know where the hell Wausau County is.

According to Keegan, who had been working what he called the Bug Game on and off for almost five years, there was another reason why they didn't pay you until your shift was done. They had to confirm the signatures. Otherwise the salesmen could just write up a couple of phony orders every day, knock down a couple of hundred dollars a week, and spend all their time watching television.

"And there are some that would do just that," he told me, with a wink. "You wouldn't believe it in a fine upstanding business like this one, Chip my lad, but there are hordes of dishonest people in this world."

I believed it.

Not that I had ever had any grave doubts on that score. But in the time I spent showing poor widow ladies my little plastic tube full of termites, I learned more about how people could be crooked without going to jail than I ever knew existed. One thing that I couldn't get out of my head was that my parents must have been real hard-core criminals. Up until then I always figured that they couldn't have been so bad if they went all their lives without getting sent to jail, but now I saw that I had been looking at it the wrong way around. If they had actually gotten themselves to a point where it looked as though they just might have to go to jail, then they were obviously a pretty criminal pair, old Mom and Dad, because you can be crooked enough to pull corks out of wine bottles with your toes and never see a cop except to say hello to, or fix a traffic ticket.

I already knew that nobody seemed to pay any attention to the law, or at least not in the way the law had in mind. In Chicago, for instance, you couldn't do commercial street photography, and even if you did you couldn't pass out handbills that way, because that constitutes an invitation to litter and means you're creating a nuisance. All of which meant that Gregor gave the patrolman on his beat ten dollars a week and never heard any more about it.

(I had always known things like this go on, but I thought, you know, that it was strictly Big Time Criminals who got involved in them. Not some plodding clod like Gregor, for Pete's sake. And I knew some cops took graft, and how it's a big temptation and all, but to take ten dollars? A rotten ten dollars from a simp like Gregor?)

Well, this happens in more places than Chicago. In every city or town our crew went to, there was a man Flickinger called the Fixer. The Fixer might be somebody in the police department or sheriff's office, or it might be a politician, or it might be some lawyer or businessman who was in good with the local government. And whoever the particular fixer might be, Flick would tell him he was bringing in a door-to-door crew and he wanted to have all the red tape handled in advance, like the permits or licenses or whatever was needed, and without the bother of filling out a lot of forms. And then Flick would slip the Fixer an envelope, and the Fixer would talk to whoever had to be talked to, and he'd keep part of what was in the envelope and pass on the rest, and none of us would have to worry about any aggravation from the police. And I don't mean just that they wouldn't give us a hard time about not having licenses. Besides that, there was always the fact that a certain number of noncustomers would call the cops and complain about us for one reason or another. But the word would be out, and when those calls came in the cop who answered the phone would say *Yeah* and *Sure, ma'am* and listen while all the information came over the wire and into his ear, but he wouldn't bother writing any of it down, and we would never even hear

about it, unless maybe someone would call Flick private-
ly and ask him to for Christ's sake ask his boys to be a
little more diplomatic in their dealings with the natives.

Don't ask how much was in the envelope. One of the
reasons Flick got that fifteen dollars a sale extra was that
he knew what it would take to fix each particular fixer.

I went out into the hall and got a Coke out of the
machine. I was leaning against the wall drinking it when
Solly came out of his room with a plastic pitcher. He
carried it to the ice machine and filled it up.

I said, "Heavy night?"

"All she wants to do is drink and screw. I wouldn't
mind only she drinks better'n she screws."

"Did you ask her if she's got a friend?"

"If she had a friend, I'd take the friend and boot this
one out on her hinder. She's a pig. You, Chip, you got the
right idea."

"I do?"

"Goddamn right."

He seemed to be more than a little looped. I said,
"What's the right idea? Coca-Cola?"

"Not Coca-fuckin'-Cola. It's bad for your teeth, you
know that?"

"Not if you use a regular bottle opener."

"Huh?" He blinked. "Smart ass. But you got the right
idea. The girls I see you out with."

"Oh."

"Whattaya mean, *oh*?" Solly became very forceful when
he drank. Not belligerent or nasty, just emphatic. "Decent
girls, pretty girls. And I never see you with the same girl
twice. Smart. The right idea."

He weaved away and plunged back to his room and
woman while I tried to think of an answer. Not that it was
worth the trouble. The girls he had seen me out with were
nice decent girls, all right. And pretty girls. And I guess I
was getting a little better at knowing what to say to them
and how to make time with them, because these weren't
girls that anybody introduced me to, and they weren't
girls who went out looking to get picked up. They were ordi-

nary run of the mill nice small-town girls that I would meet during the job or at a restaurant and that I would take to a movie and out for coffee or something like that.

If you can convince someone to sign a piece of paper agreeing to let Dynamic Termite Extermination, Inc. rid his house of termites and dendivorous vermin (that's what it said on the paper they signed, and you can look it up in your Funk and Wagnall's) for whatever fee DTE, Inc. wanted to charge, if you can do all that, you really ought to be able to convince some small-town girl to go to a movie with you.

But not to anything much more dynamic than a movie, as it happens.

I drank a second soft drink, but this time I made it an Uncola, probably because I was brainwashed by Solly telling me Coke would ruin my teeth. It probably would, but the Uncola probably would, too.

Because I was beginning to come to the conclusion that everything was a con.

Which is a hell of a conclusion to come to, for Pete's sake, especially when you happen to be descended from a long line of con men. Well, two of them anyway. And when you've decided to become a success along legitimate lines and to work hard and save your money and marry the boss's daughter and do all the other things right, too.

Why go through all that if some smooth-talking little rat could come along and stand on your stoop and twist his cap in his hands and wind up costing you a couple of hundred dollars to kill termites that weren't there to begin with, and that wouldn't hurt your house a whole lot even if they were? (Because this may be something you never thought of, in which case I'm going to be saving you a lot of money over the years, because the first thing we all learned is that maybe ninety-nine houses out of a hundred have some termites, and those houses will go on standing for a couple of hundred years without anybody doing anything about those termites. See, it takes a long time for a termite to eat a house. It even takes a long time for a lot of termites to eat a house. But you take the average idiot and show him a termite eating his house, and he figures that in another week there won't be anything left but the foundation.

(And while I'm on the subject, the second thing we all learned was that you couldn't in a million years sell an extermination job to somebody with a brick house. Flick said you can't sell them fireproofing, either, and Flick would know; he's sold everything at one time or another, and if that includes his mother and his sister I wouldn't be surprised. But people who have brick houses seem to think the brick is what holds the house together, so—

(You know, I have the feeling that I might be telling you more about termites than you really want to know. Maybe all of this will get cut out before the book gets printed, or maybe the book won't ever *get* printed, which would mean rough sledding for one Chip Harrison, but either way I'm going to cool it at this point with all this inside information about the termite business. That's a firm promise.

(In fact, I'm going to cool it on that forgettable evening, as far as that goes, because it wasn't the kind of evening you would want to read about. I rapped a little with Lester when he came in, and I let Jimmy Joe tell me the plot of the movie he and Keegan saw. And I made up a lie about having a girl in my room and banging her while they were at the movie, and Jimmy Joe made up a lie about picking up a girl after the movie. We were both lying and knew it, but it broke the monotony in a small way. And outside of having a couple more soft drinks and reading an Indianapolis newspaper—which made the Chicago *Tribune* seem like the *Daily Worker,* or close to it—that was all there was to that evening, so there's no point wasting everybody's time with it.

(It was the night after that one that might interest you, when Solly brought the redhead back to the motel and organized a gang bang. I have to admit it was more interesting than Cokes and Uncolas. And it did more damage than any termites I ever saw.)

CHAPTER SEVEN

DURING THE DAY I HAD BEEN WORKING THE same area where I'd made a sale the day before. Up until then the television weatherman had been saying it was unseasonably cool for mid-July, which meant it was reasonably comfortable. But that day it decided to get seasonable again.

I'm writing this on a cold damp rotten morning. My radiator is some slumlord's idea of decoration, completely nonfunctional. But I can get warm just remembering that day. I didn't make a sale. No one did. No one expected to. I think I worked as long as anyone, and I was back in my air-conditioned room by three-thirty. Flickinger didn't even put in a token gripe. Pointless. We could have sold air conditioners or dry ice or Japanese fans, but that was about the extent of it. It was so hot we didn't even talk about how hot it was, if that makes sense.

I skipped dinner and stretched out on my bed in my shorts and let the air conditioner blow on me. I woke up shivering, figure that one out, when Lester banged on my door. I let him in and he flopped in a chair and waited for his breath to come back. He had gone out for dinner and walked through all that heat, and looking at him made me glad I stayed around the room instead.

We talked about this and that, one thing and the other, and ultimately reached Topic A. I launched into a long story that was kind of loosely based on something that happened with Aileen, except that in this version of the story we didn't worry about being faithful to Gregor, who was a Cuban refugee dentist in the latest version. I don't know if Lester believed it or not. I don't think he cared enough to worry whether it was true or not. When you sit around swapping sex stories to keep from dying of boredom, nobody really gives a shit if they're true or not. Just so they're sufficiently interesting and/or horny to keep you awake.

"You know something?" he demanded, when I had carried Carmelita and myself to the heights of rapture. "When all is said and done, no woman really knows how to give head."

I made a noncommittal noise.

"You agree with me, Chip?"

I said something that sounded like *Rowrbazzle*. Because it was one of those questions like *Have you stopped beating your meat*? Whatever you said, you came off either more ignorant or more informed than you might want to.

Lester talked for a while, sort of saying but not saying that he was afraid he got more of a kick out of the queers than he wanted to, and hinting that if he did have a woman available on a steady basis he might miss the Greyhound Terminal set, water on the knee and all. I just made grunting sounds, which was all the situation called for. One thing I've noticed is that when you want to talk something out and get it right in your mind, all you really want the other person to do is be there with his mouth shut. It's a way of talking to yourself without feeling a little flaky about it.

He dropped the subject when Jimmy Joe came in unannounced and stuck his head in front of the air conditioner.

"Hey," he wanted to know, "am I interrupting anything?"

"We were talking about sex," Lester said.

"That's the trouble. Everybody talks about it and nobody does anything about it." And he sat down on the carpet and joined the party.

Bit by bit they all filtered in. Keegan first, and then Flickinger himself, standing at the door with a stupid look on his face and a bottle of gin in each hand. He came in and said he felt like company, and why didn't we all join him in a drink? No one could think of a reason not to. We drank gin on the rocks out of water tumblers. Keegan smacked his lips, wrinkled his nose, frowned, and said he wanted a little less vermouth next time around.

That reminded Flick of a story. I knew it would, because I had heard the story twice before, the two times I got drunk with him. Every last one of us had heard that goddamned story but nobody wanted to ruin his evening by saying anything about it.

You know, somewhere in this world Flickinger must have a drinking buddy who has the same kind of memory as Flick does. And I can just imagine the two of them sitting up night after night, lapping up the sauce and telling each other the exact same stories every single night. And each time Flick would think he was telling the story for the first time, and each time the other juicehead would think he was hearing it for the first time, and the two of them would go on and on, repeating like a decimal until the world came to an end.

Flick finished his story, finally, and poured everybody another drink whether they needed it or not, and got that look on his face that let you know another story was on its way. Before he could get his mouth in gear, Keegan said, "Why isn't Solly at our little party?"

He wasn't looking for an answer. He just wanted to throw a question in Flickinger's way. But no sooner were the words out than the door flew open, and there, drunker than the five of us put together, was Solly himself.

"Well, it's about time," he said. "Wondered where you all went to. Knocked on this door and that door and thought you were all gone, and you're all here. Goddamn good thing, too. Never forgive yourselves if you missed this."

"Somebody give him a drink," Lester suggested.

"Brought you boys a present," Solly said. He stuck out his hand and just left it hanging there, waiting for someone to put a drink in it as Lester had suggested, but that's the trouble with indefinite orders; we all waited for somebody else to give Solly a drink, and Solly's hand just stayed out in the air for a little while before he remembered where he had left it and brought it back.

"A present," he repeated, and got his hand back, and stuck it out into the hallway and brought it back in again, only now there was a girl's wrist in it, with a girl attached. A redhead with a see-through sleeveless blouse and a flaring white miniskirt that ended less than an inch short of indecent exposure.

"This is Cherry," he said, and started to laugh. "Jesus Christ in Marlboro Country, but if this here is cherry then I'm an unkey's moncle."

He tried to say it straight, and muffed it again, and fell apart laughing. Then he tried again from the beginning.

"This here is Cherry," he said. "Her name. She wants to get checked out for dendivorous insects. No, what she wants is to get laid and relayed and parlayed. Screwed, blewed and tattooed. She wants to take on everybody who's game, and I thought of my old buddies, and I thought, shit, what else do you do for kicks when it's a hundred and ten in the shade?"

Cherry was just standing there with a simple smile on her face. I guess that was the only kind she was capable of. She did look simple. There was no getting around it. She looked great, with a face that was reasonably pretty even if you didn't fall heart-stoppingly in love with her, and with a body that would have made you willing to have her around even if the face had been horrible. But there was something in that face, some quality that was part stupidity and part vacancy, in the sense that if you opened up her head you would find a sign saying that part of her mind was on a sabbatical in Europe or something. So she stood there looking dumb and desirable, and that's exactly what she was.

The rest of us were saying encouraging things like *Hey* and *Wow* and *Sounds good* and *No crap*. And Solly put one of his big hands on Cherry's little behind and gave a kind of a shove, and she took four or five little running steps into the room. Solly followed her inside and closed the door.

"Now show the boys what you got there," he said. "Get your clothes off, Cherry. Hurry it up. Any of you bastards got a deck of cards? High goes first and so on in order, and the same order for seconds and thirds, and after that we'll worry about it."

"Seconds and thirds?"

"Look at her. How often do you get a shot at something like that? You guys, I don't know, you guys get so little ass that when you jerk off you close your eyes and pretend you're jerking off. You think one shot at Cherry here is going to be all you want? Jesus, *look* at her!"

I don't know who he was talking to, because I'm pretty sure we were all looking at her. It seemed to me that she looked awfully young, but that happens with simple people. They don't have the sense to worry about things.

She took everything off, and she stood there with the same smile on her face, and I thought, well, take a good look at this one, Chip, because this is the one you'll never forget, the first girl ever for you, and nothing can stop you now.

"Ace is high. Suits are spades high, then hearts, then diamonds and then clubs. Same as in bridge, but you bastards don't play bridge. Cut the cards, dammit."

Keegan wanted to cut first to determine the cutting order. Jimmy Joe told him to for Christ's sake save the comedy for some other time. Flickinger, for once in his life, wasn't reminded of a story. Lester looked as though they could tear down every Greyhound station and throw all the faggots on the fire and he wouldn't mind for a minute. Solly cut the pack and got the seven of clubs and said something appropriate. Keegan cut the jack of diamonds. Jimmy Joe got the jack of clubs and insisted that put him ahead of Keegan. Keegan told him to piss off. Solly said diamonds were ahead of clubs. Jimmy Joe told Solly to piss off. Flickinger was sitting on a chair next to Cherry. He had one hand on her behind and was stroking up along the inside of her thigh with the other.

I was going to get an ace. I knew it. I could feel it, the way sometimes you can feel things.

Lester cut a nine, it doesn't matter which suit. Flickinger was so busy with Cherry it was hard to get his attention, but finally he cut the cards and got the queen of hearts.

Solly said, "Son of a bitch, that puts him first. He gets fifteen bucks every time one of us makes a sale, and now he gets first crack at her crack."

"Wait a minute," someone said. "It's the kid's turn."

"Flick might as well start. Queen's gonna be high."

"Aces are higher than queens," I said. I gave the words a Dean Martin drawl because I felt just that cool and confident. I reached out for the pack of cards, cut, and got the fucking four of clubs. They all laughed their heads off, except for old Flick who was too busy getting his pants off.

Lester put a glass of gin in my hand. "No sweat," he said. "Somebody's gotta be last. Just five guys ahead of you. The condition everybody's in, you'll be in the saddle in fifteen minutes. If it takes that long."

"Shit," I said. I drank the gin in one swallow. I don't ever do that, not even with a normal sized drink, and this was a whole glass of gin. I had already swallowed it before I realized what I had done, and even then I didn't give a damn.

"A girl like this, she'll just be warming up when you get her."

"I'll bet."

"Look at her face. Jesus, look at the old bull socking it to her, and she just lies there with that grin on her face. Like she's enjoying herself but it isn't really reaching her. You get a girl like that who wants to pull a train, you'd think of her as basically hot, right? But look at her. Cool as ice. That's the thing. It takes her three or four men just to put her in the mood. God almighty, but will you look at Flickinger. I didn't know he had it in him. Hung like a stud horse, too. If she can't feel what he's throwing her she must have a bun full of novocaine. He's gonna ruin her for the rest of us if he don't hurry up and get it over with."

"He'll ruin her for the entire human race," someone else said. "She won't be fit for anything but donkeys and horses. Take it easy, Flick!"

"And get it over with, Flick, you mother!"

Flickinger got it over with, and almost got himself over with in the process. He finished roaring, and collapsed on the girl, and whether it was the sex or the liquor or what I don't know, but he went out like a light. We had to roll him off of her, and Keegan kept saying that he was probably dead, but he wasn't. We got him into a chair and let him sit there by himself while Keegan took over for him.

Somebody handed me the bottle. I knew what I was doing this time, but all the same I took a drink. Just a short one, though. Not that I was afraid I wouldn't be able to do anything. I knew I would be able to do anything I wanted to do. But what worried me was that I might be like Flickinger and have a blackout. If I finally got laid after all this time and then couldn't even remember it, for Pete's sake, I might as well kill myself.

I wondered if Flickinger would remember. Maybe he just forgot telling stories to people. I looked around to make sure he was okay. He was conscious now, but his breath was coming along pretty raggedly.

While Keegan gave her a slow rhythmic banging, the rest of us somehow automatically started taking off our own clothes. We didn't say anything but just did this. I suppose the idea was that we were getting ready so that no time would be lost, but it didn't make any real sense for me, for example, to be in such a mad rush to get out of my clothes when there were still four men who were going to have her before my turn came.

What it was, I suppose, was that we were all knocked out enough by the heat and the air conditioning and the sexual excitement of the scene that the usual inhibitions were gone and the raunchier the whole evening got, the better we were going to like it.

When I thought about it later, for example, I couldn't remember anyone actually *saying* that we would stand around watching while each of us took a turn with Cherry. This was never put into words, and yet once things got into gear, we all more or less took it for granted that that was how it would go. Normally I would have found that idea a little off-putting. I would have gone along with it, maybe, but I would have at least questioned it a little. You would think it would just be more natural for a group of men to want to make it with the girl in private rather than as part of a group thing. Maybe we all wanted to watch each other with Cherry, and maybe we wanted to *be* watched, but it took the special mood of the evening for all of this to come into the open and to be taken so completely for granted by all six of us.

Keegan suddenly increased the pace, and we were all sort of nodding along in rhythm with him as he hit his stride and finished. He was no sooner out than Jimmy Joe was in his place, all hunched up over Cherry so that he could nibble at her breasts as he humped away at her. I got a look at her face. Her eyes were half lidded and her jaw was slack, and she was drooling a little bit out of the corner of her mouth. That was about the extent of her participation in what was going on. She didn't even move very much, just giving her behind a slight wiggle every once in a while, maybe to prove to us that she hadn't gone and died somewhere along the way.

Jimmy Joe didn't last very long. After just a few seconds he started cursing his head off as he gave a last thrust and came. He was swearing all the way through, and he went on swearing after he withdrew, and he walked all the way across the room still cursing under his breath.

"Hey," Keegan said, pleasantly, "why don't you put a sock in it, huh? Pipe down."

"Goddamn sonofabitching—"

"Happens to everybody," Keegan said.

"What a time to turn into a rabbit."

"You got excited," I said. The world's foremost authority, Chip Harrison, passing out free advice. "You'll feel easier the second time around."

"Or the third," Keegan said.

Jimmy Joe stopped swearing. Lester was taking his turn, not lying on top of her but standing with his feet on the floor. Maybe all those hours in bus station toilets had him thinking he had to be on his feet to enjoy sex. He had Cherry arranged so that her legs hung over the edge of the bed, and then he picked up her feet and doubled them up with her knees deeply bent, and then he bent over her and got down to brass tacks. It was an interesting position and the rest of us commented on its fine points, like sportsmen checking out a thoroughbred racehorse.

"He's really getting in that way," Solly noted. "You double 'em up that way, you can about tickle their tonsils."

Someone else said he preferred to do his work lying down, and the discussion moved along, and Lester turned his head and told us to shut up, managing to do this without missing a beat.

But I was noticing something about Cherry. She was starting to get interested in what was happening. Lester had told me this would happen, but I didn't really believe him. It was true, though. There was loads of sweat on her forehead and upper lip now, and between her breasts. She was breathing hard, and her hips were bucking and twitching, and after all the time she had spent just lying there, she was gradually getting into the mood in a big way.

Which meant I was the lucky one, I thought, reaching for the bottle and knocking back another drink. I mean, they were just getting her ready for me. I was the one who was going to have the best time of it.

I guess her excitement had an effect on all of us. The talk gradually died down and stopped completely. The five of us watched in silence, eyes riveted to the two of them on the bed.

Lester finished. He dragged himself off the girl's body

and staggered over to the bathroom. Solly took his place and just stood there for a minute, looking down at the girl. I wanted to ask him what the hell he was waiting for, but I didn't break the silence.

He sighed, then put a hand down and touched her between her legs.

She moaned. I guess it was the first sound I could remember hearing her make.

He lifted his hand and looked at it. "Soaking wet," he said to himself. "Dripping, the little mink is dripping. And hot."

Come on, I thought. Come on already.

He entered her slowly, very slowly, and she moaned again, a rippling moan that was unlike any sound I'd ever heard. I was a little worried now that Solly was going to be the lucky one to make her come. It was a pretty silly thing to worry about now that I think back on it, but at the time it seemed very important that I be the one to do this. So I stood there with my hands in fists, wishing that Solly would learn Jimmy Joe's impersonation of a rabbit.

He worked slowly at first, in and out, very slowly, and my whole brain was filled up with the picture of the two of them rolling around on my bed, locked together in this slow thoughtful screw. If there's anything that looks more ridiculous than people screwing, I don't know what it is. I mean, if you stopped to think what you look like when you're doing it, the facial expressions and the position and all, you might not feel as much like going through with it. They looked foolish, but they also looked as though what they were doing was a tremendous amount of fun.

Then bit by bit the tempo picked up, with each of them working at the same pace. She spoke for the first time, begging him to do it harder and faster. She talked nonstop, and she didn't use more than five different words all in all, and three of them were obscene, which is a pretty good average if you spread it over a person's whole vocabulary. She begged him to do it, and he did it, and she wrapped her legs around him and dug her nails into him and really let herself go, kicking and screaming her head off.

Solly gave a cross between a growl and a roar. He pitched forward on her the way Flick had done earlier. But Cherry didn't stop kicking and screaming and wiggling her tail as if she didn't realize that the record was over. For a few seconds Solly just lay there being tossed around by her hips. Then he grunted and heaved himself up and away from her. She tried to hang on. He unhooked her arms from around his neck and dumped her on the bed.

"She don't know when to quit," he said to no one in particular. I started for her, but he was standing in the way, just shaking his head and saying that she was a crazy little broad who didn't know when to quit.

She was writhing on the bed, making noises like cats fighting under a full moon. "Oh, I almost made it," she said. "Oh, I'll make it this time, somebody, help, please, somebody, I'll make it this time."

Keegan started for her. I grabbed him by the shoulder and spun him around.

"My turn," I said.

"Oh," he lied, "I forgot about you."

"Sure you did."

"Easy, now. If you want to stand arguing, someone'll take your turn. That what you want?"

"You know something, Keegan? I never realized it before, but you know what you are?"

"Lad—"

"You're a son of a bitch, Keegan."

"Easy, now," Keegan said.

"Please," Cherry said. "Please please please please—"

"*Open up in there,*" a voice said.

"Please please please—"

"*Open that door.*"

The room went silent again. I had shouldered Keegan aside and was on my way to the girl. Someone grabbed my arm. I shook the hand off.

They kicked the door in. Four cops the size of the Green Bay Packers. One of them went around waving a badge and a gun at everybody, and the other three pulled me off Cherry.

I bit one of them in the leg and hit one of them in the face and kicked one of them in the family jewels. If there had just been the three of them I think I would have taken them. I really mean it. But the fourth one managed to get behind me and hit me over the head with the butt of his gun.

"Oh, you rats," I heard Cherry howling. "I almost made it. Another minute and I would of made it, you rats. I'll never let you dirty cop rats screw me again. Never, damn you. Oh, I almost made it—"

The gun butt popped me again. The lights went out and so did I.

You know, I can understand how people can become paranoid. It isn't that hard to figure out. When things have been going wrong in one particular way over and over again, it's natural to figure that there's a conspiracy against you.

Take me, for instance. (Take me! I'm yours!) No, seriously. Here I was, for Pete's sake, with just one thing I really wanted to do, and I was being turned at every thwart. I was playing the goddamned Doris Day part in one of those movies where the big question is whether or not Doris can keep her legs together until the end of the film, and the big answer is always yes.

You already know about Francine—remember? to hook your attention? the gun going off—and here I was the last man in line at an orgy and the cops came in just when my number came up.

Why shouldn't I be paranoid? Obviously those cops were just waiting in the hallway for it to be my turn. Obviously someone had switched decks of cards, so that I wound up cutting a deck where every card was the fucking four of clubs. Obviously there was a hole in the wall, or a two-way mirror, and good old Gregor was out there taking pictures and old Haskell was watching and beating off in the name of sociological research, and the Head was laughing, and the basketball coach was saying that a winner never quits and a quitter never wins, and Cherry was taking off her red wig and revealing herself as Aileen, being faithful to Gregor in her peculiar way, and Calvin was saying *Rowrbazzle,* which means *Up your ass* in Siamese, and my parents weren't really dead, they were just trying to escape from their boring mess of a kid.

I couldn't have been unconscious for very long, because the first thing I saw when I opened my eyes was a pair of baggy pants. I watched as the pants were pulled up past my face and onto Flickinger, to whom they belonged. I was lying on the floor next to the bed, and Flickinger was sitting on it, and pulling his pants on.

I stayed where I was. There were conversations going on, but my head was buzzing and I was sort of listening *through* the conversations without hearing them, the way you do when you watch an Italian movie. All I knew was that there were four cops in the room, along with the five guys from the crew. I didn't see or hear Cherry.

I guess I must have realized sort of vaguely that nobody was paying attention to me, and that this was Just As Well. So I was very careful to stay where I was, and I closed my eyes again, and I found out that with my eyes shut my ears worked again, and I listened to what they were saying.

A voice I didn't know, a coppish voice, was saying, "Boy, your ass is grass. You're gone be in jail so long you'll be able to homestead your cell. I just hope you like what you got off of that little girl tonight, because you won't get anything else off anybody else for the next twenty years. Indiana don't care about statutory rape, now. Indiana don't care for that at all."

"She did act like a statue at first," Flick said. "But she was no statue toward the end there. Without you jokers were kicking the door in, she was humping like a camel."

"Now I told you about your rights," the cop said. Or maybe it was another cop. If you've heard one cop, you've heard them all. "And about your rights to an attorney, and how statements made voluntarily may be introduced as evidence in criminal prosecutions against you. You recollect I gave you that warning."

"Cut the shit," Flick said.

"Because you're just digging your grave with your tongue, boy, and I want to make sure you know what you're about."

"Something about raping a statue," Keegan said.

He sounded as unconcerned as Flickinger, and I couldn't understand it. Neither could the cops. The guys were drunk, but it didn't seem possible that they were drunk enough to be this way.

Solly said, "That was no statue, that was my wife."

"Not funny, boy. That young lady was under the age of consent."

"That was no young lady," Lester put in. "That was my statue."

"What's the age of consent here anyway?"

"Eighteen, same as most everywhere else."

"And you mean to say that girl was seventeen?"

"No, sir," the cop said. He sounded very Jack Webb-ish. "I mean to say she was fifteen."

"Well, I declare," Lester said. "Why, the little liar swore up and down she was thirty-five."

The room rocked with laughter. I didn't laugh, and neither did the cops. They made threatening sounds and talked about going on down to the stationhouse. Jimmy Joe hummed *Dum-Da-Dum-Dum* and got a laugh. Flickinger stood up, stepped over me, and started rasping away in his No More Of This Nonsense voice. He saved it for special occasions, and it was very impressive. He told the cops that they could cut out this shit about warning us of our rights, because the same rights meant that they couldn't kick the door in without a warrant, and since we were in a private room with a closed and locked door, they had no case, and—

"We had a warrant," the cop said.

"Huh?"

"Naming you six men." He read our names. "That's you folks, isn't it?" Flickinger allowed that it was us, all right. I was relieved, for no particular reason, when he read my name as Chip Harrison. When he was going down the list I had the weirdest idea that he was going to read off *Leigh Harvey Harrison,* and that was all I needed.

"And charging you six men with fraud, attempted fraud, soliciting without a license, several counts of trespass and criminal trespass, and miscellaneous violations of the following civic ordinances—" and he read off a batch of numbers.

"Now just a minute," Flick said. He still didn't seem at all worried, and I decided he was crazy. I didn't know what any of those numbers were supposed to mean, but it sounded as though they had enough against us to put us away for hundreds and hundreds of years. And the worst part of all was that this had happened before I could get to Cherry. Whatever jail they put me in, the odds were good that there wouldn't be any women in it, which meant I'd be a male virgin until I was too old to be interested.

I shuddered, then tuned Flick in again. "Where you made your mistake," he was saying, "was that you came down here without you checked it all out with the sheriff. Now if you would of done this we wouldn't have any trouble. Now what you got to do is get on the phone and ring the sheriff and tell him what's happening, and you can let me have a couple of words with him, and we'll have this whole thing straightened out in a minute."

"You and the sheriff are close, is that right?"

"The closest. And there's no hard feelings, and to prove it there'll be something in it for you fellows, too. More or less to make it up to you for your time."

"That's attempting to bribe an arresting officer," the cop said. "Write that down, Ken."

"You'll have to spell it for him," Keegan said, and then there was an *oof* sound, as though someone (like Ken) had hit someone (for instance, Keegan) in the stomach.

"Officer," Flick said, coming down hard on the first syllable, "I think *I* have to spell it out for *you*. The fix is in."

"Is that right?"

"You talk to the sheriff and—"

"I talked to him an hour ago. That's his signature on the bottom of the warrant there, boy."

"Like hell it is."

A long pause. Then Flickinger said, "It says Harold M. Powers. Now who in the precious hell is Harold M-for-Mother Powers?"

The cops all laughed. They really enjoyed themselves. I guess when you're a cop you don't get all that many opportunities to cut loose and laugh, and they made the most of this one. *"Now who in the precious hell,"* one of them started, and they broke up for a while, and another finished, *"is Harold M-for-Mother Powers?"* and they all fell out all over again.

Until finally one of them said, "Why, I'll tell you, boy, if you're so close with him, how come you don't even recognize the sheriff's name?"

"What about Barnett Ramsey?"

"Why, we had an election some six or eight months ago, and old Barney got beat."

"He lost the election," Flickinger said. Heavily.

"After all those years. Yeah, it surprised a whole mess of folks."

"Great bleeding shit," Flickinger said. "Jesus frigging Christ with a tambourine. Holy laminated bifurcated ocellated Mother of Pearl."

"I never heard the like," one cop said softly.

"Sweet shit in a bucket," Flickinger said. "I bribed the wrong man."

Everybody started talking at once. I took a deep breath and said a quick prayer and rolled under the bed.

CHAPTER EIGHT

I DIDN'T REALLY EXPECT TO GET AWAY WITH it. But they had been doing such a great job of ignoring me that I figured I ought to give them all the encouragement I could. The easier I made it for them, the better.

So I rolled under the bed, and since I was right next to it already, and on the floor, and more or less face down, it wasn't that hard to do. In a sense I suppose *rolled* is the wrong word for it. I sort of crept on my belly like an earthworm. Sideways, though. Earthworms, as you probably know, tend to go back and forth. I don't know how you tell an earthworm's back from his forth. It was never very important to me. I don't even like to go fishing, for Pete's sake. I do know, though, that earthworms are male at one end and female at the other, so you know what they can do.

Lying under that bed, I decided that the police force of the fifth largest city in the state of Indiana could do the same thing earthworms can do, for all I cared. Because it occurred to me that they were not only going to give me the royal shaft, but they were going to give it to me for something I didn't do. In the first place I was only seventeen myself, so what I did to Cherry wasn't statutory rape, and in the second place I hadn't done anything in the first place.

Which seemed to indicate that as soon as I clued them in, they would let me go.

But I didn't think they would. So I stayed under the bed while Flickinger told everybody who would listen that it would take awhile to straighten everything out, but that he knew everything would be straightened out, because one thing you couldn't deny was that he and his men represented Dynamic Termite Extermination, Inc., and that DTE was no fly-by-night outfit but a company that had been a leader in its field for twenty-two-count-em-twenty-two years, and that was by God a lot of goddamn years.

(This was the God's honest truth, as a matter of fact. I had trouble believing it myself, but it was. The company didn't ever do a thing that was illegal. If a crew boss ran things on the shady side, they didn't want to know about it. If a crew boss ran things on the up and up, that was fine with DTE. Of course an honest crew boss couldn't possibly clear fifteen cents a month, but that was the way it went. You couldn't call the company crooked just because all its employees were crooked, could you?)

"We'll be out of this in no time at all," Flick said. "Youse guys just trust me on this without you all lose your heads and get rattled. All right, we gotta go see the Sheriff, that's what we got to do. That's all."

They finished getting dressed, and they talked about things, and they asked the cops if Cherry was really only fifteen, and the cops said she was, and Lester asked one of the cops how often Cherry generally got statutorily raped, and the cop said as often as she possibly could, and Lester asked why anybody would make a fuss over it then, and the cop said it was because it was the sort of thing the city couldn't take lying down, and Lester said that if Cherry could take it lying down, he didn't see why the city couldn't. The cop laughed and said that was sure a good

way of putting it. I think this comes under the heading of
Fraternizing With The Enemy.

And I kept waiting for somebody to say, "Hey, what
happened to the kid we had to hit over the head?"

Or for one of the guys on our side to say, "Say, what
the hell happened to Chip?"

Or for somebody, anybody, to sing out, "*Look who's
hiding under the bed!*"

But they found other things to say, and the door
opened, and they trailed out of it and left it ajar. I don't
know to this day where Cherry was during all of this. I
didn't see her or hear her, and I didn't hear anybody talk
to her, or say anything that gave the impression she was in
the room. But I didn't see how she could have been taken
anywhere because all of the cops were still in the room, so
who would have taken her away? I guess either they sent
her home by herself or a matron came for her while I was
unconscious. Or else she was what you would call a plant,
and the police had sent her over there to begin with so
that they could give us all the shaft. (I don't really believe
that last one at all. But I'm putting it in to give you an
idea of how paranoid a person can get under the right set
of circumstances. After all, somewhere out there is my old
roommate Haskell, and I want to make sure the book has
a certain amount of psychological significance so he won't
feel guilty while he reads it and turns the pages with one
hand. Hi, Haskell, you hypocritical jerk-off!)

They left the room, as I said before I got off course
again. They went out, and I heard them in the hallway,
and I got out from under the bed, still waiting for them to
wonder what had happened to the kid. I went over to the
window and yanked it open. And somebody must have
wondered about me, although they were too far away
from the room for me to hear them say so, because I heard
footsteps racing back up the hall and a voice—Jimmy
Joe, God bless him—shout out my name.

I stepped out of the window. It was the first floor,
which was the one good thing that had happened that
evening. And it was at the back of the motel, away from
the parking lot and nowhere near where the other cops

had been heading. That was the second good thing that happened that evening. And, because they come in threes, a third good thing happened that evening, which is that I ran like a cat with its tail on fire and got away without being spotted.

Which was very good.

But it could have been better. I mean, even considering the fact that my commissions were all being held for me by the Dynamic Termite Extermination, Inc. office, and that I had been doing my Coke buying and movie going out of my own savings for a couple of months, the fact remained that I had had over a hundred dollars in my wallet, along with various cards to prove I was me in case I died and they wanted to make sure the body wasn't Judge Crater or Ambrose Bierce. There was also a picture of Aileen that I kind of liked, and that I would miss.

It would have been good if I had been able to bring my wallet. And it would have been even better if I had had something to put my wallet in, because although the night was seasonably hot, it's never a good idea ro run amok in Indiana's fifth-largest city with no clothing whatsoever on your body.

I've read books where the hero suddenly gets struck naked one way or another. Or he breaks out of jail and has to get something to replace his prison uniform. Or he soaks his clothes swimming to safety and can't wait for them to dry. Or there are these telltale bloodstains telling tales all over the place.

When this happens in books, what the guy usually does is swipe clothing from an untended clothesline. The authors don't generally dwell on it too intently. They just throw something like *Dressing himself with clothes purloined from an untended clothesline, Stud Boring relentlessly took up the trail of the three pencil sharpeners.* Then they plunge right into the action without giving you time to think about it.

In the movies, they're even cooler about it. I saw this done just the night before last, as a matter of fact. This guy broke out of prison, out of a chain gang actually, and one moment you saw him running down the road with his prison clothes all shredded from the brambles and wet from the swamp he went through to throw the dogs off his trail, and then there was another shot of him getting off a bus, wearing a shirt and tie and carrying a leather suitcase. They didn't even cheat by giving you the abandoned clothesline bit. They just came right out and admitted that they didn't know how the hell Stud Boring got those clothes, and that they weren't going to try to fake their way out of it. I suppose you have to admire them for it.

The thing of it is that if you can find a clothesline in the middle of the night, tended or untended, you are better suited to this sort of thing than I was. I don't even think I'd care to look for one in the daytime, because the checking I did showed that (a) people don't leave clothes hanging out overnight and (b) most of them don't even have clotheslines nowadays. I went zipping through backyards looking for clothes and the whole thing was a large zero. No lines and certainly no clothes. I wouldn't have thought of looking in the first place except that I remembered all those dumb books. You've got to be very suspicious of everything you read.

I think I know what happened. Years ago nobody had clothes dryers, and everybody who washed clothes had to hang them out to dry, and with that many people washing clothes, there would always be a certain number who would forget to take their clothes in for the night, or who wouldn't get around to it because they were baking bread or beating rugs by hand or putting up preserves or watering the horses or any of those good old-time things that people don't do anymore. So in those days it was perfectly open and aboveboard to have Stud Boring steal clothes from a washline. (Open and aboveboard for the writer, I mean. It was still illegal for Stud Boring.)

But nowadays when a writer is trying to get old Stud out of a tight place, the first thing he thinks of is what he read somewhere else. (That's why so many books are the same. The writers all get ideas from each other.) And because they were never running around naked in the middle of the night, they don't know that they'd be better off looking for an abandoned clothes dryer, for Pete's sake, in this modern day and age.

After I figured out that I wasn't going to get clothes off a line, I sat in a dark corner of somebody's garage and tried to think what to do next. I thought about going where the clothes were. Clothes in general, I mean. Not my own clothes, which were all in my room, which was a place I knew better than to go back to. But other clothes, that I could sort of find before they were lost. The first ideas I had all involved breaking into some place or other. Somebody's house, or some store that sold clothes.

I figured if I broke in anyplace I would get caught, and if I got caught I would be worse off than ever, because in addition to fraud and statutory rape they could also put me in jail for burglary. And while I thought if worst came to worst I could probably get a suspended sentence for the other charges (assuming Flick remembered who to bribe for a change), I could see myself spending a long time in prison for burglary. I also figured anybody breaking into a house or a store stood a very good chance of getting opened up with a shotgun.

Then I thought, but not for long, about Lying In Ambush and crowning somebody with a brick or something heavy, say a traditional Blunt Instrument for example, like a saxophone. Having just been hit on the head myself, I didn't want to do the same to a stranger. Besides that, you may remember that I'm not even coordinated enough to pace the Upper Valley basketball team to a regional title, and that I get nauseous just thinking about violence for any length of time. I was violent enough with the three cops, but that's something else. I mean, I had something to fight for.

Then I tripped over a muddy shoe.

To give you an idea how brilliant I was, I looked at what I tripped over and said to myself, Oh, it's a shoe, and put it out of the way so I wouldn't trip over it again. And I must have sat around scheming for another five minutes before I remembered that shoes were things you wear on your feet, and that I wasn't wearing any at the moment, and that, therefore, a muddy shoe was better than no shoe at all, and I ought to follow the old proverb that starts out *If the shoe fits.*

Here's another proverb. *If the shoe doesn't exactly fit, wear it anyway, because shoes are almost as hard to come by as clotheslines.*

These shoes were a little loose, and down at the heels, and thin in the soles, and one of the laces had been broken and tied together again. If they'd been in better shape, the owner wouldn't have used them for gardening and I wouldn't have tripped over them, so I didn't really have any right to complain.

I didn't have time to complain, either. Because I figured out that some people had special shoes that they used for gardening or painting or any kind of yard work, and others had special pants and shirts, and that if I looked in enough garages I could probably put together a wardrobe that would get me a lot of curious glances, I'll admit, but that would, all things considered, get me less attention than my present costume of shoes and nothing else.

Some people lock their garages, but most of them don't. Most people don't have anything wearable in their garages, but some of them do. And I wasn't fussy about fit or looks or style, and garages are fairly easy to get in and out of without disturbing anybody, and to make a long story short (or at least as short as possible, at this stage of the game) I wound up wearing the muddy shoes and a pair of paint-blotched dungarees and a red-and-black plaid hunter's jacket and a little peaked gardener's cap.

And in the same garage where I found the hunter's jacket I found something else, and while it didn't take the nose of a bloodhound to ferret it out (or the nose of a ferret to bloodhound it out), I'm going to come right out and say that it was brilliant of me to take it along. Look, I've told you about all of the idiot things, so I might as well take whatever credit I can get.

It was a fishing rod. The way I was dressed, there were only two things on earth I could be—a criminal on the run or a lunatic fisherman. So I took the fishing rod and transformed myself from a Threat To Society to an All-

American Boy, and I walked right through the dippy town without a bit of trouble.

If this was a movie, the thing to do now would be to cut straight on through to September. Not for the sake of cheating, the way they do when they refuse to tell you how Stud Boring got dressed again, but just because nothing very interesting happened during the next two months. And if we just cut to two months later and fifteen hundred miles east of there, you wouldn't miss much.

But if you're like me you always want to know about things like that, like what happened during the two months it took me to get from the fifth largest city in Indiana to where I was in September, which is also where I am now. If I like a book and get interested, I want to know everything. When it comes to novels, I like the old-fashioned approach where they tell you what happened to the characters after the book ended. You know, the plot's all tied up and the story is all used up and done with, and then there's a last chapter where the author explains that Mary and Harold got married and had three children, two boys and a girl, and Harold lived to be sixty-seven when a stroke got him, and Mary survived him by twenty years and never remarried, and George went back together with his wife but they broke up again after three years, and George went to California and has never been heard from since, and his wife died of pleurisy the year after he left. I like to feel that the people are so real that they go on doing things even when the book is done with them, and sometimes I'll make up my own epilogue for a book in my head if the author didn't write one himself. It's called an epilogue when you do this.

Anyway, ever since I started writing this, in fact ever since Mr. Burger said I really ought to write it, I decided I would just act as though the person reading it was more or less like myself. With a similar way of looking at things and so on. So whenever I have to decide whether to put something in or not, I ask myself whether or not I would want to read it. That's why I put in all that crap about the termite racket, for example.

What I did for the rest of July and all of August and the first week of September was farm work, for the most part. I headed east when I left town and didn't stop walking and hitchhiking until I was in Ohio. I didn't think the police would bother sending out an alarm for me, since I wasn't exactly Public Enemy Number One. I mean I wasn't the most sought-after criminal since Arlo Guthrie dumped the garbage in Stockbridge, Mass. I was breathing fairly easy as soon as I got out of the county, but I still thought it would be good to get across the state line without taking any chances.

I kept getting lifts for a couple of miles at a time because this particular highway wasn't one that anybody would take for any great distance. But on a bigger road I would have stood out like acne with my clothes and my fishing rod. On this road people either assumed I was going to a particular fishing spot or when they asked I would just say *Down the road a piece* and they figured I was keeping the spot a secret. Fishermen do crazy things like that all the time. Then I would just sit in the car until they let me out because they were turning off.

Eventually, though, I got sick of having to talk about fishing with people who all knew more about it than I did. And I got sick of carrying the pole. So I left it on a bridge over a little creek that I happened to walk over between rides. I figured whoever found it would be able to get some use out of it right away.

Then, since I didn't have the pole, people assumed I was a drifter, which was what I was, actually. And one man said, "Bet you're looking to get work picking. Cherries is gone but early peaches is coming in, and won't be a week and they be picking summer apples, the weather the way she be."

I hadn't even thought about it. I wasn't in shape to think any further than the Ohio line, to tell the truth. But farm work sounded as good as anything else I could think of, and it turned out to be just right, considering the circumstances.

You didn't need a car or a suit or a degree or any experience whatsoever. You could walk in off the road wearing paint-smeared dungarees and muddy shoes and a hunting jacket and not get looked at twice. If they had berries or melons that needed picking, or peaches or apples or sweet corn or tomatoes, they didn't care where you went to school or who your father was or if you had a Social Security card. All they cared was if you wanted to get out in the field and pick the stuff.

Of course they didn't pay much, either. They really couldn't. Look, a pint of blueberries, say, will cost you maybe half a dollar at the supermarket, right? Suppose the farmer who grew it got half of that, which he never does, I don't think, unless he sells it himself or something. But anyway, say he gets a quarter a pint. Now if you ever picked blueberries you know that it takes forever to fill a pint container with the stupid little things. You could get the whole quarter for picking those berries and it wouldn't be exactly the highest wages in history, and that would mean the farmer was giving the berries away for nothing.

But even with the pay low, and even with being on your feet all day, and getting up early in the morning and working twelve or fourteen hours at a stretch, even with all of that, there were good things about it. Even with the backache you got from picking stuff that grew on the ground, or the bruises you got from falling off ladders while picking stuff that grows on trees, it was still a good way to cover two months and fifteen hundred miles.

For one thing, you could really eat as though food was free, because it just about was. You were expected to eat all you wanted of whatever you were picking while you picked it. (This was more of a thrill when what you were picking was red raspberries than when it happened to be summer cooking apples.) You also got three meals a day. Breakfast was three or four eggs fresh from the hen and home-baked bread and jam. All the fruits and vegetables were fresh at lunch and dinner, and they kept passing huge oval bowls full of different things around the table.

I had never eaten like that in my life. Not to say anything against my mother, but she wasn't the world's greatest cook. I suppose when you can function as a confidence woman for twenty years without ever getting caught, you can also let other people do the cooking for you. Still, I ate better at home than I did at any of the camps or schools I went to, and from the last school I had gone more or less directly to Aileen's instant coffee and nondairy creamer and TV dinners, moving on to third-rate restaurant food in Illinois and Indiana towns. I had gotten so I never cared much about food, probably because I didn't really know what good food tasted like. I always thought I hated vegetables, for instance, because the ones I ate always came out of cans or plastic bags and then sat on the stove for a couple of months.

Besides the food, the life was just generally healthy. They usually let you sleep in the barn, except a couple of times in large apple orchards in New York State where there were just more pickers than there was floor space. Even there they took care of us, though, with straw mattresses to sleep on and sheets of canvas to tie to the trees and sleep under, not just because it might rain but so that apples wouldn't drop on top of you.

What I mostly picked was apples. Supposedly you could make better money working vegetable farms, but I really hated the stooping, and I never got used to the feel of the sun on the back of my neck. An apple orchard is cool on hot days and has a great smell to it and you work standing up. Of course you have to expect to fall off the ladder once in a while. They say that anybody who doesn't fall now and then isn't picking fast enough. I won't say that you get used to falling off ladders, or that you grow to look forward to it, but in all the time I picked apples, I never got more than a bruise or saw anybody do worse than sprain a wrist. You learn how to fall after the first couple of times, and it sort of struck me, during one of the moments of philosophical reflection that you get plenty of in an apple orchard, that anybody who lived the kind of life I did really ought to learn how to fall.

The average apple knocker is in his twenties and grew up in the country and quit school young and keeps his mouth shut and likes to get in a fight when he's had a couple of drinks. The average apple knocker is a guy, and so is the unaverage apple knocker. There were no girls up in those trees or out in those barns or under those canvas ceilings.

There was always the farmer's daughter, but she was a long ways away from what she was like in the jokes. Generally she was home on vacation from college, and she would no sooner go off with a picker than she'd pick her nose in church. Her main object was to get pinned to a fraternity boy and live in a big city where he could get rich sitting at a desk.

Now and then I would manage to meet a girl. Actually a picker could make out pretty well if he happened to be good at it. In any given area there would be certain taverns and bowling alleys that all the pickers would congregate at when they were in the neighborhood. The taverns generally had either a combo or a jukebox primed with country music. The bowling alleys had balls and pins. The pickers would holler and stomp and get drunk and fight, and occasionally someone would get cut up. You wouldn't believe how casual some of these guys would be about this. A guy might have a scar from his neck to his navel, and if you asked about it he would say, "Oh, my buddy over there cut on me a touch when we were drinking." And they would still be buddies and joke about it, and eventually they would have another fight and the knives would come out again.

Girls would come to the taverns, and especially to the bowling alleys—I guess it was more respectable for a girl to go to a bowling alley, although you never saw any of them actually go so far as to bowl. And the girls who came to these places were there to get picked up by the pickers, and they knew that pickers were only interested in One Thing, and it wasn't discussions of the Great Books Of The Western World. So any girl who went with a picker was just about putting it in writing that she was willing to put out. That saved a lot of time and wasted effort on both sides, and in a business where you were never in one place very long, it made things simpler all around.

The thing was that you had to be a certain type of

person to make out under those conditions. The make-out type, you might say. And it was a type that I obviously wasn't. The guys who were best at it were basically pretty stupid guys who could carry on a conversation all night long without saying anything worth hearing. But they never had to stop and think about anything. Instead they had this loose easy style that I guess made it easy for a girl to relax or something. Whatever it was, I just didn't have it. Whenever I tried to make out at taverns, I would get involved in a conversation with a girl, and she would seem interested, and then she would say she had to go to the ladies' room. And I'd see her five minutes later going home with some other picker.

The girls I dated were girls you could talk to and girls you could have a pleasant evening with. One of them was on vacation from Fredonia State Teachers College where she was having an awful time with required science courses: she just couldn't seem to get the hang of what they were all about. Another one wanted to talk about liberal religious movements. She didn't believe in God anymore but she was afraid she wouldn't have anything to do on Sunday mornings. She sure won't want to spend them in bed unless she changes a lot, because by the time I got rid of her I needed treatment for frostbite.

There were girls I didn't get to first base with, and there were girls I did get to first base with. And some I got to second base with, and one or two who let me get all the way to third. More than one or two, maybe. But one way or another they all turned in superb clutch pitching, and no matter how many hits I got, the inning would end in a scoreless tie, with my men stranded all over the bases.

I wanted to take my bat and balls and go home.

The last apples I picked were in a small Early MacIntosh orchard in Dutchess County, New York. That's about sixty or seventy miles from New York City. When we finished picking those trees I all of a sudden knew that I didn't want to pick another apple for a very long time, or anything else. The high season was just coming on, and it was the one time of the year when a fruit picker can actually make decent money, but I was sick of it and ready for something else. I was just done and that was all.

I had around thirty dollars and two changes of clothes including one pair of heavy boots and a pair of regular shoes. I also had a whole load of money coming to me from the termite sales. I was dumb enough to send them a couple of wires asking them to send the dough. Of course I never heard from them.

One of two things happened: (a) Flickinger managed to bribe his way out of the mess, in which case he certainly wouldn't tell the office what had happened, so they would treat me like any deserter, or (b) they were all rotting in jail, and nobody ever so much as turned those signed orders in, and there was no money coming to me.

Either way, I had thirty dollars. Which means I had made a clear profit of a dollar a month since I left Upper Valley. I had a lot of vocational experience, none of which would get me a job with Opportunity For Advancement. And my cherry, like the winter apples, was still on the tree.

That's how I spent the summer. The more I think of it, the more I figure the movies have the right idea. Start with a long shot of a kid in muddy shoes and a hunter's jacket on a dusty Indiana road, and cut to a shot of the same kid finishing a hard day's work as a wiper in a car wash in Upstate New York. In a town which I won't name, because I'm still here now, writing this, and may be here forever.

It was in this very town that I met Francine.

Remember Francine?

To tell you the absolute truth, I'm having a little trouble remembering her myself. Good old Burger told me it was always a good idea to start off with something dramatic to hook the reader, and then go back and fill in the background and work up to it, but I have a feeling that would have been a better idea if I were someone who knew something about writing a book. If I were starting over again, I would just start at the beginning and go straight through to the end and the hell with hooking your attention and riveting your eye to the page. Either you're

with me or you're not. But in case you forgot about
Francine, and how things were going when I broke off to
start backing and filling, it went like this:

*And paused, because it seemed that a herd of elephants
was stampeding up the staircase and down the hall, and
voices were shouting, and Francine was roaring at me,
begging me to do it, to stick it in, and I lay there,
paralyzed, and the door to my room exploded inward, and
a man the size of a mountain charged inside. He had a
hand the size of a leg of lamb, and in that hand he had a
gun the size of a cannon.*

"You son of a bitch!" he bellowed.

And pointed the gun at me, and pulled the trigger.

CHAPTER NINE

THE GUN JAMMED.

CHAPTER TEN

WELL, WHAT DID YOU EXPECT?

Blood?

Look, a guy stuck a gun in my face and pulled the trigger. Now if the gun didn't jam then he would have blown my head off and you would be reading something else because I wouldn't be around to write this.

I mean, I can just hear you clucking like a chicken and saying, "Now how in hell is he going to get out of this one?" And then on the last page it said *The gun jammed* and you said, "Oh, shit, *the gun jammed*, what a cornball way to save him."

I didn't *plan* it that way, for Pete's sake. If you want to know something, it took me a full day to write the last chapter. One stupid page with three stupid words on it and it took me all day to write it because I couldn't figure out how to tell you that the gun jammed. And finally it came to me that there was only one way. *The gun jammed.* Period, end of chapter.

I'll tell you something. I was going to make something up instead of having the gun jam. You know, to lie to you and figure out something more convincing and satisfying than a jammed gun. (I already put two things in this book that aren't true. They're out and out lies, actually. They're both in the second chapter. If you think you know what they are, write to me. I'd be interested to see if you get it right.)

But I couldn't think of a lie. Either I'm dictating this from the grave or the gun jammed. Well, the gun jammed and that's all there is to it, and come to think of it, I don't know why in the hell I'm apologizing, because what it amounts to is I'm apologizing for being *alive,* and that doesn't make any sense.

CHAPTER ELEVEN

WHEN HE SAW THAT THE GUN WAS JAMMED, he tried wiggling the trigger with his finger. It wouldn't come back into position. I suppose that was the logical time to pick up a chair and brain him with it, while he was standing there playing with the gun and swearing at it, but I don't have those kind of reflexes. I just sat there on the bed with one hand on my knee and the other on the best part of Francine and waited for him to get the gun fixed and shoot me all over again.

Then he looked at me and said, "You're not Pivnick." His voice was very stern, as if he was *accusing* me of not being Pivnick. As though Pivnick was something everybody should be, like clean or loyal or trustworthy.

"No," I said. "I'm not."

"I was sure it was Pivnick. I would have sworn up and down it was Pivnick." He frowned. Then he looked up again and turned his eyes on Francine.

"You," he said. "You're not Marcia."

She didn't say anything. "No," I said, for her. "She's not Marcia. She's Francine."

"No wonder you're not Pivnick." He frowned again, deep in conversation, and then nodded his head emphatically. "Of course," he said. "Of course. I see it all now. That's why you're not Pivnick."

"It's the main reason."

"Then where is my wife?"

"Huh?"

"My wife," he snapped. "Marcia. My wife."

"Oh, Marcia," I said. "Well, it's obvious, isn't it?"

"Tell me."

"She must be with Pivnick."

"Ha," he said, triumphantly. "I thought so! I always thought so. But where?" He lowered his head and paced, then raised it and snapped.

"There is another apartment in this building?"

"No. Just the barbershop downstairs."

"This is One-eighteen South Main Street?"

"Yes."

"Damn it to hell," he said. "I was told I would find them at One-eighteen South Main Street. I was not told that it was Pivnick. But I was certain. And I was definitely told that it was my wife. They told me I would find her at One-eighteen South Main Street in Rhinebeck."

"This isn't Rhinebeck."

"*What*?"

"This isn't Rhinebeck," I said. And I told him the name of the town.

"Damn it to hell," he said. "I knew I had made a mistake as soon as I saw it wasn't Pivnick. But what a mistake! What an extraordinary mistake! Marcia will never believe this!"

He was glowing and bubbling. Then his face went suddenly somber, as if he had just had a power failure. "But I could have killed you," he said. "An innocent man. I could have shot you down in hot blood. And you were not even Pivnick."

"Not for a moment."

"My God," he said. He looked at the gun in his hand and shuddered. Then he jammed it into his pocket, bowed halfway to the floor, apologized to both of us for the interruption, and headed for what was left of my door. Very little was. He took two steps and the gun went off in his pocket. He lost two toes on his right foot, and it was hell getting the bleeding stopped. I thought sure the cops would come and let him go and arrest me for picking apples out of season. The cops didn't come.

"Bostonians," he said, dully, looking at his feet.

"Marcia and Pivnick?"

"The shoes! One-hundred-and-ten-dollar Bostonians!" He glared at them. "And only seven years old. The salesman swore they would last a lifetime. Bostonians!"

I considered pointing out that one of them was still in perfectly good shape, as were eight of his toes. But I kept this to myself.

Francine ripped up a pillowcase to make bandages. I fixed him up and told him he ought to go to a hospital. He said he had to go to Rhinebeck. I don't know if he ever found Pivnick or not, but if I were Marcia I would be very goddamned careful from now on.

Once we were rid of Marcia's husband, Francine remembered that she didn't have any clothes on. It was really pretty funny. Before the jerk kicked the door in, it was easy enough for her to pretend that she didn't know what was happening, or that we were just necking a little, or whatever she wanted to pretend. And while he was there waving the gun in the air and talking about Pivnick, we both had too much to worry about to think about being naked. But then he went out and closed my broken door behind him, and there we were. I turned to look at Francine, and she pulled a bed sheet over her really sensational body and tried to look everywhere but at me.

I got onto the bed and scurried over next to her.

"My," she said, "I really have to be getting home now, Chip."

"Oh, it's real early, Francine."

"What a strange man! I thought he was going to shoot you or something."

"Well, he tried."

She talked about him, the sort of brainless talk Francine was good at, and meanwhile I got a hand under the sheet and kept putting it on Francine, and she kept moving it off without missing a beat.

Then she said, "I wish you would cover yourself up, Chip."

"Huh?"

"You don't have any clothes on."

"It's a warm night."

"Be nice, Chip."

"Huh?"

She chewed her lip. "I shouldn't even be here. I don't know what got into me." Nothing, I thought. "But I guess I just got carried away because of the things you said and how sweet a boy you are. You're very sweet, Chip."

I went to kiss her, but she got her mouth out of the way very skillfully. "Be nice," she said.

"Nice? I thought we would sort of get back to what we were doing."

"I don't know what you mean by that."

"Before he walked through the door."

"I don't know what—"

"Well, just for the record, Francine, we were about to make love."

"Really, Chip, I don't—"

"I mean I was lying on top of you, for Christ's sake, and you were telling me to shove it in all the way to your neck. I mean let's not pretend we don't know our names, for Pete's sake. I mean that's what we were doing before we were so rudely interrupted, and I don't see why all of a sudden we have to pretend that we just met each other at a church picnic."

She was staring at me.

"I mean it seems pretty silly," I said.

She turned away from me. "You're a very crude boy," she said.

"A minute ago I was very sweet."

"I thought you were, but obviously I was mistaken. I shouldn't even be here."

"Well, give me a minute and I'll cut the ropes."

"What?"

"The ropes that are tying you down so you can't escape my evil clutches. I'll cut you loose and you can hurry on home."

"Chip—"

"What?"

She sighed a couple of times. Her eyes stole a look at me, moving over my body to the part of me she wanted me to pull a sheet over. She withdrew them, but they came back again of their own accord.

She said, "If you would just be a gentleman, and if you would tell me the things you said before, you know, about thinking I'm really pretty and that you like me as a person and you respect me, then everything could be the way it was before."

I made her say it again. And she said it again in just about the same words.

"That's a great idea," I said. "Say, do you suppose we should put our clothes on first so that we can start over from the beginning?"

"That would be best, Chip."

"That sure is a great idea," I said.

"I'm glad you—Chip, *what* are you *doing*?"

"What does it look like I'm doing?"

"Chip, now *stop* that!"

"It's my thing," I said. "If I want to play with it, I've got every right in the world."

"If you think I'm going to sit here and watch you, you're out of your mind!"

"Would you like to do it for me?"

"Chip, I don't know what's the matter with you."

"Go home."

"But I thought—"

"Go home."

"Chip?"

"Go home."

When she went home, I stopped playing with myself. I was only doing it to annoy her. I mean, I wouldn't want you thinking that I got any kick out of it, at least in a sexual sense. But it sure got old Francine's teeth on edge, and that was the general idea.

After she left I sat around for a while. I got dressed again and had a look at the door. If the barber saw it he was going to have a fit and if he didn't see it I didn't want him cutting my hair, because he would be likely to lop off an ear. I mean it was smashed beyond recognition. You couldn't make it look like a door again. The only way to hide it was to hang a picture over it, and I didn't know where to get one at that hour.

What I did was take the door right off its hinges and carry the whole mess downstairs. I put all the pieces back with the garbage from the drugstore two doors down. The next time Mr. Bruno asked for the rent, I asked him when he was going to bring my door back.

"Door? What door? I never tooka your door."

"Then where did it go?"

"Jeez," he said, and added something in Italian. The next day two of his sons came and hung a new door for me. The next time I saw old Bruno he said he was sorry they had taken the door off without telling me, but it needed painting. I got so I had trouble knowing whether that guy kicked my door in or not.

But all this is off the subject. I guess I'm trying to duck the obvious question, which is was I losing my mind or what?

Because Francine would have let me do it. She just about came right out and said she would let me do it if only I would play up to her the way she wanted. She spelled it out for me, just about, and I wasn't so dumb that I didn't get the message, and what did I do? I sent her home, for Pete's sake. I sat there, pulling my pud like a total dip and told her to take her whatchamacallit and go home, and kept telling her until she went.

I sat around for hours trying to figure it out. And the best I could come up with was that I had just been trying to get laid for so long that finally something snapped inside me and I just wasn't going to go through all that goddamned nonsense again. If you stop to think, ever since I left Upper Valley I had been planning on working hard and applying myself and being straightforward and open and honest and sensible, all in a heroic All-American effort to Get Ahead. And time after time I wound up being dishonest and sneaky and conniving, and floated around aimlessly and didn't save money and wasn't getting ahead, and all because the only thing I really gave a damn about was getting laid. And it might have made sense if I was making out like a maniac, but I wasn't getting any place at all, and the whole thing just wasn't worth the trouble.

And Francine wasn't worth the trouble, for Pete's sake. No matter how nice her body was, there was too thick a layer of stupidity and selfishness hovering over it. And no matter what terrific secrets she had hidden between her legs, they just couldn't be worth all the games and crap you had to go through to get to her.

I just wasn't interested.

You may have trouble believing it. I don't blame you for a minute. This is I, Chip Harrison, talking, after all, and to tell you the truth, I didn't believe it all myself. But it was true.

I went outside and walked around until I found a place to have a cup of coffee. I just walked right in and sat down at the counter without giving the place the usual carefully casual are-there-any-girls-here glance. I didn't even care. I sat at the counter, and the waitress who always served me came over and gave me the usual big phony smile and leaned forward to give me the usual cheap thrill, and I talked to her the same way I always did but without even pausing to think for a moment that I would like to bang her. I drank my coffee and ordered another cup. I told myself I might be a virgin for the rest of my life, and if that was the way it was going to be, I would just have to learn to live with it, because no matter how great Doing It felt (and I didn't suppose it would really feel a whole hell of a lot different from some of the things I had done with Aileen, as far as that goes), it still couldn't be worth making a horse's ass of yourself or building your whole life around. It just wasn't worth it.

I was having a third cup of coffee, which I don't usually do, but this wasn't my usual kind of evening, either. A voice said, "Say, is anybody sitting here?"

I turned around. It was a girl about my age, with long brown hair and very wide brown eyes. She was wearing a pair of those granny glasses and if anything they made her eyes look bigger.

"No one at all," I said.

"What I meant was, do you feel like company or are you involved with your own private thoughts?"

"Company's fine."

"Are you sure? I don't want to come on heavy or anything."

"I'm sure. I ran out of thoughts, anyway."

She parked herself on the stool next to mine. The waitress came over and showed off her breasts. The girl ordered coffee, and I said I didn't want anything, thanks just the same. The waitress gave me one of those tentative dirty looks, as though she didn't know whether to take that the wrong way or not. She brought the girl's coffee and went away.

"I think I've seen you around," the girl said.

"I've been around."

"Are you living in town?"

"For the time being. Just passing through, actually."

"I've been living here for years, but I'm on my way out now. I'm going to college tomorrow morning."

"Oh."

She stirred her coffee. "My first year. I guess I must be a little nervous about it because I couldn't sleep. I had to get out of the house. I didn't think I was nervous but I must be."

"Maybe you're just excited. That can happen."

"I guess so. Do you go to school now or did you finish?"

"I sort of dropped out."

"That's groovy. I guess I'll probably drop out. Most of the kids I know who went already, the more interesting ones, all dropped out after a year or two. But I wanted to see what it was like first."

"That's probably a good idea."

"That's what I figured." She drummed the counter top with her fingers. Her fingernails were chewed ragged and the backs of her hands were brown from the sun. "I'm a Capricorn. Open to new ideas. I believe in that, I think, but I don't know much about it. Astrology, I mean. What are you?"

"Oh. Virgo."

"My name's Hallie."

"Mine's Chip."

"That's very together. I like that." She sipped her coffee and made a face.

"It's pretty bad coffee," I said.

"The worst. But everybody's closed at this hour. Do you work or what?"

"Over at the car wash. They wash and I dry."

"That sounds fair enough."

"I don't love it, but it's a job."

"I think that's where I may have seen you. And you know, walking around."

I looked at her again. "I've seen you, too. I think. With a sort of stocky guy? With shoulders?"

"My brother."

"Oh."

"He's in the Service. The Infantry."

"Oh."

"He enlisted to get it over with and now he's sorry. He hates it."

"I can imagine."

"He thought it would get better after basic training, but he says it's the same shuck all around, and now he thinks they're going to send him overseas."

"Rough."

"You know it."

I looked at her again. She was damned attractive, although it was the kind of good lookingness that you didn't notice right off. It didn't wave and shout at you, but after you saw it a few times you began to appreciate it. She looked very clean and cool and casual, and she talked with her whole face. I mean, she didn't keep throwing smiles and winks at you and do things with her eyebrows, nothing like that. But the expression on her face always went along with what she was saying. A lot of the time a person's mouth will go off in one direction while their mind is somewhere else.

We didn't talk about anything very important. I told her about some of the apple knockers I had met, and she talked about spending summers on her uncle's farm when she was a kid. I hadn't really talked to a girl this way in I don't know how long. I used to talk to Aileen in Chicago, but that was all screwed up by the fact that I was all hung up on her sexually. With Hallie, sex didn't have anything to do with it. Not that she wouldn't have appealed to me, but that I had gone through some real changes and I wasn't the same horny kid I had been a couple of hours ago.

She had a second cup of the terrible coffee, and I kept her company and had a fourth. When she finished hers I said I thought I would probably go for a walk, and she said maybe some fresh air would do her good, help her get to sleep. We each paid for our own coffee and went outside together.

We walked two or three blocks without talking. But it was an easy silence, not one of those uncomfortable ones where you try to think of something to say and keep running different sentences through your mind. It was completely relaxed. I didn't even get lost in my own thoughts. I just walked along, hardly thinking of anything.

Then she said, "Chip?" I looked at her and for a second her eyes seemed so deep that I could see for miles into them. Then she lowered them and shifted her weight from one foot to the other.

She said, "I live at home with my folks."

"I know."

"We could go to your place."

"If you're tired of walking, sure."

"I mean if you wanted to ball or anything. Not to come on strong, but like I have to go to college tomorrow so there's no time to let things just happen. I think they would happen because I sort of dig you and everything, and even our signs are compatible, Virgo and Capricorn, or at least I think they are, but I don't really know much about it. Astrology."

"Neither do I."

"So if you don't want to, just say so." Her teeth attacked her lower lip. "Whatever you say."

"I live upstairs of Bruno's Barbershop. On the next block."

"I know where it is."

"There's no door to my room. It got broken and I had to take it off, but there's nobody else in the place at night so it doesn't really matter if there's a door or not."

"How did the door get broken?"

"A guy kicked it in. If you don't mind about there not being a door—"

"Well, it wouldn't matter if we're the only ones in the building, would it?"

"No."

"So," she said.

I took hold of her hand. It felt much smaller in mine than you would have expected. We walked to the corner, turned, went to my place and climbed the stairs. I put a light on and apologized for the mess. She said it didn't matter. She said it looked romantic, with the slanting roof and the exposed rafters. "Like a garret," she said. "You'll be a great but unknown artist dying of tuberculosis and I'll be your mistress and model, and you'll get drunk and cough and spit blood and beat me."

I kissed her. She kissed in the same fresh open way she talked, holding nothing back. We stood there kissing for a long time.

Then she took her sweatshirt off and turned around so that I could unhook her bra for her. She kicked off her sandals and stepped out of her dungarees and threw all her clothes in the corner. She stood watching eagerly as I got my clothes off and tossed them after hers. She put out her hand and touched me, and we floated down onto the bed like falling leaves.

"Oh, wow," she said. She burrowed close to me, her head tucked under my arm. "That was—"

"Uh-huh."

"Like unbelievable."

"Yeah."

"It's never been this good for me before." She rolled over on her back and folded her hands together just below her breasts. I looked at her. She said, "I wish they were bigger."

"They're beautiful."

"Tiny."

"So?"

"So I can never be an actress in Italian movies."

"I can't play basketball."

"Huh?"

"Nothing important."

She sat up, looked down at me. "That's the cutest thing," she said.

"I'm sort of attached to it."

"So am I, but in another way. It's so beautiful. Do you think it would get all embarrassed if I gave it a kiss?"

"There's only one way to find out."

She curled into a ball and nestled her head in my lap. Her hair was clean and silky all over my legs.

"Close your eyes," she said.

I closed them, but then I cheated and opened them again. It was so beautiful to watch her. She had her eyes shut and her face glowed with contentment. She looked like a baby nursing.

She stopped to say, "What a funny taste!"

"That's you."

"It is? I guess it must be. Funny."

She came up for air again to say, "It must like me. Look how big it got."

"Uh-huh."

"I really groove on sucking you. Is that terribly perverted of me?"

"Only if you don't do anything else."

"What else should I do?"

I stretched her out on her back and showed her.

Later on she was dozing lightly. I put my hand on her arm and her eyes opened.

"I don't want to scare you or anything, Hallie, but did I hurt you before?"

"I don't think so. Why?"

"Well, look." I pointed to the stain. "That must have come from one of us, and I wouldn't say anything, but if I *did* hurt you or anything—"

"Oh," she said.

"I just thought—"

"I guess I bled a little. I didn't realize."

"Is that common? I mean, oh, do you usually?"

She turned away. "Well, see—"

"What?"

"I should have told you, I guess. But we had such a good thing going and I didn't want anything to get in the way." Her eyes met mine. "I'm a virgin. I mean I was. Until just now. Chip? What's so funny?"

"Nothing."

"Then why are you laughing?"

"It's not important." I put my hands on her. "Look, when do you have to get up in the morning? What I'm getting at is how much longer can you stay?"

"I should have been asleep hours ago."

"Oh."

"But there's time, Chip, if that's what you meant. In fact, you don't even have to hurry. There's plenty of time, actually."

EPILOGUE

I ALREADY TOLD YOU THAT I LIKE EPILOGUES, and knowing what happened to the characters after the story ended. Actually there isn't too much I can put in this particular epilogue because not that much time has passed since then. And the only character I know what happened to is me, and I'm still in the same room over the same barbershop. I've got a new door, but otherwise things are about the same.

But I figured this is probably the only book I'll ever write, so when else am I ever going to get a chance to write an epilogue?

Hallie went home, and the next morning she left for college. She said she would drop a card with her address on it, and if I was ever in Wisconsin I could look her up. I haven't gotten the card yet.

Mr. Bruno replaced my door. I guess I already told you about that, though. And he didn't exactly ask about the bullet hole in his ceiling. "You a gooda boy," he said at one point, as if willing himself to believe it. "You donta

shoot anybody, and anybody donta shoota you." He
seemed vaguely frightened of me after that.

The car wash closed for the winter. This happened
almost immediately, and when they told me, I had the
crazy feeling that they were closing the car wash because
Hallie had gone to college. In a way it was sort of like
that. More people get their cars washed in the summer
than in the winter anyway, and this is especially true in
this particular city, where there are all sorts of people up
for the summer from New York City. So when the summer is over and college kids go back to school and summer people go back to the city, there's not enough business to support the car wash. I was out of a job, but since
it wasn't one with an Outstanding Opportunity For Advancement, I wasn't what you might call shattered.

Then I happened to get to talking with Mr. Burger. I
was lying around my room, reading a book and wondering
where I would go next, and what I would do when I got
there, when old Bruno came tearing up the stairs to tell
me that one of his customers had a flat tire. "You change
it, he give-a you money," he said.

I changed it and he gave-a me a dollar. The car was a
Lincoln Continental Mark III. Not that it's any more
work changing the tire on an expensive car, but if it had
been, say, a beat-up '51 Ford, then I might not have been
exactly staggered by getting a lousy dollar for changing it.
I still don't think I would have been overwhelmed,
though.

"Gee," I said, "thanks very much. Now I can go get a
hamburger and maybe some french fries. Man, I can
hardly wait."

"Sounds as though you haven't eaten in a long time,"
Mr. Burger said.

He missed the point, but I went along with it. "I'm out
of work," I said, "but through no fault of my own. The
position was temporary and the work seasonal."

"The car wash," he said, snapping his fingers. "You
were the kid who wiped the windows on the passenger
side."

"I remember your car now. You brought it in every Friday night."

"As soon as I got up from the city. That's right." He offered me a cigarette. I took it even though I don't smoke, and I told him that if it was all right with him I would save it and smoke it later, after my meal. He gave me a funny look, then said sure, he didn't care, and lit his own cigarette. "So you're out of work," he said. "Tough break, all right. I wish I could help you out, but I'm afraid I'm not in the car wash business myself."

"What business are you in?"

"Publishing."

"What type?"

"Books," he said warily. "What makes you ask?"

"No reason."

"Because I haven't got anything for a person without experience."

"Oh, I've got experience," I said. "I've got more experience than you would believe, even if it won't do me any good. I've done more things in the past nine or ten months—"

"I can imagine. When I was your age—" He shook his head. "What did I give you, a buck? Why don't you hang onto it and I'll buy you that hamburger you were drooling over and we'll talk."

"About what?"

"I don't know. Maybe we can do each other some good."

So Mr. Burger worked up a contract for my book and gave me money for living expenses and bought me a typewriter and got me a beautiful blond secretary.

Not really.

What he did, really, was listen to me talk about where I'd been and what I'd done, and nod every now and then, and smoke a lot of cigarettes, and wonder why I wouldn't smoke one but kept saving them for later. And he told me, when I was all done, that I had a hell of a story to tell and that it was the kind of story he'd like to bring to the attention of the reading public.

"You be sure you put all the sex in," he said. "What you have to do is hook the reader's attention and rivet his eyes to the page right from the start, and then you make him laugh and cry by tugging at his heart strings, but if you want to sell books, you better make sure you write something that'll give the son of a bitch a hard on."

And he said he would take a chance on me.

"I'm a gambling man," he said. "I'm willing to take a risk. Now I'll tell you what I'll do. It won't take you long to write this all up, but you'll need something to live on in the meantime. You got a typewriter?" I didn't. "Well, you got to have a typewriter and money to live on. I figure you ought to be able to get a decent typewriter for twenty dollars. And living expenses—suppose I give you fifty bucks total, and you'll see how it goes."

I finally found a typewriter for thirty-five dollars. Not a very good typewriter, but since I can't type with more than two fingers, I suppose a good typewriter would be wasted on me. That left me with fifteen dollars, plus the dollar for changing the flat tire, plus the few dollars I had set aside.

Now Mr. Burger is supposed to read this, if he remembers who I am. And if he likes it he can publish it, and then I'll get some money, I guess. I don't know exactly how it works but I must get something. I've been killing myself writing all this, though I suppose it doesn't show when you read it. I don't suppose it's very good, either. And I probably put in either too much sex or not enough, and I don't even know which. And I'm sure I told you too many things you didn't want to know and skipped things you would have wanted to hear more about, but I never did this before.

And that's the whole point, actually, now that I think about it. The first time is the hardest. There are probably other morals, too, but as sure as I like epilogues, I hate it when the author steps in at the end of the book and tells you what it was all about. Either you find it out for yourself or it's not worth knowing about. So I'll just say good-bye and thanks for reading this, and I'm sorry it wasn't better than it was.

CHIP HARRISON
SCORES AGAIN

ONE

AT FIRST I didn't pay very much attention to the guy. I was washing my hands in the men's room of a movie theater on Forty-second Street, and in a place like that it's not an especially good idea to pay too much attention to anybody or you could wind up getting more involved than you might want to. It's not that everybody is a faggot. But everybody figures everybody *else* is a faggot, so if you let your eyes roam around you could get (*a*) groped by someone who's interested or (*b*) punched in the mouth by someone who's not interested or (*c*) arrested by someone who's a cop.

If any of these things happened I would have had to leave the theatre, probably, and I didn't want to. I had already seen both movies, one of them twice, but I still didn't want to leave. It was warm in the theater. Outside it was cold, with day-old snow turning from gray to black, and once I went out there I would have to stay out there, because I had no other place to go.

(Which is not entirely true. There was this apartment on East Fifth Street between Avenues B and C where I could stay if I really had to. Some friends of mine lived there, and while it wasn't exactly a crash pad they would always let me have a section of floor to sleep on and a

163

plate of brown rice to eat. They were into this macrobiotic thing and all they ever ate was brown rice, which is very nourishing and very healthy and very boring after not very long. I could go there and eat and sleep and even talk to people, although most of the people you found there were usually too stoned to say very much, but the thing was that I only had a quarter, which is a nickel less than the subway costs. It was too cold to walk that far, and it was just about as cold inside that place as it was outside, because there was no heat. My friends had been using the stove to heat the place. That hadn't worked too well in the first place, and it worked less well when Con Ed turned off the gas and electricity for nonpayment. They burned candles for light and cooked the rice over litle cans of sterno. A couple of times Robbo had burned old furniture in the bathtub for heat, but he had more or less given this up, partly because heating the bathroom didn't do much for the rest of the apartment, and partly because there was a good chance the whole building would go up sooner or later.)

The point of this is just that I was washing my hands and not paying much attention to anything else until I happened to notice this guy take a wallet out of his pocket and start going through it. He was sort of hunched toward me, screening the wallet with his body from the washroom attendant, who I think existed to make sure that if anybody did anything dirty, they did it in one of the pay toilets. The guy with the wallet went through all the compartments of the thing, taking out money and plastic cards and things, and jamming everything into his pockets. Then he put the wallet in another pocket, took out a comb, combed his long dark hair back into a d.a., and left.

I turned and watched him, and on the way out his hand dipped into a pocket and came up with the wallet and dropped it into the wastebasket. There was this huge wastebasket on the opposite side of the door from the washroom attendant, and the guy with the d.a. did this whole number in one graceful motion, and the attendant never saw what happened.

I have to admit that it took me a minute to figure this out. Why would a guy throw his wallet away? And why be so slick about it? I mean, if you grow tired of your wallet, you have a perfect right to throw it away, right?

Oh.

It wasn't his wallet. He was a pickpocket or a mugger or something, and he had emptied the wallet, and now he wanted to get rid of it because it was Incriminating Evidence.

How about that.

My first reaction was just general excitement. Not that I had been an eyewitness to the most spectacular crime since the Brink's robbery. I would guess they get more wallets in those wastebaskets than they get paper towels. In fact, if you ever want a used wallet, that's probably the best place to go looking for one. But my own life hadn't been that thrilling lately, and it didn't take much to make my day.

The next thing that struck me was that I, Chip Harrison, had just been presented with an opportunity. A small one, perhaps, but I was as low on opportunities as I was on excitement. And that wallet was an opportunity.

It might hold important papers, for example. You might argue that people with important papers in their wallets don't spend all that much time in Forty-second Street movie houses, but one never knows for sure. Perhaps the owner would pay a reward for the return of the wallet. (Perhaps he'd call the police and have me arrested as a pickpocket.) Or perhaps there was some small change in the change compartment, if there was a change compartment. Or a subway token. Or a postage stamp. The Post Office won't redeem unused stamps, but at least I could mail a letter, if there was someone I wanted to write to. Or perhaps—

Well, there were endless possibilities.

I mulled them over in my mind while I was drying my hands on a paper towel, and I looked at the attendant and at the wastebasket, and then I went and combed my hair again. I had just done this before washing my hands in the first place and while my hair tends to need combing frequently it didn't really need it now. But I was about to Take Advantage of Opportunity, and thus I had to Think On My Feet.

I dried my hands again, and I carried the used paper towel over to the wastebasket, keeping the comb in the same hand with it, and I dropped them both into the basket.

Then I took a step or two toward the door, stopped abruptly, made a fist of one hand and hit the palm of the other hand with it.

"Oh, shit," I said. "I dropped my comb in the wastebasket."

"I seen you," the attendant said.

"All the stupid things."

"You want another comb, there's a machine over on the side."

"I want *that* comb," I said.

"Prob'ly dirty by now. You wouldn't believe the crap they throw in those baskets."

"I think I can get it." I was leaning into the basket and pawing around through old Kleenex and paper towels. The wallet had plummeted through them to the bottom, and I was having a hell of a time finding it.

"Over there," the clown said helpfully. "You see it?"

I did, damn him. I pawed at some paper towels and made the comb slip away. "Almost had it," I said, and went diving for it again. I had my feet off the ground and was balanced rather precariously, with the edge of the can pushing my belt buckle through my stomach. I had visions of losing my balance and winding up headfirst in the trashcan, which might provide some people with some laughs but which wouldn't provide me with the wallet, the comb, or much in the way of self-respect.

And self-respect, at that point of time, was as hard to come by as excitement, opportunity, and money.

I kept my balance and after another few shots I got the wallet. I can't swear that it's the same wallet I saw go in. For all I know there were a dozen of them somewhere down there. I got *a* wallet, palmed it off, and slipped it inside my shirt, and then I had to go through the charade of getting the fucking comb. It just didn't seem right to leave it there.

On my way through the lobby I dumped the comb in yet another wastebasket. And did it very surreptitiously, as if I were, well, a pickpocket ditching a wallet. Which is nothing but stupid.

I went outside and walked down to Broadway and watched the news flashing on the Allied Chemical Tower. It was cold, and there was a miserable wind blowing off the Hudson. I stood there shivering. I was out in the cold with no way of getting back into the warm, and I had traded a perfectly adequate pocket comb for a wallet that someone else had already gone through once, and I wasn't entirely certain I had come out ahead on the deal.

The papers in that wallet weren't important enough to wrap fish in. There were a couple of cash register receipts from unidentified stores and a Chinese laundry ticket. There was a head-and-shoulders snapshot of an ugly high school girl signed *Your Pal, Mary Beth Hawkins*. Judging by the hair style, Mary Beth was either (*a*) the squarest teen-ager in America or (b) forty-five-years old by now. Either way, I would have rather had my comb than her picture.

There were a few other things, but none of them mattered except for the bus ticket. It was in one of the secret compartments, and I guess that had kept it a secret from the pickpocket. A Greyhound bus ticket, good for one-way passage in either direction between Boston, Massachusetts, and Bordentown, South Carolina. It said it was valid anytime within one year from the date stamped on the back. The date was March something, and it was now December something, so the ticket had another three months to go before it became even more worthless than it already was.

I got rid of the rest of the wallet, Mary Beth's picture and all. I dumped it in a trashcan—what else?—and I was as slick as possible about this, because I didn't want any other poor clown to waste his time doing what I had just done. If you're going to steal a wallet, you ought to get it from its original owner. After that the depreciation is fantastic.

Then I walked around for a while, which kept me warmer than standing still, if just barely. Now and then I would take the ticket out and stare at it. It was that or stare at the quarter. Sensational, I thought. If I happen to be in Boston between now and March, I can catch a bus to Bordentown. Or, should I some fine morning find myself in Bordentown, I can hop on a Greyhound for Boston. Wonderful.

I wound up on Broadway looking at whores. Not in a particularly acquisitive way. Not that I wasn't tempted. I had been in New York for almost three months, and my sex life during that time could have been inscribed on the head of a pin with plenty of room left for the Lord's Prayer and as many angels as felt like dancing there.

(I had been living with a girl for one of those months, but she had just had a baby and couldn't do anything for six weeks, and by the time the six weeks were up she had gone away. At least she took the baby with her.)

I have always had these ethical objections to patronizing a prostitute, but in this case I might have overcome these objections if I'd had more than twenty-five cents to overcome them with. We'll never know.

So I went window-shopping, and the girls seemed to know it. They would look me up and down, and disapproval would glint in their eyes, and they would turn away, as if there was nothing so obvious as the fact that I couldn't possibly afford them. None of this was very ego-building.

And then one girl, who was either less experienced or a poorer judge of character, gave me a smile. An actual smile. So I stopped dead and smiled back at her, and she asked me if I'd like to go to her apartment.

"Is it warm there?"

"Honey," she said, "where I am, it's always warm."

I told her it sounded great. She asked me if I could spend twenty-five dollars.

"No way."

"Well, see, I like you. Could you spend twenty?"

"I wish I could."

"Well, shit. What *can* you spend?"

I could spend twenty-five cents, but I was damned if I was going to tell her that. I said, "Where are you from?"

"What do you want to know that for?"

"I just wondered."

"Well, I have this place on Fifty-fifth Street. How much can—"

"I mean originally," I said. "You're not from New York, are you?"

"From Memphis," she said. "And never goin' back there again, thanks all the same."

"Oh," I said.

"Why?"

"I thought maybe you were from Bordentown, South Carolina," I said. "Or maybe from Boston."

"You been drinkin', honey?"

"Because I have this bus ticket," I said, and showed it to her. "So if you had any interest in going to Boston or Bordentown—"

"That good?"

I showed her the date. "Perfectly good," I said.

"You want to come home with me?"

"To Memphis?"

"Shit. I tol' you. Fifty-fifth Street. You want to come?"

I tried on a smile. "All I really have is this ticket," I said. "I don't have any money. Just twenty-five cents and this ticket. I'm sorry for wasting your time—"

But she had my arm tucked under hers. "You know something? I like you. I really do. What's your name?"

"Chip."

"Yeah? I'm Mary Beth. What's the matter?"

"Nothing. I knew a girl named Mary Beth. I had a picture of her in a wallet that I carried for a while."

"Girl here in New York?"

"No," I said. "I think she lives in Bordentown. Or in Boston. Or she used to."

"You sure you all right?"

"I'm fine," I said. She was still holding onto my arm, and we seemed to be walking uptown, sort of toward Fifty-fifth Street, actually.

"I do like you, Chip," she was saying. "You just come home with me and I'll do you like you never been done. You ever had something called the Waterloo? That's a specialty of mine. What I take is a mouthful of warm water, see—"

She told me quite a bit about the Waterloo, and while she talked we walked, and while we walked she held onto my arm and rubbed it against her breast. My pants began getting very cramped.

"You just forget about no money," she said. "Don't make no never mind."

Oh, Jesus, I thought. I can't believe this.

Because I couldn't. I mean, it wasn't as though I hadn't had thoughts along this line before. I don't suppose it's the rarest fantasy ever. The ultimate sexual ego trip—that a prostitute, a girl who spends her life getting paid to have sex, will find you so overwhelmingly attractive that she'll want to give it to you for free. And she would know tricks you never dreamed of, and do all these fantastic things, and do them all for love.

Who ever thought it would actually happen?

Her apartment was pleasant in a sort of dull way. I couldn't tell whether or not it was a typical prostitute's apartment, but it seemed to me then that it couldn't be, because it seemed to me then that she was by no means a typical prostitute. By the time we got there I had already decided that she wasn't basically a whore at all. Just because a girl was whoring didn't make her a whore. After all, in the past year I had sold termite extermination service, picked fruit, posed for pornographic pictures and written a book, and I didn't think of myself as a writer or fruitpicker or any of those things. Life deals unpredictable cards, and you have to play each hand as it lays, and little Mary Beth might be walking the streets but that didn't make her a streetwalker. It might not make her the Virgin Mary, either, but it didn't make her a whore.

I really had things all figured out. I would Take Her Away From All This. She already loved me, and by the time I got done balling her she would love me to distraction, and at that point the idea of ever having sex with anyone but Chip Harrison would positively turn her stomach. And I would live with her and land a Job With A Future, and we would screw incessantly while I made my way in the world, and we would, uh, Live Happily Ever After.

The things is, see, that when a fantasy starts coming true before your eyes, it's natural to go on taking the fantasy to its logical (?) conclusion. Did I really expect all of this would happen? Not really, but remember that I never expected it to start happening in the first place. If someone goes and repeals the Law of Gravity and you find yourself flying to the Moon, it's no more unreasonable to plan on flying clear through to Mars.

I stood there working all of this out while she closed the door and turned four or five locks. Doesn't want us to be interrupted, I thought happily. We might be here for days. Weeks. And she wants to make sure we have privacy.

"Well," she said. "Not much, but it's home."

"Mary Beth," I said.

"Hi, Chip."

"Mary Beth." And I put my hands on her shoulders and drew her close. Somewhere along the way her head turned to the side and I was kissing a gold hoop ear-ring.

"Uh-uh," she said.

"Huh?"

She rubbed her breasts against my chest and bounced her groin playfully against mine. I had this tight feeling in my chest.

"I don't kiss on the mouth," she said.

"Huh?"

She gave me another happy bounce, then moved away. "Just something I don't do," she said. "Kiss you anywheres else, kiss you like nobody ever, but not on the mouth."

"But that's silly."

"Shit—"

"But—"

I remembered reading that some prostitutes refused to kiss their clients mouth-to-mouth. They would do anything else, but they reserved that intimacy for the men they loved. It had never made much sense to me at the time, because if you stop and think about it, well, it's pretty ridiculous. Especially since I had spent the past

year with a lot of girls who would kiss you mouth-to-
mouth until Rome fell but wouldn't do anything more
exciting than that. It seemed as though the whores had
their value system turned upside down.

But what I couldn't understand was what this had to do
with me and Mary Beth. She didn't want money from me.
She was doing this for love, so by rights she should be
particularly keen on kissing me on the mouth.

And then I got it. The poor kid, I realized, had never
really had any sex life to speak of outside of prostitution.
So naturally that was her frame of reference. Here she
wanted to ball me for the sheer unadulterated pleasure of
it, but her mind was so conditioned by the life she led that
she had to act with me in much the same way as she acted
with her paying customers. It was weird, and sort of
disheartening in a way, but there was also something sort
of sweet and pathetic about it.

She has never known love, I told myself. But I shall
change her. I shall fulfill her.

"Well, now," she said. "And what have we here?"

That must have been a rhetorical question, because
what we had there was something she came into contact
with quite frequently in her profession, and where we had
it was in her hand. She had opened my fly and taken me
firmly in hand, and she was stroking me rhythmically. Her
wrist did everything; the rest of her arm stayed motion-
less.

"You come with me," she said. "We'll just wash you up
first."

We stood at the bathroom sink and washed me up. The
editorial *we* was bugging me a little. Nurses talk like
that—"How are we feeling this morning?"—but I never
figured whores did, too. Anyway, she soaped me up and
rinsed me off, and it was sort of pleasant and unpleasant
both at once, pleasant in that it felt good, and unpleasant
in that it sort of implied that I was fundamentally too

dirty to deal with otherwise. But then I thought of some of
the things she had in mind, and some of the things she
had done with other people, and I decided I was just as
glad that she tended to wash this portion of a person
beforehand, and also, to tell the truth, just as pleased that
she didn't believe in mouth-to-mouth kissing.

When she was done she filled a glass with hot water and
carried it into the bedroom. "For the Waterloo," she explained. "You're gonna love this."

"Uh."

"Don't you want to take off your clothes, Chip?"

"Uh, sure," I said, and started undressing. I was feeling
unbelievably dizzy and stupid, and it wasn't just the excitement. That was a part of it. But another part was the
feeling that none of this was really happening. It all
seemed so thoroughly unreal. I took off all my clothes and
looked up and she was just standing there, with her
clothes on.

"Your clothes," I said.

"Huh?"

"Why don't you, uh, get undressed?"

"You want me to?"

"Well, sure."

She shrugged. A very strange girl, I decided. Maybe it
wasn't just that she hadn't had any real sex life outside of
prostitution. Maybe she was equally inexperienced *in*
prostitution. Maybe she just read about the Waterloo in a
book or something.

I stood there watching while she got undressed. She
didn't make the process particularly seductive, just
shucked off her clothes and draped them over a chair. Her
body was skimpy everywhere but the breasts, which were
on the large size. I haven't described her too much because I have trouble picturing her now in my mind. She
was sort of mousy, really, hair somewhere between blond
and brown. I suppose she was around my age, although

she seemed older, maybe because she was more at home in this scene than I was.

She left on her stockings and garter belt. I asked her if she didn't want to take them off and get comfortable, and she gave me an impatient look. "Most men like 'em on," she said. "Don't you think they look pretty?"

I thought they looked like something out of those whip-and-chain movies, but I said sure, they were pretty.

"Because it's wasting time, you know, taking 'em off, putting 'em on."

"Then leave them on," I said, and she nodded, and I reached out for her and drew her in close. I went to kiss her again, out of habit, but she turned away automatically and I didn't press the point. I sort of felt like apologizing but couldn't think of an intelligent way to do that, so I kept my mouth shut and let my fingers do the walking. I felt various parts of her, and she did a little deep breathing and such, but nothing that really assured me I was driving her out of her skull.

"Let me," she said, disengaging herself. "You just lay down, Chip, and let me do you up."

I got on the bed. She reached for the glass of water, then stopped with it halfway to her lips. "You tell me if it's too hot," she said.

Then she took a mouthful of water and bent over me.

It was really very nice. She just did it for a second or so, then pulled away and looked at me. I was waiting for her to ask me whatever the hell it was she was going to ask me, and then I realized that she wasn't going to ask me anything because she couldn't because she had her mouth full of hot water.

"It's not too hot," I said. "It's just right."

She nodded and started doing it again. And, as before, it was really very nice indeed. It was strange, too, because I felt totally unconnected with the whole process. I decided that it was a great technique, and it was really great that she knew these great techniques, but that it would be infinitely better when I taught her how to put some love into the whole process. Or at least to make it obvious to me that she was enjoying what she was doing.

Then she stopped again.

"Believe me, it's not too hot," I said, and started to push her head back in place. But her head wouldn't push. She leaned over and spat the water out onto the linoleum.

"The ticket," she said.

"Huh?"

She looked impatient again. "The bus ticket, man. You better give it to me now. I want to make sure it's still good."

"The bus ticket?"

She sat up and stared at me. "Shit, the *bus* ticket," she said. "What's the matter with you? You got to give it to me and I got to make sure I can cash it before we do any more. All I need is—"

"Cash the bus ticket?"

"Take it over to Port Authority and cash it," she said. "I told you you didn't need money. Just the ticket is all. If it's good I'll get twenty-thirty dollars out of that ticket."

I suppose you saw it coming all along, but I'm not going to apologize for my stupidity. After all, it was *my* fantasy that we were acting out.

The Waterloo, I thought. I had already had the hot water part, and now I was getting the cold water. Buckets of it, all over all my enthusiasm for little old Mary Beth.

"Hey! Where you goin'?"

I was putting on my clothes. Not too quickly, not too slowly. Very mechanically, actually. Tucking the shirt into the pants, getting my socks right-side out and then putting them on, then the shoes—

"You crazy?"

"I have to go," I said.

"Go? Where to?"

"The bus station," I said. "I have to cash the ticket."

"Shit, I said I would cash it. Just hand it on over here."

"Fuck you," I said.

"Are you out of your *mind?*"

I turned toward her, and I guess I must have wanted to kill her, or at least I looked as though I wanted to kill her, because her face drained of color and she backed off fast. I turned away from her again and went to the door.

The whore with the heart of gold. You didn't need money. All you needed was a negotiable bus ticket.

I almost went crazy unlocking all those locks. She never said a word, which was lucky for her. I'm normally about as non-violent as it's possible to get, but I wasn't feeling very normal just then. Nothing makes you hate a person quite so much as being made an absolute asshole out of.

The last lock cleared just as I was about to give up and kick the door down.

It was as cold as ever out there, but I walked three blocks before I even noticed it.

Two thoughts kept me from running around and screaming. One was that, if and when I calmed down, I was certain to see the humor in the situation. I didn't see any humor in it now, but I knew I would sooner or later.

The other comforting thought, and it was the more comforting of the two, was that I had that bus ticket in my pocket. And I could cash it in.

TWO

THIS IS sort of a problem.

See, I was going to open the book by saying who I am and my background and all the rest of it and get that out of the way right at the start. But the thing is that I wrote one book before this. It was called *No Score*, and it just came out last month. Gold Medal published it. *No Score*, by Chip Harrison. That wasn't what I wanted to call it, but forget what I wanted to call it because they changed it. I think *No Score* is a pretty good title, catchy, and probably a lot better than what I had in mind.

The point is that some of you already read *No Score* and some of you didn't, and if you did read it maybe you still remember it and maybe you don't. I remember it very clearly, but that's different.

See, if you read *No Score*, I don't want to bore you by feeding you all that stuff here and there throughout this book. If you didn't read it, I want to tell you as much as you have to know about it, but at the same time I don't want to spoil it for you in case you by some chance enjoy this book and want to read *No Score* later on. Of course the best thing would be if you ran out right now and got a copy of *No Score* and read it first and then came back to this book, but obviously not everybody can do that. If they happen to be reading this on a plane, for instance.

So what I think I'll do is put down some of it right here and now to tell you as much as you have to know about me, and possibly more than you want to know, as far as that goes. If you did read *No Score,* you can skip ahead right now to the next chapter, because none of this will be news to you.

My name is Chip Harrison. I guess you know that. My legal name was originally Leigh Harvey Harrison, but Chip was my nickname from early childhood, and my parents decided in November of 1963 that it might be sensible to forget my legal name and concentrate on Chip, Leigh Harvey being a liability in the name market at that point in time.

Of course, that was so many assassinations ago I don't suppose it matters any more.

No Score opened when I was seventeen and in my last semester at Upper Valley Prep School. I found out then that my parents had been confidence swindlers, and they were about to go to prison, and they committed suicide. I wasn't allowed to finish school, partly because of the scandal and partly because there was no money to pay my bills and I wasn't a good enough basketball player to make a difference, although I was fairly tall for my age.

So I went out to seek my fortune. I went to Chicago and got a job passing out slingers for a sidewalk photographer, and not quite sleeping with his wife, and then I went down through Illinois and Indiana with a termite inspection crew, and almost went to jail for statutory rape, which would have been really weird because (*a*) I was underage myself and (*b*) I didn't get to do anything. Then I wound up picking berries and apples across Ohio and New York, and almost got shot by a jealous husband, which also would have been ironic because (*a*) it wasn't his wife and (*b*) I didn't get to do anything.

In a way, not getting to do anything was what *No Score* was all about. That did work itself out, though, with a surprise touchdown in the final minutes of play. And then I happened to meet Mr. Knox Burger, and he bought me a hamburger because I helped him change a tire on his car, and I got to talking about my experiences and he suggested writing a book. He even gave me fifty dollars so that I could buy a typewriter and live on Maine sardines and day-old bread while I wrote the book. That book turned out to be *No Score,* and when it was done I took it to New York, and in September of 1970 it finally came out. I got some money when I finished the book but not as much as I thought and it didn't last long. It lasted until December, actually, at which time I had twenty-five cents left.

(I don't want to get hung up in time sequences, but let me get the chronology of this down for you. I started writing *No Score* in September of 1969 and finished it about a month later. From October to December of 1969 I was living in New York in the East Village, partly with the girl I mentioned who had just had a baby, and partly here and partly there, and partly at the sort of crash pad where they had all the brown rice and burned chairs in the bathtub. That's when the action in this book starts, in December of 1969. Then in September of 1970 *No Score* was finally published—I don't know why those things take so long, really—and it is now October of 1970 and I am sitting here writing *this* book, which you are reading. God knows when it will be when you get to read it. 1984, probably. In fact it may be close to then by the time I finish this chapter, because it's really very difficult trying to get all this together.

(Actually it may not come out at all, because Mr. Burger doesn't even work there any more. He left, probably because of the nervous strain of editing *No Score*. There's a Mr. Walter Fultz there now, and he gave me about the same advice Mr. Burger did. Keep it moving, he said. Keep it warm and sensitive and perceptive and lively, and most of all—make sure there's sex in it.

(I don't know how well it's moving. Not too well in this chapter because of all the boring recapitulation. I really hope most of you already read *No Score* and were able to skip all of this crap. But I promise the pace will pick up in the next chapter. It would almost have to.

(And I also promise that there will be plenty of sex in it. There really can't help being plenty of sex in it. That's why I decided to start this book in December instead of picking up where *No Score* left off. There were those three months when nothing happened, so I decided to skip them and start right when things started to happen.)

So that's who I am. Not the seventeen-year-old virgin who was there for the start of *No Score,* but an eighteen-year-old virgin-once-removed. A Virgo, with Gemini rising and Moon in Leo, if you pay attention to things like that. Sort of tall and sort of thin and sort of ordinary-looking, and walking full speed through the slush to the Port Authority Bus Terminal.

THREE

THE PORT AUTHORITY Bus Terminal is a well-lighted and spacious modern building, and if you walk through it quickly in the daytime it just looks like a bank or an airport. But at night it's depressing. All bus stations are. It's the people. Half of them are only there because they don't have enough money to fly or take a train, and the other half are there because it's reasonably warm and the benches are reasonably comfortable and you can steal a nap there and other people will think maybe you're waiting for a bus, and will leave you alone. Sooner or later, though, some uniformed old fart will ask you for a ticket, and when you don't have one they tell you to go away.

I didn't have any trouble cashing the ticket. I was in line behind a fat woman whose luggage was a matched set of shopping bags. She wanted to go someplace in Missouri, and she and the clerk had a hell of a job working out the details. This gave me time to figure out various reasons why I was cashing the ticket, but when my turn came I just pushed the ticket through the window and asked for cash. The clerk looked at it as if he suspected I was part of a gang of counterfeiters specializing in old bus tickets. But it passed.

You know, if it hadn't, I really would have been irritated. I mean, the ticket would at least have gotten me Mary Beth.

Instead it got me thirty-seven dollars and eighty-three cents. I went to one of the benches and sat down and counted the money over and over again. Then I put different amounts in different pockets. I was somehow more conscious of pickpockets than ever before. It occurred to me that I could have kept the wallet, and if I had then I'd now have something to put the money in.

Thirty-seven dollars and eighty-three cents. I sat there with different portions of the money in different pockets for a long time, thinking of one thing and another. Then I went to the john. The free stall was in use so I had to use one of the pay toilets, but the attendant wasn't there so I crawled under it. (Under the door. Not under the toilet.)

There should be a law against pay toilets.

I did some more thinking, in addition to doing what I had gone there to do, and I bought a comb for a quarter and combed my hair. The comb lost a couple teeth in the process. It was really shoddy compared to the one I'd thrown away.

Then I went back to the ticket window. "Bordentown, South Carolina," I said. "One way."

The clerk started hunting for the Bordentown tickets, then did an elaborate double take. "You were just here a minute ago," he said.

"Well, maybe fifteen minutes."

"You cashed in a ticket. A Bordentown ticket."

"I know."

"And now you want to buy it back?"

"That was a Boston-to-Bordentown ticket," I said. "What I want is a New York-to-Bordentown ticket."

"Whyntcha just trade it in in the first place and save me the aggravation?"

"I didn't realize that I wanted to go to Bordentown."

"What are you, a wise guy?"

"Can't I just buy a ticket?"

"You people. I don't know. Think everybody's got all the time in the world."

The fare from New York to Bordentown was thirty-three dollars and four cents, and I had to go through various pockets until I got that sum together. While I did this, he talked to himself. He wouldn't tell me when the next bus left. I had to use one of the house phones and call Information. They told me there was a bus leaving in two and a half hours. It made express stops from New York to Raleigh, then made local stops all the way to Miami. It would put me in Bordentown in a little over forty hours.

The only thing I knew about Bordentown was that it was in South Carolina, and that somebody named Mary Beth Hawkins probably lived there once. And that I evidently wanted to go there.

I had four dollars and seventy-nine cents left. That was a lot less than thirty-three dollars and four cents, but it was a lot more than a quarter, so I was ahead of the game and playing on the house's money.

I was also starving. I found a lunch counter in the building and had two hamburgers and an order of french fries and three cups of coffee. It certainly wasn't a macrobiotic meal. It wasn't even very good, but that didn't seem to matter. I ate everything but the napkin.

Why Bordentown?

That's a good question. I don't know if I can find an answer that's as good as the question.

See, what happened was that I sat, first on the bench and then on the toilet, and I thought about the money and tried to think of something to do with it. And none of the things that involved staying in New York seemed like very good ideas, and I came to the conclusion that I had bombed out in New York and it was time to go somewhere else. Nothing against the city. Any city or town is as good or as bad as what you're doing and the people you're doing it with. And for one reason or another I had never quite managed to get it together in New York. There were some good times in among the bad times, and I was glad I had come, but it was time to split.

(I have this tendency to go someplace else whenever I don't like where I am. I never really had a home that I can remember. When I was with my parents we would stay at a different expensive hotel in a different city every couple of months, and when I was at school it was a different boarding school every year, and the pattern hasn't changed since. Sometimes I think it's weakness of character to pick up and run whenever things turn sour. But why stay where you don't want to be? For Pete's sake, there's a whole world out there. I suppose there are things to be said for settling down and sinking roots, but someone else will have to say them.)

The thing is, it's not enough to have someplace to go away from. You also need someplace to go away *to*. And I didn't have one. There were places I had already been, but I couldn't see any point in going back to any of them. Chicago was vaguely possible, I had had reasonably good times there, but I thought about that wind coming off Lake Michigan and schussing through the Loop and imagined what that wind would be like in January, and that ruled out Chicago. Besides, it was too big, it would be too much like what I was leaving.

There was a girl named Hallie with whom I had traded virginities on the very best night of my life. She was in college in Wisconsin. I had sent her a postcard before coming to New York, and since then I had written her three or four stupid letters but never mailed any of them, maybe because I wasn't quite sure what I wanted to say to her. I decided that it would be nice to see Hallie again, and then I decided it would be even nicer to see Hallie when I was a little clearer on how I felt about her and what I wanted to do about it. It would also be nicer if I could see her with clean clothes on me and money in my pocket and a little firmer sense of direction.

And then it came to me.

Bordentown.

Maybe you've noticed that when you've gone without sleep and food for a long time, and without really talking to anybody, you start to get messages from God. That's a little less crazy than it sounds. What happens is that a lot of minor things start taking on tremendous significance, and you start reading vital messages into them.

Like the whole bit with the wallet. And what was in the wallet—a picture of Mary Beth Hawkins and a bus ticket. And the first person I met after that was also named Mary Beth, which may be less remarkable in the cold light of dispassionate analysis but which seemed extraordinary at the time. The way all these things seemed to add up was that it was meant for me to get that bus ticket. It was destiny. And for me to cash in the ticket and spend the money was spitting in destiny's face. Obviously the thing to do with that ticket was to use it and go where it went.

Which still gave me two choices, actually. Boston or Bordentown. But I never seriously considered Boston. It would have been copping out. I mean, the ticket was about eighty-five percent New York-to-Bordentown and fifteen percent New York-to-Boston.

Besides, Boston would be as cold as New York, maybe even colder. And Bordentown was in South Carolina—I knew that much about it, dammit. It would be warm. And it would be a small town, it would have to be fairly small or I probably would have heard of it at one time or another. So if I was looking for a change from New York, I really didn't have to look any farther.

For Pete's sake, I've gone lots of places on less reason than that.

The bus ride started off horrible. Then it became very boring for a while, and then it got wonderful.

The horrible part was brief, from New York to Philadelphia. It was horrible because there were four men two rows back drinking wine and singing, and a third of the way to Philadelphia one of them threw up, and a few miles later so did the rest of them. It was horrible because the woman across the aisle from me was carrying a baby who cried all the way from New York to Philadelphia. The woman didn't seem to mind. Me, I minded. It was horrible because the man in the seat next to me was fat enough to take up all of his seat and a good deal of mine as well. He didn't use Dial, and I don't guess he cared if anybody else did, either.

The four drunks got off in Trenton. The woman with the brat got off in Philadelphia. The smelly fat man was riding clear down to Miami, but when we got to Philadelphia I was able to change my seat. So that ended the horrible part.

The boring part was just boring. Nothing much to be said about it, really. I took crumby naps and woke up and went to the john and came back and sat down and looked out the window and waited for something to happen. Now and then the bus stopped somewhere and we all got off it and went to a terrible lunch counter, and I would have a Coke and a package of those little orange crackers with cheese and peanut butter between them.

(I knew a speed freak in New York who lived on nothing but Cokes and those sandwich crackers. Three packs of the crackers a day and six Cokes. He weighed about eighty-three pounds and the circles under his eyes looked as though they'd been painted on with shoe polish. "Speed doesn't kill," he told me. "That's the lie they feed you. It's the malnutrition that does you in. I figure I've got six months before my liver goes. Once your liver goes you've had it."

("Then why don't you start eating right?"

("Priorities, man. I need to speed to get my head together. Once my head is together I'll kick the speed and stabilize myself with tranks and downs, and then I'll get into eating right. High-protein, fertile eggs, the whole organic foods trip. And I want to get into body-building. I've been getting all these catalogues of barbell equipment. But first I have to get my head together. I figure I can get my head together in six months. I figure my liver can make it that long."

(Sure.)

The wonderful part, the part that was not at all horrible or boring, started sometime in the late afternoon and somewhere south of Washington. I don't know the time because I wasn't wearing a watch, and I don't know the name of the town or even the state because I wasn't paying all that much attention to where we were when she joined us. We stopped at some station and I didn't feel like another Coke so I stayed in my seat with my eyes closed. Then just as the bus was starting up a voice said, "Pardon me?" and I looked up and there she was.

She was a little thing, with yellow hair to her shoulders and large round brown eyes and a pointed chin. She was wearing a plaid mini skirt that got halfway to her knee and a cardigan sweater the color of her hair. She had a coat over one arm and was carrying a little suitcase.

At first glance she looked about sixteen. When you looked a little closer at her eyes and the corners of her mouth you could add maybe ten years to that. Say twenty-five.

"Could y'all tell me if this seat is taken?"

It wasn't. Neither were half the seats on the bus, which had emptied out a good deal in Washington. She could have had a whole double seat to herself, actually.

"And could I ask you to help me with this suitcase here?"

It was small and light. I put it in the overhead rack, and then she took a book and a package of cigarettes from her coat pocket and gave me the coat, and I put it alongside the suitcase. I sat down again and she sat down next to me. She didn't have any makeup on except maybe a trace of lipstick, but she was wearing quite a bit of perfume. She smelled very nice, actually. It made me think of Mary Beth, the bus-ticket hooker. Mary Beth had been wearing perfume and hadn't smelled very terrific at all. There's perfume and there's perfume.

"Well, now! I thought we might have rain, but it's turned a nice day after all, hasn't it?"

"Just so there's no snow."

"You from up No'th?"

"I'm not exactly from anywhere," I said. "I was in New York for the past few months."

"And what place do you call home?"

"Wherever I am."

Her face lit up. "Now that's exciting," she said. What she said was *excitin'*, actually, but I hate it when writers spell everything phonetically to get across the fact that somebody has an accent. I'll just say now that she had an accent thicker than spoonbread and you can bear that in mind when you run her dialogue through your head.

"When you don't have one home in particular, why, it's like you're never *away!* Me, I'm an old homebody. My aunt has the pleurisy and I was up doing for her for onto ten days, but except when she has it bad I never get away from home."

"Where's home?"

"Georgia. Mud Kettle, Georgia. Ever been there?"

"No."

"Well, it's not that you missed much." This I believed. The name wasn't Mud Kettle, by the way, but I looked up the town she mentioned in an atlas just now and the population is less than twenty-five hundred, so I changed the name to Mud Kettle because otherwise somebody could probably figure out who she was, and it might shake up the old folks at home. "Not missing much at all. Well, here I am, little old Willie Em Weeks from Mud Kettle, G-A. Lordy!"

"What does the *M* stand for?" I mean, girls don't usually announce middle initials.

"Emily," she said.

"Emily starts with an *E*," I said.

"Doesn't stand for, it's *short* for! You silly. Willamina Emily Weeks, and isn't that a handle."

Then she waited expectantly, and it occurred to me to tell her my name. She had never met anyone named Chip before, and I had never met any Willie Em, and we got what conversational mileage we could out of that. Which wasn't much.

Then she said, "Chip? Would you mind awfully if I asked you a favor? Would you change seats with me?"

If she wanted to sit by a window, there were windows all over the place she could pick. I didn't tell her this. I changed seats with her, and our bodies bumped a little in passing. Nothing fantastic, just enough to put ideas in my head.

Which was ridiculous, I thought, sitting down again. She would be fun to talk to, someone to break the monotony of the trip, but that was obviously as far as it was going to go. I was getting off in South Carolina and she was riding clear on to Georgia. And anyway she was married, there was a ring on her finger. And besides that we were on a *bus,* for Pete's sake, in the middle of the afternoon, and all you can do on a bus is sweat and sleep, with sweating considerably more likely than sleeping.

We talked a little more. She asked if I minded if she smoked, and I said I didn't, and she lit a cigarette and opened her book and I settled back in my seat and closed my eyes. I was just as glad she was reading because she

wasn't that outstanding to talk to. It was nice watching her
and listening to her voice, a very pleasant voice, but it was
very hard to concentrate on what she was saying.

So I thought I would doze off again into that sort of
half sleep that's possible on a bus, but I couldn't manage
it. It was her, the perfume, the presence. I was aware of
her. Somehow I was more aware of her now when she
wasn't talking and I wasn't looking at her than I had been
before.

After a while she said, "Chip? Are you asleep?"

"No."

"Could you do me a favor?"

She was very large on favors. I opened my eyes.
"Sure," I said.

She handed me her book, her finger indicating a place
on the page. "Starting right here," she said. "Could you
just read that scene?"

"Out loud?"

"No, silly."

I took the book and started to read, and the first thing I
did was start blinking furiously. The book was called
either *The Swinging Swappers* or *The Swapping Swingers*.
It hardly matters which. And the scene she had given me
involved six people in a sexual tangle, with everybody
doing everything to everybody else, and all in the crudest
and most explicit sort of writing. Absolute hard-core pornography. The scene went on for God knows how many
pages. I stopped after two and a half of them, and it was
just gathering momentum.

And so was I.

I don't know whether I actually blush or not, but if I
do, I was doing it then. I closed the book and turned very
very slowly to look at her. The expression on her face
surprised me. Very serious and matter-of-fact, with a little
vertical furrow in the center of her forehead.

"Did you read it?"

"Uh, a couple of pages, yeah."

"You read fast. Could y'all tell me something?"

"What?"

"Was that there an erotic scene? Was it exciting?"

"Yes."

"It was?"

"Uh, yeah. Yes, I would say that you would have to call that an erotic scene. Yes."

Her face relaxed and she gave a little sigh. "Well, that's good news," she said. "See, I thought maybe it was just the bus that was getting to me. I always get so randy on buses. I swear I get like a mare in heat just from riding on a bus. I don't rightly know what it is that does it. The rhythm of the wheels?"

"Maybe."

"You think that could be it?"

"I suppose."

She nodded thoughtfully. "I can feel it right now," she said. "The rhythm of the wheels on my backside."

From her tone of voice we could have been discussing the weather. *Think it'll rain? Oh, most likely not. Course we're due for a little rain. Yes, and I always get so randy on buses.* Christ almighty.

She said, "Feel my heart, Chip," and she took my hand and placed it on her left breast.

"Can you feel it?"

I couldn't feel her heart beat, perhaps because my own had suddenly grown so loud. I could certainly feel her breast, though. I felt it through the thicknesses of sweater and bra, felt the nipple poking against my palm.

I cupped her breast, stroked with my fingers. It was as warm and soft as a little bird. I kept the little bird in my hand and dreamed of giving her two in the bush.

Our mouths found one another. She tasted of cigarettes. I don't like to smoke but I like that taste on a girl's mouth. We slid into an all-out kiss right off the bat. She was very goddamned good at kissing. We kissed for miles, and I held her breast as if I was afraid it would fly away if I let it go. I wasn't about to take any chances.

When we broke the kiss she sagged back in her seat with her eyes closed and her jaw slack. Her breathing was really ragged. I was a little shook up myself but she was way out ahead of me.

Finally she said, "Get my coat, Chip."

"You can't leave now. I mean, the least you have to do is wait until the bus stops."

"*Leave?* Who's leaving?"

"Not me. I thought you wanted your coat."

She sighed and tsssted at me. "Don't you have no sense?" she whispered. "To put over us. To neck under. So nobody sees us."

"Oh."

"Because I'm not about to stop now. Chip, I told you how I get on buses, and then reading that scene with them . . . and then you messing around with me, I mean I'm not about to stop now."

"Fine by me."

"Now fetch my coat."

I fetched her coat and draped it over us. While I was getting it I checked out the other people in the area. If any of them were checking us out in return they were doing a good job of hiding it. The seats across the aisle were empty, and most of our other neighbors were asleep.

As soon as I was seated beside her she grabbed my hand and tucked it up under her mini skirt. She was wearing panties. Very moist panties.

I said, "Willie Em—"

"Shhhh!" she whispered. "No more talking, Chip. Oh, Lord have mercy, I'm so hot I could *burn!* But don't talk, don't say anything. Just get me off. God, please get me *off*—"

The thing is, she kept getting off and climbing right

back on again. There was only so much we could do. I played with her and that was about the extent of it. She was unbelievably responsive. Each orgasm just seemed to make her that much more anxious for the next one.

This went on for maybe half an hour, and I could see where it was destined to go on all the way to Bordentown unless I happened to run out of fingers somewhere along the way. And I was going to get off the bus in Bordentown with testicles the size of basketballs, and they were going to hurt like hell, and that was just too damned bad because I had already decided it was worth it.

Maybe she wasn't the only one who got horny on buses. Maybe it was the other people around, or maybe it was the build-up and letdown I'd gotten earlier from Mary Beth, or maybe it was just Willamina Emily Weeks herself, but whatever it was, it was worth six Waterloos and an Armageddon. I mean it was very goddamned exciting, believe me.

God knows how many little orgasms she had. I couldn't keep score. But she finally got the big one and collapsed like a tubercular lung.

In less than two minutes we pulled off the highway and stopped for a ten-minute rest break in Erewhon, North Carolina.

I swear she planned it that way.

She said, "Get my suitcase down, Chip. And put your jacket over those two seats across the aisle, and leave my coat here. And when we come back you sit over there and sort of take up both seats until the bus moves. So no one sits across from us, you hear?"

I heard and I did. I didn't know why she wanted her suitcase, or why we had to get off the bus and back on again, or any of those things, really. I would have understood the bit about the coats even if she hadn't explained it to me, although I'll admit I wouldn't have thought of it on my own, not just then.

But I wasn't going to bug her about any of this. I mean, it was pretty obvious this wasn't the first time she ever got randy on a bus, and it wasn't the first time she ever decided to do anything about it. This bus fetish was something she had indulged in before. And probably often. Which was why she sat down next to me to begin with. And why she wanted the window seat—partly so that we could bump bottoms while changing places, and partly because she would be better shielded from observation if she sat away from the aisle.

I didn't really want to get off the bus and back on again. Walking presented certain logistical problems that would be even more obvious to spectators if I had to leave my jacket on the bus. But I got off and I forced myself to drink a Coke and munch a pack of those peanut butter and cheese things. I waited until she emerged from the ladies' room and got on board the bus before I followed her. She put her suitcase on the seat beside her so that no one could sit there, and I sprawled over the two opposite seats and looked as unkempt as possible so that no one would want to sit next to me. She waited until the bus was back on the highway before giving me a nod, and I came over and put her suitcase overhead and sat down next to her.

We huddled together under her coat and kissed briefly. Then I said, "Why the suitcase?"

"Can't you guess?"

The only thing that had occurred to me was that she wanted to put her diaphragm on, but I couldn't believe that. This was a bus, after all, and it wasn't particularly comfortable or roomy even if all you wanted to do was sit in it. I know people screw in the most unlikely places, but only midgets and contortionists could possibly do it on a bus.

I had already decided that the best I could hope for was to shoot in my pants, if you'll forgive me for being crude about it. (I can't really think of any other way to say it.) And I wasn't all that sure I wanted to do that. I don't suppose I really cared about getting off myself. I just wanted to go on thrilling Willie Em.

"No," I said, "I can't guess."

"Did that old suitcase feel heavier this time?"

"No."

"It was, though."

"It was?"

She grinned impishly. "Something in it that wasn't in it before."

What? A roll of toilet paper? A Coke? What?

"What?"

"You have to find out for yourself. But I'll bet you appreciate the change."

"I think you lost me."

"Why, I surely hope not! Now why don't you shut your mouth and start loving me up instead of asking all those questions?"

I had no argument there. I kissed her and put a hand on her breast. It felt softer than ever. I petted it and light dawned.

"Oh."

"Uh-huh. And that's just the half of it."

I could guess the other half, but I sent my hand on an expedition to make sure. I slipped it under her skirt and there were no panties there. The panties, like the bra, were currently in her suitcase.

I hope she wrung them out first.

It certainly did make things easier. We snuggled under her coat and unbuttoned her cardigan and pulled her skirt all the way up, and all of a sudden there was a lot more to do. She had wonderfully soft skin and nice firm little breasts. The perfume she was wearing mixed nicely with the musk of her.

I was going to put down a whole description of just what we did over the next couple of hours, but I've been thinking about it and I decided the hell with it. Partly because I think that would just be too much sex. And despite what Mr. Fultz said, I think there is such a thing as too much sex.

Because when all you have is a description of what happened, who did what and where and how and all of that, then all you've got is the kind of book Willie Em was reading, *The Swinging Swappers* or *The Swapping Swingers*. And that sort of thing may be exciting in small doses, but it's also pretty disgusting, actually.

What's important, really, is what it was like and where everybody's head was at while it was going on, or otherwise it's just bodies with no people attached to them. And anyway we kept on like this for a couple of hours, and I couldn't honestly remember the whole thing piece by piece. It would be easy enough to fake it and get the tone right the same way I fake some of the dialogue because I can't actually remember every stupid conversation I ever had word for word. Let's just say that I kept doing things to her and she kept enjoying them and let's let it go at that. I figure that if all you wanted in the way of a book was something to get off with you would have stopped reading before now and gone on to the swinging switching swapping swill.

Three times in the course of all this I took her hand and put it on me. Twice she gave a little squeeze and murmured *"Later."* The third time she repeated this and added, "When it gets dark, Chip."

You know, I wonder how often she did this. I mean, she had the whole thing choreographed, for Pete's sake. Sometimes when I think about her I picture her spending her entire life riding north and south on Greyhound buses. Maybe her aunt doesn't even *have* pleurisy. Maybe she doesn't even have an *aunt*. Maybe Greyhound gives her a commuter's rate. Maybe they let her ride free because it's such great public relations for them. Maybe—

When it got dark, I didn't even have to reach for her hand. It came over of its own accord and quickly found what it was looking for. She gave a few affectionate squeezes, worked a zipper, reached in, and brought her hand quickly back out again.

She put her lips to my ear and whispered, "Why don't you go to the lavatory and take off your shorts?"

I guess I should have done this at the rest stop. God knows it would have been a lot easier. The lavatory wasn't really spacious enough to change clothes in. It was barely big enough to take a leak in, actually.

I came back with my shorts in my pocket and got under the coat again. Then she decided we should change places, with me sitting in the window seat and her on the outside, and somehow we managed to do this without getting out from under the coat. Don't ask me how.

"Poor old Chip," she murmured. "Getting me off about a hundred times"—at the very least, I thought—"and you never getting off once your own self. But we'll fix that."

And I sat there with her head in my lap and my hand bunched up in all that yellow hair and she fixed everything in the world. She fixed things that weren't even broken.

Wow.

Afterward, while I waited for the top of my skull to come back down where it belonged, she nestled her sweet and talented little head on my shoulder. After a while she said, "Happy?"

"Mmmmm."

"You like being loved up that way?"

"Mmmmm."

"They tell me girls up North don't like to do that. Damned if I know why. First time I did that I wasn't but fourteen years old and at a drive-in movie and too dumb to know about keeping my teeth out of the way, and the good old boy I was with was too dumb to tell me." She giggled. "You like that kind of loving, you're gonna enjoy yourself down South. Southern girls are decent, see. And they know that one thing that's not decent is getting pregnant before you're married, and another thing they know is no girl ever got a big belly from it."

From her tone of voice she could have been talking about crop rotation and soil erosion. It was really weird.

I said, "The purity of Southern womanhood."

"You better believe it. Next Southern girl you meet and get friendly with, you tell her to try it with a mouthful of warm water. Of course you couldn't do that on a bus."

"The Waterloo," I said.

"You know about that?"

"Uh-huh."

"They know about that up North?"

"Not exactly."

"You ever have it done?"

"Not exactly."

"What do you mean, 'Not exactly'?"

"It's hard to explain."

"Well—?"

"I read about it."

"In a *book?*"

"Uh-huh."

"Like the kind of book I was reading before? One of those randy books?"

"More or less."

"Lordy," she said. "I'll usually get a book like that to read if, oh, if I happen to have to take a long trip on a bus." I could believe it. "I've read my share of them, I guess. Never read anything about the Waterloo in any old book."

"Maybe it was written by a Southern girl," I suggested.

"No maybe about it. It must have been."

"Maybe a girl from Tennessee."

"Georgia," she said.

FOUR

THE BUS STATION in Bordentown was just an Atlantic gas station that sold bus tickets. They had a Coke machine, but I passed it up. I was down to about two and a half dollars and I didn't know where I was going to get a room, or how much it would cost. I figured the Y was the best bet, and I asked an old guy at the station how to get to it.

He scratched his head and said, "Why?"

"Because I need a place to stay."

"But you asked—"

"The Y," I said. He was still puzzled. "The YMCA," I said.

"Oh, the YMCA. Let me just think. I believe they have one over to Savolia, but I couldn't say for sure."

"How far is that?"

"Oh, I guess I'd put it at twenty-eight miles. Say thirty at the outside."

There was a hotel in Bordentown, he told me. It was called the Bordentown Hotel, which seemed logical enough, and it was on Main Street, which wasn't all that much of a surprise either. Salesmen would stay there, if they had to be in Bordentown overnight, and if they wanted to save money, because those motels over on the highway all ranged from eight to twelve dollars a room, whereas you could stay at the hotel for five dollars, or seven-fifty with a private bath. And then there were some single people who lived there year-round, widowers for the most part, and they paid by the month, which made it considerably cheaper.

"Of course you wouldn't be wanting to spend a month in Bordentown," he said.

I had the feeling he might be right. Anyway, I couldn't afford to pay by the month. I couldn't even afford to pay by the night. I asked if there were any less expensive places. He said there were some women who took in tourists for two or three dollars a night, but it was too late to go knocking on their doors.

"How would it be if I slept in the back here?" I suggested. "It would just be for tonight."

"Company wouldn't allow that."

I said I wouldn't tell them if he didn't, but he didn't even bother answering that. He didn't get exactly hostile, just sort of turned away. I had the feeling that he didn't see much point in wasting any more time on me, and I could understand his point of view.

I must have spent half an hour walking through the main part of town, and that was enough to cover it pretty thoroughly. There really wasn't a lot there. It was about then that I started wondering if coming to Bordentown might not have been something of a mistake. Of course, it was the middle of the night. You couldn't really expect a small town to be lit up like Times Square.

Until now, though, I had been very much into the idea of going to Bordentown. The weirdness of it, finding the bus ticket and using it, had a special beauty of its own. In the normal course of things I might have spent the last few hours of the bus trip thinking about what I would do after I got off the bus, making plans and working things out in my mind. But you know how I spent the last few hours of the bus trip. I spent the last few hours of the bus trip with Willie Em, and the company of Willie Em tends to make one live very much in the Now.

As a matter of fact, the *memory* of Willie Em tends to make one live very much in the Past, and while I walked around downtown Bordentown, such as it was, I found myself thinking as much about her as about my future. I couldn't really get into anything like long-term planning at all. Just short-term goals, like getting a place to sleep and finding some kind of job, were the only things I could really handle.

The place to sleep was the hard part. At that hour it seemed impossible. The only place I could go was the hotel, and I couldn't afford it. If I had only had a suitcase it would have been all right, because I could tell them I was staying for a week, and if things went well I would have enough money at the end of the week to pay what I owed. On the other hand, if things went badly I could leave them the suitcase at the end of the week and go someplace else, and all that would mean was that I could never go back to Bordentown again, which didn't sound that terrible anyway.

No suitcase, though. Nothing but the clothes on my back, which had seen cleaner days. So any hotel would be sure to ask for cash in advance. The fact that I was poor but honest wouldn't help. They'd rather have someone who's rich but crooked.

It's funny how problems solve themselves, though, when you just let things happen. I had more or less resigned myself to finding some diner and sitting up drinking coffee until morning, at which time I could get some old lady to rent me a room that I could afford, when I got a place to sleep that didn't cost me a dime.

The Bordentown Jail.

I was walking along when this car pulled up and a

voice said, "Git over here, boy." And when I got over there I knew who the guy was without him saying another word. I recognized him right away from all those Dodge commercials.

He never did advise me of my rights, but I don't guess he had to because he never exactly arrested me, either. He just told me to get in the car with him, and he drove over to a little concrete block building a few blocks from where he picked me up, and he asked me a lot of questions and took my fingerprints and put me in a cell. He took my belt and my shoelaces and my comb. I was getting sick of losing combs, and I hadn't been eating much lately and my pants, without the belt, tended to fall down a lot. But I didn't complain.

I didn't complain about any of this, actually. I was at a tremendous psychological disadvantage, especially when he made me empty my pockets and I had to take out that pair of undershorts and put them on the desk. Maybe some people can do that without feeling stupid. Not me.

He said, "No identification, no visible means of support, no clothing. You say you're from New York, boy? What you think you're doing here?"

I don't remember what I said.

"You an agitator? Come down to make trouble? Or a runaway? You wanted up North? Get your prints and description to Washington and see if there isn't somebody looking for you."

There was something about the way the cell door closed that left me feeling it would never open again. I walked around the cell, which was a lot like walking around Bordentown except that it didn't take quite so long. There was a kind of a toilet, which I'm just as glad I didn't have to use, and a corn husk mattress that was more comfortable than it looked.

During the summer some of my fellow apple-knockers had told me stories about Southern jails. About getting caught in a speed trap and being fined the amount they had on them, and then winding up on the chain gang on a vagrancy charge because they didn't have any money. About trying to hitchhike through Georgia and getting sentenced to three months of chopping weeds with a road crew.

I remembered all this now, and I really didn't think I was going to get much sleep. But I must have been more exhausted than I realized.

I woke up when the sun came through the bars. I just lay there for about an hour before the Sheriff turned up, trying to put together pieces of a story that would keep me off the chain gang.

At first I decided to tell him the truth. I must have read a hundred murder stories where some poor idiot is suspected of a crime, and if he had just played things absolutely straight from the beginning it would have worked out with no trouble, but instead he tells one little lie or holds something back and gets in deeper trouble, until he has to go out and find the real killer himself. Of course, if he played things absolutely straight there wouldn't have been any book, so I can understand why writers do it that way, but the moral always seemed to be that the truth shall make you free.

But it seemed to me that the truth in my case would make me very much unfree. In the first place, nobody was going to believe it. If I said I found a wallet that somebody had already stolen, anyone with half a brain would decide that I had stolen it. And if I said I came to Bordentown because I had a ticket that made it a toss-up between Bordentown and Boston, and Bordentown was warmer, and I didn't want to spit in the face of destiny, and how one Mary Beth could lead to another, well, all that would do was keep me off the chain gang and land me in the insane asylum.

The trouble with the truth was that it just didn't sound true enough. And by the time he unlocked my cell door and came on in, I had thought up a few ways to improve it.

"Well, now," he said. "I guess you ain't precisely Johnny Dillinger after all. Your fingerprints didn't ring any bells and nobody up in Washington got too excited about your description."

I had been a little worried that I might still be wanted in Indiana for statutory rape, but I guess that got straightened out somewhere along the way. I knew my fingerprints had never gotten on file.

(Until now.)

"But that seems to make you what they call an unknown quantity, boy." He clucked his tongue. "Chip Harrison. That some kind of a nickname?"

"It's my real name."

"Your folks handed you that, did they? Where are they now?"

"They were killed in an auto crash a little over a year ago."

"Any other kinfolk?"

"None."

"And no way on earth to prove your who you say you are. No identification at all."

"My wallet was stolen. In New York."

He looked at me.

"They got my wallet and my suitcase. I was on my way to Florida. To Miami, I couldn't stand it in New York with the weather and the kind of people you meet up there. I had my ticket bought and I was on my way to the bus station when they jumped me."

"Jumped you?"

"Three big buck niggers," I said. "One of them held a razor to my throat. I think you can still see the nick. Then one of the others hit me a few times in the stomach. They got my watch and my wallet and my suitcase, they even got the change out of my pocket. I had the ticket in my shoe."

"That was good thinking," he said. "You go to the police?"

"In New York? What good would that do?"

"I hear tell it's another country up there."

"More like another world. If you tell those New York police you've been robbed, they act like you're wasting their time." Which was true enough, incidentally. When I had a place in the East Village, somebody kicked the door in one day and robbed me, which was actually one big reason why I didn't have anything but the clothes on my back. I wasn't there at the time, and there had never been anyone holding a razor to my throat, but you can see that the story had elements of truth to it. It was sort of a matter of arranging the truth so that it made sense.

"So all I had was the ticket," I went on. "I had sixty-two dollars left after I bought my ticket, but they got it when they got the wallet. I figured it would be plenty to keep me going until I found work in Miami. A fellow was telling me there were plenty of jobs down there. At those hotels."

"That the kind of work you did in New York?"

"No, I was bussing tables in a cafeteria." I actually did that for a day once, in a cafeteria on Second Avenue. That job ended when I dropped a tray. They took it for granted that you would drop a tray now and then, but not on a customer. "But from what I heard you didn't need much experience to hire on as a bellhop or something."

He was nodding. He didn't really look like that Dodge commercial any more.

"After they robbed me," I said, "I didn't know what to do. I just knew I had to get out of New York."

"No place for a white man."

"That's the truth," I said. "Dope addicts and niggers

and long-haired radicals and I don't know what else. And being robbed and all, I just wanted to get away from there. But I didn't want to go to Miami with no money at all. I figured I'd starve before I got settled. So I worked out how much money I would need and traded my ticket so that I could get as close as possible to Miami and still have a few dollars left to live on."

"And that's how you picked Bordentown. I was wondering about that."

"I guess it would have been better to stop further north. In North Carolina, say, because that would have left me with more money. But I wanted to get as far as I could, and anyway my mother was from South Carolina originally—"

"Is that a fact?"

"She was born in Charleston. Her maiden name was Ryder. But there's no family left now."

"I didn't think you seemed like the typical Yankee."

"Well, I've always lived in the North. But I never felt, you know, that it was really home to me."

We went on like this for a while, and he got less and less like that Dodge commercial and I got more and more. South Carolina into my voice. I didn't want to get carried away and lay it on too thick, but as long as it was going over well I figured it was worth staying with. He wanted to know about my plans. I said I would just try to find work in Bordentown. There weren't many jobs, he said. Ever since the space people closed their operations in Savolia, jobs were tight all over the area. Especially in the winter, when there was no farm work to speak of. I said I was willing to do just about anything, and as soon as I had money saved I could go on down to Miami.

"Don't want to go anywhere without some identification," he said. "You'd get the same reception anywhere. First police officer who set eyes on you wouldn't have no choice but to lock you up. I suspect you can write away for certain things. Driver's license, for example."

"I never had one."

"Draft card, for certain. This day and age you don't want to go anywhere without a draft card."

"I'm only seventeen," I said. On my eighteenth birthday I had decided that it wouldn't hurt to stay seventeen as long as possible. It seemed to me that if you didn't get around to registering for the draft you wouldn't have to make any Big Decision as to whether or not you would burn your draft card.

"Need a social security card," he said. "You must of had one, I guess. Recollect the number?"

I didn't.

"Easier to go ahead and get a new one, then. You try writing to them for a replacement and those fellows in Washington, they'll be a year getting back to you. I could tell you stories about those people up there. What else you'll need is a Sheriff's ID Card. I'll fix you up with one of those. At least we can do that without going through a passel of red tape. You just apply for a social security card down to the courthouse, and on the form you put that you never had one before. That's the easiest way to go about it. Not entirely legal, but in police work you learn that there's laws and there's laws. Know what I mean?"

"Laws to help people and laws to get in people's way?"

"I guess you understand my meaning, boy." He looked at me and I looked back at him, deciding that he was a pretty nice guy. He clucked his tongue again. "Reckon you could do with a bath and a change of clothes," he said. "Or with running what clothes you got through the washing machine. The wife can do that while you're in the tub." I almost said I didn't have a wife. Then I realized we were talking about his wife, and his washing machine, and his tub.

"Like to had me wondering when you pulled those drawers out of your pocket last night. I sat up wondering what kind of damned fool pervert carries his underwear in his pocket. Guess they must of been chafing you some on that bus ride. How long were you on that bus?"

"On to forty hours."

He clucked again. "And eating in those greasy diners, were you? Fifty cents for a hamburger sandwich and you have to hunt for the meat, and fifteen cents for coffee that's not but brown water. Never had a real Southern breakfast up there, did you?"

"No."

"Grits and eggs and fries and sausage and coffee that the spoon stands up in? I guess they don't know how to eat up there. What's that Northern food like?"

I didn't mention brown rice. "Like a machine made it," I said.

"You come on now," he said, beaming. He led me out of the cell. "I'll just get you set with a sheriff's card, and then we'll take a run over to my home and see if you got the kind of appetite that would have made your mother proud. Look at the way those pants are falling off of you. I swear the wife's gone take one look at you and run straight for the kitchen. Nothing brings out her cooking like someone who looks like he could profit from it." He patted his belly, of which there was quite a lot. "She feels guilty, feeding me. But you'll be a real challenge to her."

I said, "This is awfully nice of you," or something like that.

"Oh, just put it down to Southern hospitality," he said, grinning. "We don't cotton to everybody. But we take care of our own kind, boy."

FIVE

BY THE END of the week I had a Sheriff's ID Card, a social security card, and a South Carolina driver's license. I also had two jobs, one of which paid me fifteen dollars a week and my lunches, and the other of which brought in five dollars a week, breakfasts, dinners, and a room of my own. Sheriff Tyles fixed me up with the license and one of the jobs, and his wife Minnie got me the other one.

(I had to take a road test for the license. I had never done much in the way of driving, and I don't know that I had any natural talent for it, but the test was no great problem. When you take the test in the official sheriff's car, there aren't a hell of a lot of inspectors who are likely to fail you. I didn't hit anybody, so I passed.)

Minnie Tyles took to me right off. I hadn't been that confident she would be thrilled when her husband brought me home. Forty hours on a bus and a night in a jail cell hadn't improved my appearance that much. But when we walked in the door he boomed out, "Minnie, this here boy hasn't had a decent meal in three days and his mother was a Charleston Ryder." I don't know which part of the sentence went over the heaviest. I was a little lost myself, and for a minute there I thought he was saying that my mother was a member of some South Carolina version of the Hell's Angels.

I had about four meals, and I had them all at once. And then I had a bath while my clothes washed and dried, and then I had a big piece of pie and another couple of cups of coffee. The more I ate the happier that woman got. It was really something to watch.

"Of course he'll sleep here until he finds some place," she told the Sheriff. "Won't be any trouble to fix up the spare room for him." I said something about not wanting to impose, and they both acted as though they hadn't heard me, which was fine with me.

The job situation didn't look very promising. There wasn't much available, and most of the high school kids left town when they graduated, unless their fathers had businesses for them to go into. I spent a couple of days looking for work and couldn't get anywhere. "I couldn't ask you to work for what-all I can afford to pay you," one shopkeeper said. "Easier to hire a nigger for fifty cents an hour, and I wouldn't let you work for that kind of wages even if you said you would. And with business the way it is I couldn't pay you more."

Then Minnie came up with something. "Now I'll tell you right off it isn't so much of a job," she said. "But Reverend Lathrop has been poorly lately that's at the church we go to, and with his wife gone two years in May it's all he can do to look after himself. Lucille that's his daughter cooks his meals for him and does the cleaning, what she can keep up with; some of the women from the church do his ironing and all, but if there was someone who would come in a few hours a day, because with it being an old house and all and things always breaking down, and the yard to keep up and the trash to be taken out, and what with one thing or another, and him getting along in years, he was twenty years older than Helen that

SIX

GERALDINE shook her head. "You're in trouble now, Chip."

"I am?"

"Bad trouble."

"I don't see it."

Her hand, thin with a tracing of blue veins, moved quickly and decisively. She lifted a pawn of mine, set her bishop in it's place.

"Check," she said.

"Oh."

"Think it out if you want, but I can speed it up for you. If you play King takes Bishop, I play Queen to King Eight—Checkmate. If you play King to Bishop One, I play Bishop takes Queen."

I looked at the board for a minute, and she was right. She generally was. I nodded slowly.

"You resign?"

"Uh-huh."

"Want another game?"

"Not right now. I have a feeling I'm never going to learn this game."

"You're getting better."

"I can't keep my mind on it the way you can, that's the

thing. I used to play in New York and I would win most of the time because I could see a move or so in advance, and that was better than the guys I played against. I even thought I was pretty good, because of generally winning."

"You're not so bad."

"Thanks," I said. I gathered the pieces and put them back in the cigar box. We were in the barroom, and there were three beer-drinkers in the bar. Geraldine went to see if they wanted refills. They didn't. It was around eleven, the middle of the week, and business couldn't have been much slower. Geraldine came back with a cold Coke for me and her usual glass of banana liqueur.

We talked about this and that, and then Geraldine was starting to say, "That tobacco farmer's been a long time with Claureen," when I looked up and Claureen was standing there in a pink wrapper and house slippers.

She said, "Chip? Could you come on up for a minute?"

"Trouble?"

"Just that he's asleep and I can't wake him and I was afraid if I did wake him and he woke up nasty like they will sometimes—"

"He's not a regular," Geraldine said. "This is his first time." This meant he wasn't a treasured customer, so if it would simplify things to beat his brains in I should just go ahead and do it.

I got to my feet. Geraldine said something about the kind of men who fall asleep the minute they finish. Claureen took my hand and we walked to the stairs.

On the staircase she said, "It's not like she said."

"What isn't?"

"I declare it's too embarrassing to say. He didn't fall asleep after. He fell asleep while."

"While what?"

"What do you think?"

"Oh. Too much to drink, probably."

"No, that's not it. I know when they can't because they

been drinking. It's not he can't. Oh, you'll see what I mean."

In her room I saw what she meant. The tobacco farmer was stretched out on his back with his eyes closed and his arms at his sides. He had his socks and shoes on and nothing else.

"You see how he is, Chip? He's still hard."

"Uh, yeah. So he is."

"He just sprawled out like that and I started doing him, you know, and he got like that right away. Just lying still like that, and hard as a bar of iron. And I did him and did him and did him and nothing happened. And I got to thinking, all right, you silly old son of a bitch, just how long is it gone take before you get where you're going? But I just kept on and then I wasn't even thinking about what I was doing, I thought about getting my hair done and I don't know what-all, and the time just went on by—"

"Geraldine was saying he was taking a long time."

"—and finally I thought maybe he was one of those who couldn't finish that way, and I looked up to ask him, and he was like you see him, and I talked to him, and nothing; he was dead to the world."

"You tried to wake him?"

"A little. I was scared, you know, to try too much."

I went over and put a hand on the man's shoulder. I gave him a shake.

Nothing happened.

"I even put water on his face," Claureen said.

"No reaction?"

"Nothing."

"I wonder if he's dead."

She grabbed my arm. "Oh, Holy Jesus! Chip, don't you even go and *say* a thing like that!"

"Did you check?"

"No, but—"

"Because it's possible, you know."

"Would it stay like that after you were dead?"

"I don't know."

"What a horrible thing!"

"I don't know. If you gotta go—"

"Oh, Mother of Pearl," she said. She was trembling. "Imagine me doing that to a dead man. Oh, I'm just shaking fit to die myself!"

I picked up his wrist and looked around for his pulse. It took me a little while, but ultimately I found what I was looking for and told Claureen she wasn't a murderess.

"I thought I Frenched him to death," she said. "Oh, Mercy."

"You may have Frenched him into a coma," I told her. "His pulse is there but it's very slow. It's as if he was in some kind of hypnotic trance."

"I hypnotized him? I didn't say anything like, 'Look into my eyes,' or any of that. All I did was—"

"I know what you did," I said, quickly. "Maybe I'd better tell Geraldine to call the doctor."

"At this hour?"

"I don't know what'll happen if we wait until morning. Suppose he comes to in the middle of the night? With nobody around?" I put my ear to his face. "Or suppose he *does* die, for that matter. He's breathing, but it's so faint you wouldn't believe it."

"What'll we do?"

"Maybe an orgasm would wake him."

"That's what I *tried*, Chip. That's what took so long. I did everything I could think of. Even the vibrator."

"And nothing worked?"

"Nothing. If it worked, he wouldn't be here."

"That's a point."

"What'll we do?"

"I'm going to tell Geraldine."

"She'll kill me," Claureen said.

"Don't be ridiculous. It's not your fault."

I went downstairs and told Geraldine what the problem was. Rita was sitting with her at the time. There were just the two girls there during the week, Rita and Claureen. They both had rooms upstairs that they slept in after working hours. On weekends or particularly busy nights another girl would work the busy hours, usually Jo Lee or Marguerite.

Rita just stared while I was talking. "I never heard the like," she said.

"I have," Geraldine said. "Never saw it, but heard of it. Heard of men overdosing with sleeping pills and then going with a girl, and they never wake up afterward, but that's something else because they don't stay hard like that. But I've heard of this, too. What you have to do is get their rocks off and then they wake up."

"Claureen hasn't been able to," I said. "And she tried everything."

"Don't even ask me," Rita said.

"Oh, I won't." Geraldine thought for a moment.

"Claureen's young," she said, and went silent again. Then she said, "God damn it to hell, you just never get to retire in this business. You think you're retired and you find out you're not. God damn it to hell."

She got up and went to the stairs. Rita and I sat and looked at each other.

I said, "I never heard her swear before."

"Neither did I. And I've been here for almost three years. Geraldine wouldn't say shit if she had a mouthful. I can't believe it, Chip."

"What happens now?"

"I don't know."

What happened was that Claureen came downstairs. She was wearing a dress and shoes instead of the wrapper and slippers. We stared at her. She came over and sat down at our table.

"She cursed," she said, hollowly. "Geraldine cursed."

"Did she curse *you,* honey?"

She shook her head. "She just cursed generally, like. She said, 'God damn it to hell.' "

"She said it down here. Twice."

"And then she told me to put a dress on and come downstairs. I didn't want to just go and leave her there with that, uh, with *him,* and I said I don't know what-all, and she just turned and looked at me. And I just put on the dress and the shoes and I came down here."

"You look so pale, girl."

"Look at how I'm shaking—"

Rita said, "Was she doin' anything?"

"What do you mean?"

"With that farmer."

"Oh. She made me leave the room. She wouldn't even look at him until I left the room, and then—"

"What?"

"She locked the door. You know what she always said, that you never lock the door unless you-all are alone in the room. Geraldine locked the door."

I started to say something, then stopped. The girls saw the expression on my face and followed my eyes to the staircase. The tobacco farmer was coming down it, neatly dressed, an absolutely blank look in his eyes. He came down and he walked out and the door closed behind him.

Maybe two minutes later Geraldine came down. She passed our table without a glance and drew a couple of beers for the drinkers at the bar. One of them said something and she joked back with them the way she always did. Then she came back to our table.

For the longest time in the world nobody said anything. It was really weird. We were all waiting for Geraldine to talk up, and she was off in some other world.

Finally she said, "You never really retire. You just can't, want to or not."

Claureen or Rita said, "What happened?"

"He came and went. Or he'd be there still, saluting the ceiling."

Claureen or Rita said, "But what did you—"

There was a pause on the order of the Grand Canyon during which a whole load of expressions flashed over Geraldine's face. You couldn't really read any of them because none of them were there long enough.

Then all at once her whole face smiled. I can't remember ever seeing a smile like that one before or since, and certainly not from Geraldine. A sour grin was more her usual speed. But this smile was the real thing, with lights going on and everything.

And she said, "I'm not going to tell you."

And she never did.

That was a whole lot more excitement than we usually had. Most of the time nothing much happened. You know, if someone had told me I was going to be a Deputy Sheriff in a South Carolina whorehouse I would have thought he was crazy, but if he'd gone on to tell me I'd be generally bored with the job I would have *known* he was crazy. I mean, what could be boring about it?

The thing is, there wasn't much to do. Five days a week there wasn't much for any of us to do, and it was a big night if Claureen and Rita turned half a dozen tricks between them. Fridays and Saturdays were busier, particularly Saturdays, when the workers drew their pay and the farmers came into town to do their trading. I never tried to keep count, but on a decent Saturday the girls would be pretty busy all through the night, with hardly any time at all to sit around and talk. There was also pretty good bar business on Saturday—less on Friday—and there was an average of two fights every Saturday night. One a little before midnight, usually, and the other between one-thirty and two. Geraldine told me at the beginning that that would be the pattern and it usually came out just about that way.

The fights were a pain in the neck but I got so I looked forward to them. I knew they were going to happen sooner or later and I wanted to get them over with. They were the same damned sort of fights the apple pickers used to have in upstate New York. Two guys who were lifelong buddies would try to beat the hell out of each other after a few drinks, and the next week they'd be buddies again.

I had a club to settle fights with but I hardly ever had to use it. See, with most of the guys, they would get drunk enough to start a fight, but not so drunk that they didn't know what they were doing. And one thing they were careful not to forget was that all they had to do was pull a knife or break something and Geraldine would bar them from the Lighthouse forever. Which meant they would be limited in terms of sex to their hands and their sheep and their sisters. They might chance getting killed in a fight, but they sure as hell didn't want to be barred.

So what I learned to do was sort of let it be their idea to take the fight outside. I'd walk through the room calling out, "Awright now, all you boys, let's clear the way for these two. They're trying to take it outside and you better stand back and make a path for them."

Now nine times out of ten there would already be a path for them big enough to drive a tank through, because as soon as one guy yanked a chair back everybody but the guy he was squaring off against would get the hell out of the way. But since the others would be backing off at the same time that I was doing my number, it sort of looked as though they were following my orders and opening a path to the doorway. And the fighters were left with the notion that *they* were the ones who wanted to go outside and the crowd had been stopping them.

So out they went.

I never followed them outside. Others would, and would form a ring around them, and the watchers more or less made sure that nobody got too cute with a knife or kept on going after the fight was supposed to be over. There were two reasons why Geraldine didn't want me to do anything more than get them out. For one thing, she was afraid a whole crowd might turn on anybody who did too thorough a job of policing an outside fight. For another, she didn't really give a damn if they killed each other six ways and backwards, as long as they did it outside.

A couple of times I had to hit guys. My club was a steel bar with a thick wrapping of leather, and it scared the hell out of me. If I hit someone too hard I could easily kill him and if I hit too soft I could get a knife in my ribs. Since I am (a) basically non-violent and (b) a coward, I didn't want either of these things to happen. Sheriff Tyles had given me lessons on just how much force to use and said I had the touch down pat, but I figured there was a difference between the rifle range and the field of battle, and I wasn't all that confident I would do it right.

The first time was when a kid about my age knocked the neck off a beer bottle and started after another kid. I missed his head. He got a broken collarbone out of the deal and I got an extra ten bucks from Geraldine.

Another time one guy pulled a knife and started moving in on his cousin, I think it was. I managed to come up behind him, which helped me keep my cool. I gave him the right kind of tap on the head and it worked just the way it was supposed to.

Now both of those times were exciting enough so that I would just as soon never have them happen again, but that still doesn't change the fact that they were rain on the desert.

I mean, nothing else really happened.

"I'm not really a bouncer," I told Geraldine once. "Not

if you figure my occupation by the amount of time I spend on various chores. You know what I am?"

"What?"

"A hired chess player. And you ought to be able to hire somebody who could beat you once in a while."

"I like to win, Chip. And I don't suppose I could hire Sammy Reshevsky for five dollars a week."

"And room and board."

"You don't eat much. And the room is there, I have four more rooms than I have a use for. Would you believe this was a seven-girl house when I opened it? There's not enough weekday trade now to support the two I've got. But if you just have one girl in a house it's a joke, and if a man has to have the same girl every single time he might as well marry her. I used to have seven and I used to collect twenty dollars on Saturdays. Now it's ten every day of the week. Everything costs more at every store in the county and what's the one thing that's dropped in price?"

"The Chamber of Commerce ought to advertise that. As a tourist attraction."

"Tourists? You wouldn't get tourists here if you gave it away. Bordentown. I never heard of anyone coming to Bordentown by choice."

I could have named one.

"Anyway," she said, "it's worth five dollars a week for a game of chess now and then."

So I played chess, and sent fights outside, and sat around a lot, and talked to Claureen and Rita, and ate eggs and grits and sausages for breakfast and hamburgers for supper, and around two or three or four in the morning Geraldine closed up and I went upstairs to my room and got undressed and hopped into bed and went to sleep

Alone.

I suppose you find that hard to believe. So do I, now that I think about it. I mean, you may have gotten the idea by now that sex is usually in the forefront of my mind, and if you didn't get that idea you get a low score in reading comprehension. Because it usually is. In fact it just about always is.

But I never once had either Rita or Claureen, and I never once had any of the weekend girls. (I never really got to know the weekend girls, as far as that goes; they were always busy then, and so was I.) And obviously I never had Geraldine. The tobacco farmer was the only one who did all the time I was there. I'm sure she could have given me the equivalent of a college education, and I certainly liked her as a person, but the only game I ever thought of playing with her was chess.

But what stopped me with Claureen and Rita?

Well, I wasn't interested.

It wasn't that they were unattractive. They were pretty enough, but not in any meaningful way. The best way I can think of to explain it is that you could sit and talk with them for an hour or so, and then when you left the room you would have a little trouble remembering what they looked like. I suppose that could be an advantage with a prostitute. I don't know.

But the thing is that the Mary Beth who wanted my bus ticket had turned me off prostitutes in general, and any of the fantasies I had toyed with about whores with various organs of gold just didn't hold up for me any more. And even if they had, for Pete's sake, I was sitting there every night while these girls went upstairs with men and then came back down and yawned and joked about it. I got to like them a lot in certain ways, especially Claureen. The two of them put together didn't have enough brains to make one reasonably intelligent girl, but I liked them. And they would have come to bed with me if I asked, either of them would have, and they more or less let me know this in a quiet way, but we all knew it would have made it awkward between us afterward. It wouldn't have been so awkward that I wouldn't have been willing to live with it if I had really wanted to ball them, but I didn't, so nothing ever happened.

Besides, after the first week or so I had my hands full with Lucille.

SEVEN

THE FIRST TIME I met Lucille was the first day I worked at her house. Minnie took me over that morning after Lucille had already left for school and introduced me to Rev. Lathrop, which was a little like being introduced to a tree or a mountain. I started in on chores and worked up to lunchtime, when Lucille came home to do the honors.

(One thing I'm evidently never going to get right is this business of calling meals by the right name. I grew up with the idea that what you had around noon was lunch, and what you had in the evening was dinner. In Bordentown they called it dinner at lunchtime and what they had at dinnertime was called supper or evening meal. I got this down pat while I was there but it's hard to keep it straight from a distance.)

Anyway, whatever you want to call it, Lucille came home from school and cooked something. And I introduced myself to her and she introduced herself to me (because her father was already too far gone to introduce us, assuming he remembered my name. Or her name, for that matter.) And I looked at Lucille, and Lucille looked at me, and all of a sudden there was enough electricity in the air to cause a power failure.

She was the cleanest, healthiest, prettiest little thing I ever saw in my life. She was really a shock after the East Village. See, for the past three months I had gotten used to girls who would live in a pair of dungarees and a surplus navy jacket. I'm not putting that down, because some of the girls I knew in New York were really beautiful, and with some of them you could sit and talk for hours at a time, really rapping on and on about everything. You could really relate to them as people, which is what it's all about and which makes everything much better.

But Lucille was something completely different. Short blonde hair all neatly cut and combed, and a short navy blue skirt and a powder blue sweater and blue knee socks and saddle shoes and a touch of lipstick on her mouth and a perfect complexion. One look at her and you knew that (*a*) she took two baths a day, seven days a week, and (*b*) she never got dirty in between, never even perspired.

When I think about it now, I can't stop thinking that there was nothing on earth a whole lot squarer than Lucille. Knee socks and saddle shoes, for Pete's sake. One look at her and you could hear Bill Haley and the Comets playing in the background. I mean, she looked like a cheerleader, which as it turned out she was, and in this day and age the idea of a girl hopping around like an idiot and doing the sis-boom-bah number for the basketball team is about as unhip as you can get.

Even the cleanliness thing, really, is overdoing it. Not that I'm in favor of being dirty, but there's a point where it gets ridiculous and you wind up with this feminine ideal of a girl who's been carefully wrapped in plastic wrap and never touched by the world. Girls are people, too, and it's more fun for everybody if you don't lose sight of this.

But I was really ready for Lucille, knee socks and saddle shoes and sis-boom-bah and all. It occurred to me that she looked pretty square, but it didn't occur to me that there was anything wrong with this. All I knew was that she looked good enough to eat, and it didn't matter much whether you called it lunch or dinner or coffee break.

Even so, it took me close to a week to do anything about it. It wasn't that she looked too pure to approach, because I could tell right away that she was reacting to me the same way I was reacting to her. But for awhile I had this feeling that if I so much as touched her hand I would be back in jail again, and this time it wouldn't be anywhere near as easy to get out again. I suppose this was partly because she was a minister's daughter and partly because I still felt like some sort of fugitive from justice. The trouble with getting by with a lie is that it's very hard not to go on worrying that the lie will catch up with you. I hadn't really done anything but change the truth a little in a few unimportant ways. Even so, it took me a while to be comfortable with myself. I felt, oh, as though I was on probation, I guess.

Another thing was that Lucille and I would spend an hour talking while her father was putting his food away in the back parlor. And the conversation was all things like how much trouble she was having with geometry, and how the basketball team was doing, and how her steady boyfriend was taking her to this dance, and how her friend Jeanie saw this really cool sweater in a department store in Charleston, and how Joan Crawford was her favorite actress, and things like that.

It's amazing the conversations didn't bore the hell out of me. I think if I had tapes of them I could use them to put myself asleep on bad nights.

I didn't get bored, though. I probably must have listened with only half of my head. One thing that helped, I think, was that she was younger than I was, and less experienced, and I wasn't used to this. The girls I knew were generally older and brighter and hipper than I was (which it isn't all that hard to be, actually).

I'm sure I would have gotten bored sooner or later. But after about six days of this, with our conversations never getting the least bit personal or intimate and never even beginning to make the transition from talking to rapping, I came up behind her while she was carrying some dishes to the sink, and when she turned around I lowered my mouth to hers and kissed her.

The first time I took her bra off she made so much noise I thought her father was going to come upstairs. It was only the second time we had gone upstairs. She had a small bedroom furnished largely in stuffed animals and pictures of movie stars. The day before we took her sweater off, and today we had her bra off.

Her breasts were large, milk-white, creamy pink at their tips. I don't know why in hell she thought she had to wear a bra. I can't really understand why any woman would harness herself up that way, and Lucille was so firmly built that she certainly didn't need the support.

Of course I suppose a cheerleader without a bra would really bounce all over the place, but what's wrong with that? It would just increase the crowd at the basketball games.

"Oh, Chip," she said. "We shouldn't be up here."

I was too busy kissing her to answer her.

"You make me feel so funny. I never felt like this before. And you're so *fast*!"

There's a word you don't hear much any more.

" 'Cause I been dating Jimmie Butler for three years and steady dating him for two years in April and in all that time he never got as far with me as you did in a week. I'll let him take off my sweater and reach in under the bra but not take it off, that's as much as I'll let him do, and you went and skipped over that step completely, and how long have we known each other? Two weeks?"

The next day she made the old man's dinner in five minutes flat and went upstairs without being asked. I paid a few minutes' attention to her breasts and then put a hand under her skirt.

She pushed my hand away, snapped her legs together, sat bolt upright and crossed her arms over her breasts. She looked so frightened that at first I thought her old man had walked into the room or something.

She said, "Chip, I never should have let you kiss me. At first I thought you were never going to get around to trying, and then you did, and right then I should have known what was going to happen."

"Nothing happened, Lucille."

"What you just tried to do."

"I wanted to touch you. That's all."

"You wanted to touch me under my skirt."

"Uh-huh."

"Oh, my *God!*"

"Hey," I said. I put a hand on her bare shoulder and she jumped. "Hey, calm down," I said. "Take it easy."

"Jimmie Butler doesn't even *try* touching me there. He knows if he tries that I just won't let him touch me at all. We'll go out every Friday and Saturday and park in his car for hours and he never so much as tries to do that."

The past Saturday, Jimmie Butler had been a customer at the Lighthouse. He had three quick beers for courage and went upstairs and spent ten dollars with Jo Lee. That worked out to about five dollars a minute. "All the rabbits ain't out in the fields," Jo Lee said afterward.

"Because he knows I won't let him do anything if he tries to touch me there," Lucille was saying.

"Why?"

She looked at me, wide-eyed.

"Why won't you let him?"

"I won't let anybody."

"Why not?"

"Because I want to be *pure,* Chip."

I looked into those wide blue eyes, and then I closed my own, and when I opened them she was still there.

"I want to be pure on my wedding night," she said. "The way you look at me—"

I said, "What does a hand up your skirt have to do with being pure?"

"Chip!"

"Because it doesn't make sense to me, Lucille."

"One thing can lead to another."

"One thing's supposed to lead to another. That's what life is all about. Life is just one damn thing leading to another."

"Chip, nobody *ever* touched me there."

"How about you?"

"Me?"

"Don't you ever touch yourself there, Lucille?"

Her face had gotten gradually whiter during the course of the conversation. Now all the color that had drained out came back in a rush, until most of the blood in her body must have been in her head. She looked like a sunburn ad.

She hugged her breasts. There were tears in her eyes, and I felt awful.

"Hey," I said. "Easy, honey."

"Oh, Chip," she said, and buried her face in my chest. I put my arms around her and rocked her gently. She was sobbing her heart out.

"Easy," I said. "Baby, it's completely normal. Everybody does it."

"It's a sin."

"Lots of things are, if you believe everything they tell you. But the thing is that it feels good."

"I—"

"And makes a person more relaxed."

She drew back, looked at me with pain in her eyes. "I hardly ever used to do it," she said. "Just a little once in a while before I went to bed, if I was feeling dreamy. And I would stop before anything happened. But these past few days—"

"Take it easy, honey."

"—I'm just so *terrible*! And I'm so ashamed of myself. I go back to school and I can't sit in my seat, and I go to the bathroom, and I, I, I, oh, *Chip*!"

"It makes you feel better, doesn't it?" She hesitated, then nodded miserably. "It feels good, doesn't it? And then it relaxes you."

Another nod.

"But you feel bad about it because you think it's a sin."

"Well, it is."

"Then everybody's a sinner," I said. And I told her that everybody did it except for people who were too stupid to figure out how, and that people scratched other parts of their bodies when they itched, and rubbed their muscles when they hurt, and what was the difference? By the time I was finished I sounded like a commercial for self-abuse, but she was sort of nodding along with me towards the end, and the panic scene was over.

So I just held onto her and kissed her a little in a friendly and nonsexual way, and then she remembered that it was time to go back to school, she would be late. She put her clothes back on and brushed her hair and lipsticked her mouth and went on her way, and I went downstairs and did the dinner dishes.

The next day I stayed above the waist and didn't say anything about yesterday's conversation. And out of the blue she said, "I did it again yesterday. Went to the bathroom and touched myself."

"So did I."

"You did?"

"Uh-huh."

"Do you always?"

"Sometimes."

(Actually that was the first time I had followed a session with Lucille with a session with myself. I had never really felt the need—our petting hadn't been all that frustrating, really. But after the conversation we had had and the little speech I gave her, it seemed to me it would be almost a matter of copping out if I didn't.)

"I never thought about that."

"I thought about you," I said. I petted her breast absently. "As a matter of fact, while I was doing it I pictured you in my mind. Doing it."

"Oh, that's just *awful*!"

"Actually it was kind of nice." I propped myself up on an elbow and looked down at her. "You know," I said, "since we're both going to do it, why should we hide out in separate bathrooms? We could just do it here in your room before you go back to school."

She stared.

"It would be fun," I said. "We could watch each other."

"Chip, you are the most terrible boy I ever met."

I looked at her and her face went through some interesting changes. "Oh," she said, in a small, desperate voice, and I kissed her. She gave the kiss everything she had.

"I guess I'm terrible, too," she said.

"I'll tell you something that's even nicer, Lucille. Let me do it for you."

"Chip, don't talk that way."

"If you're going to do it anyway," I said reasonably, "it can't be any more of a sin if you use somebody else's hand. All you have to do is lie back and close your eyes and let your mind go anywhere it wants to. It's a lot better when someone else does it for you, you know."

"Is it?"

"And you feel a lot better afterward. You feel together inside instead of feeling all apart by yourself."

"That's how I felt yesterday. I felt tingly and I felt relaxed and I felt I was the only person in the world."

I lifted her skirt and put my hand on her thigh. She was so soft there.

"Chip, I'm afraid."

"Don't be."

"But I am, I am. Look how far we're going already and it's such a short time and, oh, you're not even my boy friend. Here I'm going steady with a boy I don't do half of this with, and I'm doing all this with you."

"It's what we both want, Lucille."

"I graduate high school a year from June. And after graduation I'll marry Jimmie Butler, and I want to be pure for him. I want to be a virgin, Chip."

"All I'll do is touch you."

"You promise?"

"Yes."

"I don't know if I can trust you."

"You can trust me, Lucille."

"Ohhh," she said.

I raised her skirt all the way and took off her panties. She didn't help and she didn't struggle either. Her face was so unhappy I almost felt like calling the whole thing off, but that would have been even worse for her.

I kissed her mouth, then her breasts, and I put my hand on her belly and let it move down to her. She was all soft and moist and warm.

She didn't get excited right away. I guess part of her was fighting it, but the other part of her won eventually and she panted and squirmed and made beautiful little sounds. She got almost there and hovered on the edge for a long time, trying to make it and trying not to make it, and I was starting to worry that it wouldn't work and she would wind up deciding that bathrooms were better than beds.

But then she got there, got all the way there, and in my mind I was there with her, feeling what she felt. I held her for a long time before I raised myself up and looked at her face.

She was glowing and she looked impossibly beautiful and I felt a lot like God.

EIGHT

THE FUNNY THING is that I kept getting more and more involved with Lucille without really getting involved with her at all. We spent about fifty minutes out of every lunch hour in her bedroom, but outside of that we didn't see each other at all. I never stayed around after she got home from school, and on Saturdays she would generally manage to spend the day with a girlfriend. We never went to a movie or for a walk or anything.

My job at the Lighthouse had something to do with this. I was working during dating hours, and the one night she could go out on dates was the one night I really had things to do there. But once I asked her if she'd like to catch a movie during the week and she said she couldn't.

"I have to stay with my father," she said. "You know that, Chip."

"He manages well enough Friday and Saturday nights, doesn't he?"

"Well, those are the only nights I can go out. I'm not allowed to date during the week."

"You could ask permission."

"Asking's not getting. Oh, Chip, I can't go out with you anyway. I'm going steady with Jimmie Butler, you know that, I told you a thousand times."

I said something about going steady being a Mickey Mouse institution.

She looked at me. "Do you think I ought to break off with Jimmie?"

"I guess not," I said.

That was the only time I ever asked her for a date, and I was just as glad she turned me down. I guess I wanted to keep this a lunchtime thing and not let it get very intense.

There were a couple of reasons for this. One of them makes me look like Mr. Nice Guy, so I'll throw it in first, and it was just that it wouldn't have been fair of me to take up all that much of Lucille's time. Because what Lucille wanted out of life was to get married as soon as she was done with high school and start having babies and spend the rest of her life there. And while that might not sound like something worth wanting, it was what she wanted, and it was probably what would be best for her. (Especially if Jimmie Butler developed a little control by doing the multiplication tables in his head or something.)

Anyway, Lucille wanted to be Mrs. Somebody. Maybe she would have been just as happy to be Mrs. Harrison as Mrs. Butler, but I really wasn't ready for that. She just wasn't that important to me, so I didn't want to become all that important to her.

The other reason was more selfish.

See, I was just having too much fun the way things were going. It was a fantastic ego trip for me, the whole thing, and even knowing something is an ego trip isn't enough to take the enjoyment out of it. For once in my life I was the teacher and she was the pupil, and I was getting a tremendous charge out of it. Instead of feeling like some utterly hopeless dope of a kid, I was the wise old man and she was the little innocent one. And every time I took her upstairs and let the stuffed animals watch me teach her something new and con her into doing it, well, it made me feel as if I was really somebody sensational.

(Which was another reason, I guess, that I had no desire to get in bed with Claureen or Rita. There was no way on earth I could feel like the wise old man with either of those two, and I guess I knew it would just bring me down in a bad way.)

By only seeing Lucille at lunch hour, I made that part of it be our entire relationship. And because we had so little time together we could just keep on going forward a little at a time instead of rushing straight into all-the-way sex. I didn't realize at the time that this was something I wanted. Instead I told myself it wasn't fair to rush her, that I wanted to let everything come at its own pace so it would be natural and good for her. But that was bullshit, really. Utter bullshit.

"You're like a drug to me, Chip," she said one day. "I just need more and more of you."

"Must be a good kind of drug. You look prettier every day."

"The girls ask me about you."

"What do they ask?"

"What you're like. Everybody knows about that place you work at. Some of them sort of want to go out with you. They want to come home with me and meet you. But they're scared of you at the same time."

"Scared of me?"

She nodded. "They think you must know things other boys don't. The things I could tell them! And sometimes I just could die for wanting to tell someone. I feel I could burst from holding it all inside me."

"I don't think it would be a very good idea to tell anybody."

"I know. I just say we hardly talk at all. That you don't even know I'm alive."

"Oh, I can tell you're alive, all right."

"Ohhhh—"

And a little later she said, "I'm scared of you, too, Chip."

"Oh, come on. You must know by now you can trust me."

"I know. But it used to be I could trust myself, and now I can't. I never knew I was like this."

"Aren't you glad you found out?"

"I don't know."

"Huh?"

"I just, oh, I don't know." Her face clouded, then suddenly brightened and she giggled. I asked her what was so funny.

"I was thinking about Jimmie."

"What about him?"

"If he could see us now."

If he could have seen us right then he would have come on the spot and saved himself ten dollars.

"He asked about you."

"What did you tell him?"

"Same as I told the girls. Not even that much. But I was thinking what would happen if I told him about you and me and all."

"He would probably kill one of us," I said. And if he had to choose, I thought, he would pick her. I had never mentioned to her that I had seen Jimmie now and than at the Lighthouse, so I couldn't tell her that he tended to back down pretty easily from fights. I didn't hold this against him, though. In fact I preferred him that way.

Her hand dropped onto me. "The other night," she said, "he wanted me to touch him."

"Did you?"

"'Course not. I asked him what kind of a girl he thought I was."

"What did he say?"

"He apologized," she said, and giggled again. "He's just a baby, I guess. I never used to think so. Not until I met you."

Ego food.

At the beginning I thought I was going to get tired of her, maybe because she was so square. I suppose this would have happened if we had seen each other more dates and long conversations, or if I had met her friends or anything like that. But she left the boring part of her personality outside the bedroom, and once she stopped fighting the whole idea of sex she turned out to have quite a natural aptitude for it.

For a long time she spent half her time being passionate and the other half feeling guilty about it. At first she was very uptight every time we did something new, as if we were taking still another step along the road to Hell. This was fun in a way—first I taught her something new, and than I assured her it wasn't awful.

It wasn't long, though, before she wanted to do new things and came to bed looking forward to it. I guess what happened was that her mind finally realized I wasn't going to make her have regular intercourse, so she set that up in her mind as the one absolute sin and decided it was perfectly all right to do absolutely anything else.

So I taught her things I had done before, of which there were not too many, and things I had heard about or read about, of which there were a ton, and some things that I more or less invented. I'm not saying that I thought of things no one had thought of before because I'm not sure there are any of those things left, but they were new to me.

"My God," she would say. "When did you have time to learn all these things, Chip?"

She didn't know we were learning some of them together.

And she liked everything we did. Everything. I did oral things to her and taught her to do them to me, and she lived up to what Willie Em had told me about Southern girls.

And we tried anal things, which I hadn't done before. She didn't like the idea at the beginning, and she thought it would be painful and disgusting, and when we were done she said it was painful and disgusting and cried a little and I told her we wouldn't do it again.

And the next day she wanted to do it again and never said another word about it being painful or disgusting.

One day I brought a vibrator from the Lighthouse. I didn't tell Geraldine I was borrowing it. I didn't tell Lucille where it was from, either, but of course she would have had to know.

And finally one day we got our clothes off and got into bed and she asked me what I wanted to do, and I said we would just see what happened. And after a lot of things had happened she was lying on her back with her eyes closed and I was on top of her and our flesh touched.

She opened her eyes and asked me what I was doing.

I said, "I'm going to fuck you."

"All right," she said, and closed her eyes again.

Afterward she said, "I guess I should have let you do it right off. I knew it would happen the first day you kissed me. I knew it and I never forgot it and I was right, and we might just as well been doing it all along."

"Are you sorry?"

"Yes. No. I don't know."

"Did I hurt you?"

"Not enough to talk about. You hurt me worse other times and I never minded it. Will I get a baby now, Chip?"

"No."

"How come you're sure?"

I showed her the condom.

"It looks so silly," she said. "Did you buy it in a store or what?"

"I took it from—"

"From that place. I guess if Jimmie doesn't marry me I can always work there, can't I?"

"Don't talk like that."

"Knowing all you taught me. Unless you don't think I'm pretty enough."

"You're beautiful."

"I wonder do I look different now."

"No."

"I guess I'll call the school in a few minutes and say I can't come back today because my father needs me. I used to do that before you were working here."

"You don't have to worry, Lucille. No one can tell anything from looking at you."

"That's not why." She stretched and wriggled her toes. "I guess I don't want to get up and go putting on clothes again. I guess I liked what we did. I guess I want to do it again."

"Oh." I said.

"Do you have any more of those little things?"

"Uh, no."

"Can you use them more than once?"

"It's not a very good idea."

"Oh, well," she said. "There's other things we can do, I guess. An old boy named Chip taught me a whole roomful of them."

"You're an angel."

"I'm a devil is what I am. But I just don't care."

That was on a Friday afternoon in early March. I didn't see her at all over the weekend. I was hoping Jimmie Butler would come to the Lighthouse Saturday night and start a fight so that I could brain him with the club. Don't ask me why. Anyway, he didn't show up.

I almost went to church the next morning. Just a nutty impulse.

Monday morning I helped myself to a box of a dozen rubbers on my way out of the Lighthouse. We used one of them that lunch hour, and afterward she told me she almost broke up with Jimmie Saturday night.

"But I didn't. I wanted to, but I thought I'll wait until the proms are over and all, because he'd have to find somebody to take and everything, and it's easier to go along the way it is. And if I stopped going steady with him other boys might want to take me out, and at least I'm used to Jimmie. And I know I can handle him."

"Why did you want to break up?"

"Oh, I don't know. I just don't like being with him is all. And I hate it when he touches me. I just don't feel a thing. Sometimes I'll pretend I like it but I don't and it never does anything to me. He just keeps going with me now because it's a habit. He doesn't like it that I won't let him do any more than he used to do, but if he went out with anybody else he'd have to start all over at the beginning, so I guess he thinks I'm better than nothing."

"I think you're better than anything."

"I wouldn't marry him, anyway. Even if he wanted. I don't love him."

"Did you love him before?"

"No, but I didn't know it. I didn't know anything. Not knowing what I was missing, I guess."

I felt kind of weird. I had more than I had started out wanting in the first place, and I didn't know whether or not I wanted it now, or what I was going to do about it.

She said, "I love you, Chip."

I just wouldn't tell her that I loved her. She never asked for the words, not once, not even by throwing out hopeful pauses which you were supposed to fill with the words. And I just wouldn't say them.

I don't know why I made such a big deal out of it. I mean, *I love you* doesn't mean all that much. Nine times out of ten it's a polite way of saying *I want to ball you*, and you know it and the girl you say it to knows it and just saying the words doesn't send anyone out shopping for engagement rings.

The really dumb thing about it is that I could have said the words and meant them, because I *did* love her, whether or not I knew it at the time. I didn't want to spend the rest of my life with her, but that's not what the words mean anyway. I dug her and I cared about her and I enjoyed being with her and I wanted good things to happen to her and I, well, I loved her.

But instead of saying the words I even managed to keep them out of my own mind. I would ask myself things like, *Well, Chip kid, how will you get yourself out of this one? After all, old man, you've got to be gentle with the kid. You don't want to break her little heart.*

(I'll tell you something, I really hate writing all this down, because until just this minute I never realized what a complete asshole I was. I felt so goddamned adult with Lucille, and when I look back at it all now I can't believe I ever could have acted like such a shitty little snotnose. And I suppose a year from now I'll be apologizing to myself for being such an immature moron now.)

Of course I loved her, for Pete's sake. I loved her a lot more than she loved me, if you come right down to it, because I at least knew who she was and all, and what she knew about me was more lies than truth. She fell in love with me, or thought she did, because I taught her what her body was for.

Maybe I loved her for about the same reason. Oh, the hell with it.

But figure this out. The day she told me she loved me, I sent a postcard to Hallie in Wisconsin.

NINE

SHERIFF TYLES said, "Well, I hear tell you got a salary increase, boy. I hear you're coming up in the world."

"Oh, I'm getting rich."

"Reckon Geraldine thinks a lot of you."

"It was because I finally won a game of chess," I said. "So she decided I ought to have an extra five dollars a week."

"You wouldn't be getting it if she didn't like the way you were doing the job."

"There's not much job to do. Playing chess with her is about three-quarters of the job." I took a sip of Coke. "Anyway, I don't guess it's enough to retire on."

He clucked. "Well, it's all in how you look at it, isn't it? An extra five dollars a week, look at it that way and I'll admit that it ain't so much. But since you were only getting five dollars to start with, what you got amounts to a hunded percent increase, and I never heard of anybody kicking at a one hundred percent increase that they didn't even have to go and ask for. Even a goddamn nigger labor union ought to be happy about a hundred percent increase."

"I never thought of it that way."

He winked. "You keep doubling up that way, you'll be rich in no time."

"Guess you're right."

"On the subject," he said, "how you making out as far as money is concerned? You able to get by all right?"

"Oh, sure," I said. I had been buying clothes from time to time, and other things, and I was only making twenty a week from the two jobs—well, twenty-five now—but there was really nothing to spend money on. I even got my books free from the local public library, not because I was too cheap to buy a paperback but because the only ones in town were at the Atlantic station, and all they had were four shelves of swinging swapper garbage and one rack of Brian Garfield westerns. Every once in a while I would go back to see if they got something new, but they never did. I guess they were waiting until they sold the ones they had.

The library had a lot of good books. The only trouble was that they had all come out before the Second World War. This was okay as far as the fiction was concerned, I could get into old stuff well enough, but when I wanted to figure out how to fix the Lathrop television set I ran into a stone wall. There was nothing in the card catalog under *Television*.

"I've even been putting some money aside," I told him.

"Thought you might be. Probably got more than enough for the fare to Miami, I'd say."

"Oh," I said. "Well, probably."

"Be summer in a few months," he went on. "Florida weather's no attraction that time of year. Not that it's a bargain here. Myself, I don't mind the heat one way or the other. I'll sweat on a hot day, but I never minded sweating. Must do a man good. Otherwise you wouldn't do it, the way I see it."

I said something bright, like "Uh-huh."

"Heat bother you much?"

"Not usually."

"Didn't think so. A Yankee, your typical Yankee, the heat'll get him and he won't mind the cold. With folks down here it's the other way around. The way some of us were complaining about the first week in February, and it wasn't all that cold. Of course our heat isn't the kind you'll get in a big city, where the buildings hold it in. Makes somewhat of a difference."

I nodded.

"Minnie was saying you really made a good impression on the Reverend. She'll see him Sundays after the service and as like as not he'll have a good word for you."

"I hardly ever talk to him."

"Well, I wouldn't let on in front of Minnie, but I wouldn't be all that surprised if that's what the drunken old sonofabitch likes about you. Last thing he wanted was for those old hens to saddle him with a nursemaid. Imagine the kind of person they'd be apt to pick. Some Salvation Army jackass with a ramrod up his ass who'd either be watering the old sonofabitch's whiskey or praying all over the place. Just for the sake of somebody leaving him alone, I don't suppose the Reverend would even mind if you was screwing his daughter six times a week and twice on Sundays."

I came within inches of cardiac arrest. But the Sheriff went sailing right on, and I'm sure to this day he just tried to pick the least likely example he could possibly think of. He gave me a bad moment, though.

"And Geraldine's happy with you, too. Happier than she lets on. She don't let on much, that one, but I got to know her pretty good over the years. Had a place here for the longest time. Set it up herself. There was this woman she was working for who was doing wrong by everyone— girls, customers, law enforcement people. Geraldine, she opened up on her own and got the right backing and the right girls working for her and sent the other old bitch clear out of the state. She knows what she's doing, that one."

"I can believe it."

"In her day, wasn't a better-looking woman in the county. You can believe that one, too."

"I do."

"Wasn't that bad myself, in those days. Before Minnie's cooking." And he patted his paunch and let his eyes drift off to examine old memories. *Before Minnie, too,* I thought, and wondered if Geraldine and the Sheriff still got it together once in a while for Auld Lang Syne. On holidays and birthdays, say. I sort of hoped they did.

"She thinks a lot of you," he was saying. "She thinks you're a good man to have around the place. Me, I think you make a damn fine Deputy Sheriff." He clucked again. "Well, I'm running off at the mouth again, and you better get on back if you want your supper. Just thought I'd give you a few things to think about."

A couple of days later Geraldine said, "Mate in four, starting with Knight to King Five. See it?"

I studied it for a long time, then nodded and started picking up the pieces.

"Interesting thing happened in the next county over," she said. "Used to be two regular gambling places there. About a year ago Ewell Rodgers had a second coronary, and you generally only get three of them, and he closed up and went and sat on his rocking chair. The other place was run by a man named Morgan from East Tennessee. He was getting all of Ewell's crowd, and success must have gone to his head. He rubbed some people the wrong way that he shouldn't have. He got raided and arrested, and while he was sitting in jail waiting for someone to put up bail money, his place somehow or other caught on fire, and the fire department just happened to take a wrong turn getting there. Not a stick left. Morgan took the insurance money and bought the fastest car he could find and drove all the way back to East Tennessee with the gas pedal on the floor."

She got up and went behind the bar and came back with a Coke for me and her bottle of banana liqueur. I couldn't remember her ever bringing the bottle to the table before. Usually she took her glass back each time and refilled it.

She said, "I used to have gambling in here, you know. I must have told you that."

"I think you mentioned it."

"Did very well with the gambling. Then there was an election and I was let know that there wouldn't be any trouble if the tables and slots and all went, so they went. By the time it was all right to replace them, it just wasn't worth it. Ewell and that Morgan were doing good business and everything was off around here, I was down from seven girls to two, and I couldn't be bothered. When Ewell retired I don't mind telling you it gave me ideas. There was that much business open, and I was sure to get a good portion of it. And then when Morgan's place went up in smoke—"

She picked up her glass, looked at it, and drank it down. This was as surprising as the time I heard her swear. She always took the stuff in little sips, and a drink would last her so long that I doubt she actually drank more than half of it; the rest evaporated.

"I would have six tables for cards," she said. "No more than that. Five tables of poker and one of blackjack. On the poker you let the deal pass and just charge so much an hour to sit in the game. No cutting the pot. Morgan was cutting pots there at the end.

"On the blackjack, you would have to have a dealer. I could deal it myself, as far as that goes. Any fool can. The only problem is if you have a dealer working for you and you can't trust him, because a blackjack dealer can think of fifteen different ways to cheat the house and you'll be forever trying to keep up with him."

She poured herself another drink. And drank it right down.

"And one craps table," she said. "That's all you would need. You let the players run the game, same as the poker. Then what I would do is slap slot machines all over the place. You make a ton on slot machines and all you have to do is take out the money and put a drop of Three-In-One Oil in the works once a month. No one ever lost money on a slot machine. Except the damned fools who play them."

"Where would you put all of this?"

"Right here in this room. It's big enough so there'd be space left over, no one would be crowded."

"What about the drinkers?"

She filled her glass but left it on the table. "Over on the right. Nobody ever goes in that room and you wouldn't know it's there, but it wouldn't be anything to put a bar in there."

"I don't know," I said. "You'd never fit our Saturday crowd in there unless you packed them like sardines."

"Chip, you wouldn't want that kind of crowd if you had gambling. I don't even want them now, but there's not enough money just in the girls and I have to have every drink sale I can get. Put in tables and the idea would be to cut that crowd to a third of what it is. Maybe less than that, maybe a fifth, say, on Saturdays."

"Some of those drinkers wind up going upstairs."

"And most of them don't. Instead they make noise and start fights, and that's the last thing you can tolerate when you have gambling tables."

"How would you cut the drinking crowd?"

"Easiest thing in the world. Leave out the beer taps. Sell imported beer by the bottle at seventy or eighty cents. Push the hard liquor price up to a dollar a drink, nothing cheaper. The way it is now, we're selling girls to men who come here to drink. The other way, we'd be selling whiskey to men who come here for girls and gambling. And when a man's gambling he doesn't mind paying high prices for whiskey, and when he wins he likes to celebrate with a girl."

"You've got it all figured out," I said.

She drained her glass. "It's not something that just came to me in a flash. I've been thinking about it."

"Without the d iking crowd, I guess you wouldn't have much need for a bouncer."

She didn't seem to hear me. "There won't be anybody opening up over the county line. And there won't be anybody else opening up here as long as Claude Tyles is Sheriff, and they won't get him out without burying him. Nobody even bothered running against Claude in the last election. He's well liked, Claude is. Not that he likes that many people himself. It's a rare person that Claude Tyles takes a shine to.

"Nobody else opening up, and all the gambling trade in this county and the next one. The drink business would go down but the profits would go up, and less aggravation involved. Be a five-girl house in no time at all, maybe go all the way up to seven girls if it worked that way. And with gambling, business spreads out more. It doesn't all concentrate on Saturday night. Might even raise the price on the girls to fifteen dollars. And they'd be making tips on top of that with the right kind of crowd."

She poured herself another drink. If it was affecting her, I couldn't see how.

"Make more money on drinks and more money on girls, and that's not counting what the gambling brings in. I haven't made that kind of money in so long I have trouble recollecting what it feels like."

She drank her drink.

"Only one thing wrong," she said.

"What's that?"

Her eyes locked with mine. "I'm too old to be bothered with it. It means all that work and concentration, and I ask myself what's the point? Would you like a drink instead of that Coke, Chip?"

"No, thanks."

"What I should be doing is cutting down, not building up. I'm not ready to pack it all in yet. Not this year. If I closed up now I'd die of boredom. But you feel yourself slowing down, you know. You feel yourself getting sick of people. The customers. You don't have the patience to put up with them. Little signs like that. Another couple of years, next year or the year after that, and it won't be a bad idea to get out of here and live in a big hotel in Puerto Rico and let people fetch me things. I have money saved. Not enough to do it in style, but more than a little."

She gave her head a shake. "But if I expanded I'd have all I need and then some. Thing is, I'd have things just about ideal by the time I wanted to retire. And who in the world would take it over? Rita and Claureen between them couldn't run a pool hall. They couldn't run a race. Two days of operating this place and the whole thing would fall apart.

"In fact, they couldn't even help me out enough in getting things organized. I'd need a man, and he would have to be somebody smart and sure of himself, somebody who could get on good with Claude Tyles, somebody who wouldn't rub the girls the wrong way or be after them all the time. And assuming I had the luck to turn up someone like that in this part of the country, which is as likely as mucking out a stable and finding an emerald, why, what chance in the world would there be that he'd be someone I can trust?"

"I see what you mean," I said.

Her eyes challenged me. "Do you?"

"Well, uh, sure."

"I wonder if you do. You think about it, Chip. You think about it, and one of these days I'll bring up the subject and then we'll talk about it some more. Meanwhile you just give my problem some thought, will you?"

The thing is, subtlety generally sails right on past me. When Geraldine first started opening up that night I wondered why she was telling me all this, and I decided she just wanted somebody to use for a sounding board, bouncing words off me when she was actually talking to herself. And I figured she picked me for the same reason that she played chess with me—I was working for her, and I didn't have anything better to do.

She closed for the night as soon as we finished talking, and I went upstairs and got undressed for bed. And I stretched out and put my head on the pillow and closed my eyes, and then I immediately opened them and sat up and switched the light on.

She hadn't just been talking *to* me. She had been talking *about* me.

(Of course when you read this it's probably pretty obvious all along, especially because I put her conversation right after the one with the Sheriff. But that other conversation wasn't even in my mind when I sat listening to Geraldine, so maybe it should have been obvious to me anyway, but not as obvious as seems.)

Anyway, I sat up in bed and figured out what it was all about. Sheriff Tyles thought I should stay in Bordentown, and said that Geraldine thought the world of me. And Geraldine wanted to expand the business but couldn't do it without the help of some man who was capable and honest and had an in with the Sheriff, someone she liked and trusted, someone who could take over the whole operation when she was ready for complete retirement.

Which meant that I had found the one thing I never even thought to look for in Bordentown.

A Job With A Future.

I got up and walked around the room a little. I had that sensation in my mind and body of having had too much coffee and all I had was one cup with supper. I just kept pacing, and then I went down the hall to the bathroom only to find out that I didn't really have to go after all. Just nerves, I told myself nervously, and went back to my room and paced the floor again.

A Job With A Future. A Position With Real Opportunities For Advancement.

I couldn't believe it.

Because, after all, that was the one thing I had been looking for ever since they booted me out of Upper Valley Preparatory Academy. I left that stupid school determined to make my way in the world and do all the good old Horatio Alger type things and work my way up in the world. And I never got anywhere. In fact I never got close to getting anywhere, because I kept getting idiotic jobs and drifting into idiotic situations.

Until finally the most idiotic situation of all brought me to Bordentown, a town that barely offered opportunities for stagnation, let alone advancement. And instead of one idiotic job I got two of them, and instead of trying to make my mark in the world I just tried to stay alive and let time pass, figuring that sooner or later I would get up and get out of Bordentown, but not even being in any rush to do that because the whole idea of getting ahead in the world seemed like something I was never going to get around to.

(If you really knock yourself out trying not to end sentences with prepositions, that last sentence would wind up *seemed like something around to which I was never going to get.* I mean, it's an awkward sentence anyway, just sprawling all over the place, but I think it would be even worse if it didn't end with a preposition. Or two prepositions, actually.)

Some of the kids I knew in New York were very much into Zen, and one girl made me read a description of Zen Archery, in which you don't exactly aim the arrow at the target and don't exactly ever let go of it. You just become part of the bow and arrow and let yourself happen along with the bow and the arrow, and somewhere along the line the arrow goes from your fingertips to the target. It read very nicely, but I wasn't sure if it made any sense. The girl said it was easier to understand if you were stoned. I tried to get stoned a couple of times but nothing happened. Now though, I was beginning to understand.

Because this seemed to me like a case of Zen Advancement, of Zen Making-One's-Way-In-The-World. I hadn't tried to do anything, just sort of becoming part of Borden town and letting the rest happen, not even pointing myself at the target, not even letting go of the string.

Bull's-eye!

TEN

"YOU SEEM different," Lucille said.

"I do?"

"Maybe not," she said. She yawned and stretched. She was lying on her back with one arm at her side and her other hand tucked palm-up under her head. I touched her armpit. (It's a shame there isn't a better word for it. When you hear the word *armpit* you think of deodorant. When I touched Lucille's, all secretly smooth and hairless, I didn't think of deodorant. I thought of other warm private places, and of better things to do with an armpit than rub deodorant on it.) I touched hers now, rubbing a little with the tip of my finger.

"Maybe it's me," she said.

"Maybe what is?"

"I don't know."

It was the middle of the week and the lunch hour was only twenty minutes over with. We had another half hour to ourselves and had already done what we did during lunch hours. Usually we would take our time, but this afternoon she didn't want to pause along the way and admire the view. She just wanted to get there full speed ahead, and she did and I did, and it was very nice.

But now she was in a mood, and it was something I wasn't used to with her. I asked her what was the matter.

"Oh, nothing," she said. "Just that you seem all wrapped up in thoughts lately, and you might as well be a hundred miles away."

"I'm right here," I said, and touched her to prove it.

She moved my hand away. "Have you been thinking things, Chip?"

"Nothing in particular."

"Oh."

"I always think things," I said. "I mean, I'm alone a lot, so I'll let my mind just wander off on its own some of the time."

"You like doing that?"

"It beats talking to yourself."

"I do that sometimes. Talk to myself. I don't think much, though."

"Uh."

"I guess you must think I'm awful simple."

"What makes you say that, Lucille?"

"I don't know. Maybe on account of it's true."

"I don't think so."

"Just an old preacher's daughter. Never been anywhere and never done anything."

"You've done a few things."

She sat up suddenly and put her legs over the side of the bed. Without looking at me she said, "Do you know what it's like when you start thinking things and you can't stop? You don't want to think them but there they all are in your head and you can't make them stop?"

"I know."

"Does it sometimes happen to you?"

"A lot of the time."

"It never happened to me before. I would just, oh, you know, I would just go along. Hardly thinking about anything, and if I ever had a thought that bothered me I would just whisk it off out of my head and not think about it any more. Like a program on the television that you don't want to watch so you turn it off. But now I can't do that."

"What's bothering you?"

"You know what it's like? Like having that bad television program going on in a set that's inside of your head, and there's no way you can turn it off or pull the plug or change the channel, so what do you do?"

"Pray for a commercial," I suggested.

"Oh, you don't see what I mean."

"Yes, I do. I'm sorry, Lucille. It was just a dumb joke."

"No commercials and the program's never through, it just goes on. I reckon that's why Daddy drinks. You know he told me about it once. He said one day he looked into his soul and saw something there that he couldn't bear the sight of, and drink kept him from seeing it. And I always thought, well, why didn't he think on something else. I knew what he was saying but I thought if something like that ever happened to me I would just make the thought go away, but you can't, can you?"

"You want to talk about it, Lucille?"

"I guess not."

I put my arms around her and turned her face toward me. There were tears in the corners of her eyes.

"I said, "Hey."

"Lemme be, Chip."

"If something's bothering you—"

"Oh, I'm making something out of nothing is all. Never had a thought in my head before and I'm just not used to it. Just a mood I'm in that I'll get over."

"Maybe it's your period coming on."

"You think so?"

"I don't know."

"Maybe that's what it is," she said.

What it probably was, I felt, was that she had gotten a contact high from my own moods. Because I couldn't stop thinking about what Geraldine and I had not quite discussed and what Sheriff Tyles and I had not quite talked over. Which was that I would stay in Bordentown and share the management of the Lighthouse with Geraldine, and together we would expand the operation and hire more girls and put in gambling tables, and in a year or two when she was ready to spend the rest of her days sipping banana liqueur in Puerto Rico, the Lighthouse would be mine.

And I could see it all happening just that way.

I got a paper and pencil and did a little rough figuring, and then I threw the paper away because the numbers I was using were just ones I was picking out of the blue. And the numbers didn't matter, anyway, because you didn't need them to realize that the Lighthouse, run the way Geraldine was talking about running it, couldn't help but make a fortune.

I mean, it wasn't just a matter of being secure and established and successful.

I'd get rich.

It wouldn't be hard, either. At first I thought that Geraldine only thought I was right for it for the same reason that she thought I was fit to play chess with. There just weren't that many people around to choose from. But I had to admit it went further than that. I *was* honest, and I *did* get along well with the girls, and I seemed to have a feeling for handling the customers, and Sheriff Tyles, who she said didn't take to many people, had done everything on earth short of adopting me. On top of all that, I kind of liked the business itself. I had always thought that the only reason anyone would want to go and live in a whorehouse was so he could have his pick of the whores, but I hadn't picked one of them yet and I really liked living there. I mean, I felt at home there.

And as far as the gambling part of it was concerned, I suppose I was suited for that, too. I had played cards a few times without getting caught up in it, and I couldn't imagine ever risking anything important on whether two pair was the best hand at the table or what number would come up on the next roll of dice. And why anyone would drop a perfectly good quarter in a slot machine was beyond me.

Now it seems to me that the one thing you wouldn't want to be if you ran a gambling operation is a gambler. It was like a blackout alcoholic owning a liquor store, or a sex maniac running a whorehouse. You would just eat up all the profits. And at the time I was kind of interested in gambling in a spectator-type way. I mean, as long as it's not my money, the excitement's fine.

I would be rich, and I would be comfortable with what I was doing, and I would be good at it. The whole thing would be officially illegal, but there are laws and laws. And even if Sheriff Tyles stopped being sheriff sooner or later, by then I would be one of the important men in Bordentown. It doesn't take all that much to be one of the important men in Bordentown, it's not like being President of the United States. I would be important.

I kept just playing all of this through my mind. It was like Lucille had said, a television set in your head that you can't turn off.

The thing was, I liked the program.

Of course thinking about all this made me think about Lucille, too, because she was part of it. Until I talked with Geraldine (or listened to her, because she was the one who did all the talking) I took it for granted that I was going to leave Bordentown sooner or later. I was in no rush, and I had more or less forgotten all that business about Miami, until the Sheriff reminded me, but I would be leaving sooner or later.

And, although I didn't like to dwell on it, when I left Bordentown I would also be leaving Lucille.

Oh, once in a while I would play around with the thought of taking her with me. But I don't think I ever gave that any serious consideration. In Bordentown, for an hour a day five days a week, she was perfect. In the rest of the world, and on a full-time basis, she just wouldn't work out. (Maybe that line makes me sound like a shit, but it's honest. She wouldn't work out for me and I wouldn't work out for her and it's silly to pretend otherwise.)

But if I stayed in Bordentown, that meant I would eventually marry Lucille.

In that kind of situation, she would be perfect, actually. It was her home town and she belonged there. The idea of the preacher's daughter marrying the keeper of the cathouse sounds pretty ridiculous, but I can't think of anybody who would have gotten really uptight about it. Except maybe her father, but who was going to tell him? And why should he pay attention?

It would be perfect for Lucille, and in that situation she would be the perfect wife for me. And what I always wanted was a job with a future and a girl who loved to have me make love to her. Which meant I would be getting everything I always wanted.

That was the whole trouble.

I once read a book by Fredric Brown called *The Screaming Mimi*. (I also read about twenty other books by Fredric Brown, and there wasn't one I didn't like. I like lots of books, but I don't always finish one feeling that I'd really like to meet the author sometime. I always feel that way about Fredric Brown.)

Anyway, this book starts with two drunks sitting on a bench, and one of them says that you can always have what you want as long as you want it badly enough. (The catch is that, when you don't get it, that just goes to show that you didn't want it badly enough.) The other guy sees a beautiful girl pass by and says that what *he* really wants is to spend a night with her, and for her to be stark naked.

Well, this happens at the end, only it isn't quite the way he hoped. (I don't want to spoil the book for you.) But the ultimate point, the philosophical point, is that if you want something badly enough you *will* get it, sooner or later, and then you'll find out that you don't want it any more, and maybe you never really wanted it in the first place.

So this is what kept going through my mind, not steadily but off and on. It was all there, and all I had to do was reach out and take it.

But did I still want it?

I liked Bordentown, but I wasn't sure I wanted to live there permanently. I mean, I like swimming, but I'd hate to spend the next fifty years in the middle of the ocean. And more important, there was this major question of identity that was suddenly bothering me. I liked the idea of running the Lighthouse and putting down roots there and all, but I wasn't convinced that it was me.

Oh, even the way I was talking, the South Carolina accent. I wasn't consciously putting it on. I talked that way without thinking because everybody else talked that way and I tend to fall into the patterns of wherever I am. But if you woke me up in the middle of the night I wouldn't sound that way. So it felt natural when I did it but it really wasn't, not inside.

And the attitudes I had. Like being against long-haired hippies and black people and Yankees and everything else. It didn't particularly bother me to act that way, or to use the word *nigger,* for example, because as far as I was concerned it was just part of doing the Bordentown thing for as long as I happened to be there.

But if I was there forever I would be doing all of that

business forever, and when you do something long enough either it becomes real for you, which might be bad, or else you spend your whole life living a lie, which might be worse.

If I stayed in Bordentown, it meant I would probably never in my life rap with anybody the way I had rapped with some friends in the East Village, the way I rapped with Hallie the one night I spent with her. I might make a lot of friends, and I might get to know them very well, but they would never really get to know me.

Even Lucille. I could marry her and live with her for the rest of my life, and she would never really know who I was. Even if I didn't try to keep anything from her, even if I opened up completely. There was no way for me to get through to her that completely.

And sooner or later that part of me that no one knew about wouldn't even be there any more. Because I would be the only one who knew about it, and I would tend to forget.

This scared the hell out of me.

The trouble with writing all this down is that there's no real way to get across exactly how I felt from day to day. See, it was never a constant thing. It was a seesaw, really. I would feel very strongly one way on one day, and the next day I would feel very strongly the other way. And after a little while of this I would be aware of the pattern myself, I would know while I was feeling like staying in Bordentown that the next day I would feel like running for my life. When you get like that it's really terrible because you're afraid to trust yourself. You don't dare make a decision because you know that whatever you decide will seem like the wrong choice in a day or two.

If I left, that was the end of it. I could never come back, and I would probably never have a chance like this for the rest of my life. And if I stayed I would gradually get in deeper and deeper, and we would expand the Lighthouse, and I would marry Lucille, and by the time I realized I should have left, I would be too tied down and it would be too late, and I would spend the rest of my life regretting that I didn't get out while I had the chance. What I wanted to do was keep my options open as long as possible, but you can't, really, not for very long.

Lucille helped keep me sane, or as close to sane as I was. My moods kept switching and she was vaguely aware of this but she had her own moods to contend with. And no matter what mood either of us was in, those lunch hours in her bedroom helped. I always wanted to make love to her, and she always wanted me to, and it always worked. Sex isn't the only thing in the world, despite what you might read in *The Swinging Swappers*. But when it's good it can do a lot to take your mind off the other things.

Until finally one afternoon I got so groovily lost in her warm body, so completely out of myself and away from myself, that when the world settled together again all I could think of was how much I owed her. Not what I felt for her, or what future I wanted with her or without her, but how much I owed her.

I wanted to give her something, and it seemed to me that I wasn't giving her enough. I wasn't even sharing thoughts with her, and I couldn't do that, not yet, but there was one thing I could give her, one phrase I had been holding back all along for no good reason at all. There were words I could say that she had been waiting to hear, and I could say them whether they were true or not.

I turned and looked into her eyes, and she looked back into mine. And I said the three words she had been waiting so long to hear:

"I love you."

And she looked back at me, drinking the words, her

eyes widening as she heard them. And she opened her mouth hesitantly, and I heard the echo of my own words in my head and waited for her to speak.

And she said three words back to me:

ELEVEN

"Chip, I'm pregnant."

TWELVE

"GERALDINE? There was this thing I was sort of wondering about."

"What we talked about awhile ago? I thought you might have been thinking about it."

"Well, I was sort of doing some heavy thinking about the business. And then this one little point got stuck in my head, and I thought I would just ask."

"Be my guest."

"Well, I was sort of wondering what you would do if one of the girls, if Rita or Claureen, if one of them got pregnant."

"I'd be powerfully surprised," she said. "Rita's step-aunt did a knitting needle abortion on her when she was fourteen, and they had to take out some of the parts you need if you want to have a baby. And Claureen had to go to the hospital for a scraping a year and a half ago and while he was in there the doc tied off her tubes."

"Well, Jo Lee or Marguerite, then. I mean, you know, any girl who happened to work here."

"Just any girl."

"That's right."

"Any girl at all."

"Uh-huh."

"Like Lucille Lathrop, even."

"___"

"Chip, I'm an old woman. I've been years in the same business and seen every kind of man there is to see, and I can tell whether a man's getting it or not, or if he's the kind of man who wants it or not. And I know you're getting it, and getting it regular, and I know you like what you're getting. And you're not getting it here where it's all over the place for the taking, and you're not out catting around, so where else *would* you be getting it?"

"You've known all along?"

"Took it for granted."

"Does anyone else—"

"Claude Tyles asked what you were doing for love, and I imagine I led him to think you were alternating between Rita and Claureen. When did you find out she was pregnant?"

"This afternoon."

"How long gone is she?"

"Almost two months."

"She's sure about it?"

"She seems to be."

"Instead of stealing rubbers from around here, you should have told me and I would have gotten pills for her. You can't count on rubbers, don't you know that? Well, that's under the bridge. What do you want to do?"

"I don't know."

"Marry the girl? Have an abortion? What?"

"I don't know."

She did something odd. She put her hand on top of mine for a minute, then gave a squeeze and took her own hand back.

She said, "Chip, if she just told you today then you're in a bad way. You sure she didn't tell you a week ago?"

"No. Why?"

"You didn't suspect until today?"

"Never."

"Because you've been walking round in grand confusion for better than a week, and if it's not that it's something else, and now with this on top of it you must be in a bad way."

"I guess I am."

"Chip, I'm too old to get shocked or disappointed or anything but older, and I can't even get that too much. I'm not much for questions. But you got something that you got to tell to somebody, and I guess I can do a better job of listening than most. You can just put it straight out and not stop first to think how it'll sound."

I didn't say anything.

"Or you can tell me to forget it and I will. I'm good at forgetting. I can forget just about anything."

"No," I said. "I was just trying to figure out where to start."

The words were all there waiting, and once I opened the valve they poured out. A couple of times she filled in with a question but she didn't have to do that very often. I just went ahead and talked until there were no words left. I probably said the same thing half a dozen times in different ways. If I repeated myself, she pretended not to notice. She sat there and took it all in until I was done.

Then she went to the bar and came back with a water glass full of something. She handed it to me and I looked at it.

"Just plain corn," she said. For a minute I thought she was referring to what I had said. "Corn whiskey," she said. "Drink it."

"The whole thing? It'll kill me."

"The state you're in, it would take a quart before you'd feel a thing. All this'll do is settle you some. Go ahead and drink it."

I finished it in three gulps. It went down like fire. I guess it settled me some.

"Now I'll tell you a story, Chip. Story about a girl like Rita or Claureen, just a down-home girl who wasn't much and wound up going with men for money. Her pa ran off when she wasn't more than a bit of a girl and all she ever had from him was a postcard once in a while. Maybe she built him up a little in her mind but not all that much. Then one day after she's been hustling for a time she hears from one of her aunts that got a telegram from Norfolk. My . . . this girl's father was in a fight in a waterfront bar and some sailor broke a bottle over his head and he's in the hospital with his skull fractured.

"So this girl goes to Norfolk to see her pa, and he's in a hospital there. She visits him but he's in a coma, and after a week he dies without ever coming out of it. And she makes arrangements to ship the body back here to be buried next to my mother.

"Now while this girl was in Norfolk . . that's two slips so far, I suspect you could put a name to this girl if you were pressed, couldn't you? Doesn't matter. This girl, while she's in Norfolk, she meets this man and one thing leads to another. This man is in naval stores in Baltimore. A good family. He wants her to marry him and come on back to Baltimore.

"And it's like a dream to her. This man, he's rich, and he's a good man, and he wants her to marry him. But she thinks, Now, how can I marry up with him when I've got all this in my past? And what if he finds out?

"So she decides to tell him, and she tells him. And he says what does he care, because that's something that happened in South Carolina and what does it have to do with Baltimore, and as far as he's concerned it never happened at all, and it doesn't bother him one bit, and if it bothers her then she's a fool, and he knows she's not a fool.

"And she thinks, well, it'll bother him in the years to come. But if it ever does she never knows about it, he never once throws it back to her, as it turns out.

"So she goes to Baltimore, and they're married, and there were all these things she was afraid of, how his family would take to her and what his friends would think, and none of the things she worries about ever come to pass. She thinks maybe she'll meet someone from her past and it'll ruin everything, but none of this ever happens. There are all of these things she worries about and it turns out she needn't have worried about any of them, because none of them ever come to pass.

"And she's an intelligent girl, Chip. She has a good mind. She always educated herself and paid some mind to how people talked, and she goes on doing this in Baltimore, and his family and friends like her. They accept her completely. Completely. They never even think he married beneath him because they get to thinking that she comes from quality people down in South Carolina.

"She's there for three years, and in that space of time she sees that the things that worried her are nothing at all. And she has a child. A little boy."

She stopped talking and her eyes were focused into the distance at a point somewhere over my shoulder. Whatever she was looking at was in some other room.

"And one day she said *I'm not me no more*. And she put a few weeks into thinking on that, and one morning she left the baby with the maid and took a taxi downtown to the railroad station. She wouldn't look out that train window for fear she might get off at the next stop. She just sat there, this fine lady in these expensive clothes, and she stared straight ahead and didn't see a thing.

"She never looked back, ever.

"Whether they looked for her or not she never knew. She left him a note saying she was running off with another man. She figured if you want to hurt somebod you do it quick and clean, and if you want to do one thing decent it's to have the guts to make people hate you if it'll be easier for them that way. Because the hate won't reach you because you'll be out of it, and if it'll sear another person's wounds . . ."

She was silent for a long time, but I didn't say anything because I knew she hadn't finished.

Then she said, "Of course, she wasn't the same girl who went off to Norfolk three years earlier. She saw things in a way she never would have seen them before. She knew how to talk like a lady. She knew manners. But she could let them slide off and nobody knew the difference. Except for what she knew of herself.

"She was lonely, but she would have been that anywhere. She was where she deep-down belonged, whether it was better or worse for her to belong there. She never regretted it. She would be sad sometimes, and she would wonder what happened to that man in Baltimore, and to that baby. . . ."

In another voice she said, "Somewhere along the way it gets determined just what a person is, and for the rest of his life he's stuck with it. Whoever else he may try to be is just play-acting. I guess you know you'll have to go, Chip."

"I know."

"I guess you knew it all along."

"I guess I did."

"Once you got to do something, there's nothing but to do it. Tonight is better than tomorrow. You'll take my car."

"I can't—"

"It's no use to me. I haven't driven it myself in ten years. It's almost as old as you are. I don't guess it has as many miles on it, though. You can drive, can't you?"

"I have a license. I've used the Reverend's car a couple of times on errands."

"This has a stick shift. You know how to work it?"

"In a sort of academic way."

"You'll get the hang of it. I'll make the registration over to you. Oh, now, it's not so much. A 1954 Cadillac, what would I get selling it? Not even an antique yet. That star of yours will guarantee against a ticket anywhere in the state, and by then you'll be comfortable driving it. I let the girls use it. It runs all right. It's still a Cadillac. Always will be, old as it gets."

I said, "Lucille."

"You want to take her along?"

"I don't know."

"She would go."

"I know. I keep feeling I ought to take her."

"You could take her with you. But she'd never really *be* with you. No more than you could stay here. Listen to me. You can hurt her now quickly or spend fifty years killing her by halves. Because whether you stay here or take her with you one thing is sure, and that's that she will never complete you. And you would never tell her that but she would always know, and never know why."

I swallowed.

"The Sheriff will get a report and he'll tell her about it. You had an accident on a road out of town. You were driving my car, and you were in a wreck and were killed, and the body was shipped north for burial with your parents."

"The Sheriff—"

"Claude will tell her that. He'll get that report."

"How?"

"From me."

"Oh."

"Claude Tyles knows all a man has to know about who you have to be whether you want to or not. Sometimes what you have to do is stay. Not in a place, necessarily, but with a person. He had to, and he did, and he knows. For my part, I'll see she gets the baby taken care of. Whichever she wants, having it and then getting shut of it or just getting shut of it. If she's even pregnant in the first place, which we're none of us sure of. Chip?"

"What?"

"You can feel as guilty as you want to, but all it is is foolishness. What the two of you had was good for the two of you. Nobody can ask more than that. It's no kindness to take something good and keep it going when it's no good no more. She had a beautiful young romance and her lover died. Why, you'll be more in her memory than you ever could have been in her life."

She gave me a couple old suitcases of hers. I packed everything and put the suitcases in the trunk. I went back to say goodbye to her and she looked as though she wished I hadn't.

"You send me a card from time to time. Just so I'll have an idea of where you're at. No need to sign it or the snoops at the Post Office'll have something to talk about. I don't get that much mail," she said. "I guess I'll know who it's from."

THIRTEEN

THERE WAS a stretch of time then when nothing happened you would want to read about. I didn't do much but drive, and I didn't work too hard at that, either. I would push the old Cadillac until I came to a town that looked decent enough and pick out one of the large Victorian houses with a sign in front that said TOURISTS or ROOMS or something of the sort. They would generally be run by a widow living alone, or two old maids, or a widow and her old maid sister, and the rooms were clean and comfortable and only cost two or three dollars a night, which was less than half what the cheapest motel would charge. Sometimes they included breakfast, or sold it to you for something ridiculous like fifty cents.

I stayed in so many of those places I have trouble remembering which was which. They were all the same in so many ways. There would always be a small portable television set, and it would be the only piece of furniture in the house that was less than thirty years old. There was usually a spinet piano in the parlor that no one had played in almost that long, and if I stayed more than a night the woman would ask wistfully if I played the piano, and would be sad to hear that I didn't.

"No one ever does," she would say. "I suppose I ought

to sell it for all the use it is, but I cannot bear to, Mr. Harrison. I just cannot bear to sell that piano."

If they all sell them all at once, the market for second-hand pianos is going to collapse overnight.

There were always framed photographs on the piano, and on the carved sideboard in the hallway. You could tell the frames were silver because they were usually slightly tarnished. And there was generally a vase of cut flowers on the sideboard next to the photographs, and there were potted plants all over the place. The plants were usually green and healthy.

Sometimes there would be a cat or a dog. More cats than dogs, all in all. The cats tended to keep to themselves. The dogs tended to be very small, and bark a lot, primarily at me.

I couldn't tell you just how many houses like this I stayed in, or how much time I spent this way. I wasn't very much involved in time, for some reason. I would be very conscious of the time of day because as soon as it was nine or ten at night I could go to bed and not think about anything until it was time to get up the next morning. But I didn't bother with days of the week, or what month it was, or that sort of thing. I didn't read newspapers or look at television. I knew there was a whole world out there but I didn't want to think about it. I had a bath every night and put on clean clothes every morning and when my clean clothes began to run short I did a load of wash in my current landlady's washing machine. Some of them didn't have washing machines of their own but knew a neighbor who would let me use theirs.

Sometimes I stayed one night and then left, particularly if there was a yipping dog in the house, or if there were other boarders. If I felt like staying, I would have a look around the house for something that needed fixing. Usually I didn't have to look very hard because the woman would apologize for whatever it is.

"You'll have to forgive the appearance of that room because it needs repapering, Mr. Harrison" . . . "The boy who used to do my yard work was drafted into the Army last month, Mr. Harrison, and I just can't keep up with my rose beds" . . . "I don't know how this house can go another year without painting, Mr. Harrison, but I had a man out to give me an estimate and, land, the price he asked!"

I changed a lot of faucet washers and replaced a lot of broken panes of glass. I cleaned out some basements and mowed and reseeded lawns and trimmed shrubbery and hauled trash. I patched plaster, which wasn't as hard as I thought it would be, and I put up wallpaper, which was. In Columbia, Missouri, I painted a whole house without falling off the ladder once. I guess that summer of apple-picking was valuable.

That was for the woman who hadn't known how the house could go another year without painting. She told me this at breakfast, and it was a breakfast that came free with my three-dollar room rent, and it was such a good breakfast and such a clean comfortable house that I figured I wouldn't mind spending another week or two there.

So I said, "Well, I could paint it for you."

"But I couldn't afford it. The size of this house, and he wanted nine hundred dollars."

"If you'll pay for the paint and brushes, and find out where I can borrow a ladder, I'll do it for five dollars a day and my keep."

"Why, I just can't believe that, Mr. Harrison! How can you afford to do that?"

"Well," I said, "I don't have all that much else to do, actually."

It was really very satisfying doing things like that. With that house, I saw that she bought the best paint, and I took my time and did a good job. At the beginning I'm sure she was scared to death I would fall off the ladder and kill myself. The same thing had occurred to me. But I didn't, and the house got painted, and I slept ten hours a night in my room and ate three good meals a day, and when I washed out my brush for the last time she paid me fifty dollars and couldn't believe that was all it was going to cost her.

"It looks so fine now," she said, walking around the house and admiring it from every angle. "It hasn't looked so fine since he was alive. You don't know what it's been like, Mr. Harrison, thinking I would never live to see it looking right again."

It made me feel good to leave a place in better shape than I found it. Sometimes I felt like Johnny Appleseed and other times like the Lone Ranger.

And I needed that kind of feeling, because if I let myself think about other things, about Bordentown things, I didn't feel like Johnny or Lone. I just felt like a son of a bitch.

That first night, driving the Cadillac generally north and generally east, I was too numb to feel much of anything at all. It was a good thing Geraldine sent me away right off. If I had had a night to sleep on it God only knows what I would have done, but I was on the road before I knew exactly what was happening and there was never a point where I could turn back.

I kept wanting to for the longest time. But that was the one thing I knew I couldn't do. I just couldn't go back there again.

The car was a good one, old as it was, and plain driving was a good way to get away from yourself while getting away from Bordentown. I hadn't realized they made Cadillacs with stick shifts, even back in 1954. I don't suppose they made very many of them. The ones they made, they did a good job with. I got the hang of shifting pretty quickly, and after that there was nothing to do but drive.

What I would think about while I was driving, well, the hell with all that. Nothing very brilliant, I don't guess.

I stayed at a motel the first night, and didn't sleep much. It wasn't exactly the Hilton. It was what I think they call a hot-pillow joint, and the room next door to mine was one of the ones they would rent out by the hour. If the walls had been any thinner they would have been transparent. All night long the bedsprings squeaked and groaned, and all night long different men and women told each other they loved each other, and they were all of them lying in their teeth. I don't suppose I would have slept much anyway, but this didn't help.

After that, though, it got easier. One thing the widows' houses didn't have was bedsprings wailing all night long. And I also learned that sleep was a great way to get through time without going crazy. I got so I could fall asleep right away, pulling the sleep over my head like a blanket, and I'd be good for ten hours, sometimes more. I never used to sleep that way before and never have since, just burrowing into sleep and sort of using it.

Every day Bordentown was a few miles further south and east and one day deeper in the past. You just let the past slip away from you and one day you turn around and it's out of sight.

It's that simple, and that hard.

I wrote three letters, one to Sheriff Tyles, one to Geraldine, one to Lucille. This was just a game I was playing with myself because I knew I didn't intend to mail the letters. What was interesting was that the one to Geraldine was the hardest to write. I would have thought it would be the other way around. I tore them all up when I was done, and tore the pieces into smaller pieces, as if the FBI might come around and try to put the stupid letters back together again like jigsaw puzzles.

I also wrote a letter to Hallie telling her about the whole business in Bordentown. I actually expected to mail that letter when I was done with it, and I took a lot of time trying to get it just right, and of course when it was through I tore it up, too.

I did send Geraldine a postcard. I sent her a couple of them at different times. I could never once think of anything to write, so I would leave the message part blank or else just run the address across the whole length of the card. Miss Geraldine Simms, The Lighthouse, Bordentown, South Carolina. And the zip code, which I don't remember, but I knew it at the time.

A lot of the time when I was driving there would be hitchhikers on the road, guys alone or two of them together or sometimes a guy and a girl. Back when I did a lot of hitching I would always promise myself that if I ever had a car I would never pass up a hitchhiker. And the people who gave me rides generally mentioned that they had thumbed their way around when they were younger, and that was why they felt they had to stop for me in return, even though they knew that it was supposed to be a dangerous thing to do.

Now I had a car, a big car with nothing but room in it, and there were all these people on the road, I never went a day without seeing a dozen of them, and I never once stopped. There were soldiers in uniform and hippies and straight-looking kids and older people, everything, and I passed them all up. Not because it was dangerous to stop, although I guess it is, but because I just didn't want to talk to anybody.

It was a funny stretch of time. I guess I wouldn't want to go through it again.

FOURTEEN

I HAD to write the last chapter twice. The first time I did it, I put in a six-page scene that never happened. It was the first night after I left Bordentown, when I stayed in the motel with cardboard walls. The way I wrote it the first time, there was this long scene where I listened to a couple through the wall, and the guy finished before the girl was satisfied, and he just left her there, and she was storming around the room throwing things and crying. So then I went next door and brought her back to my own room and took her to bed, and afterward she was sleeping and I heard the same thing happen again in the room next door, except this time the guy was drunk and passed out before he could do anything. Whereupon the heroic Chip Harrison went next door and found the second girl, and she was also ready to walk up the wall and across the ceiling, and good old Chipperoo brought her back, too, and balled her in the bed while the first girl was still sleeping, and then the first girl woke up, and the three of us had this wild orgy with everybody doing everything to everybody else all at once.

I filled up six pages with that crap. It was a pretty good scene, actually, and I think it would have been pretty erotic.

But I thought about it and tore it all up and did it over the way it really happened.

So I wrote that scene, and it didn't bother me while I was writing it. In fact while I was typing it all out I could actually believe it really happened. Sometimes it's a little frightening the way your imagination will take a lie and make it almost true.

Then why did I tear it up? I could say it was because I didn't want to put any lies in this book, but that's not it because there are already a couple of lies in it that I'm leaving in. Just small lies, but that doesn't make them true. The real reason, I think, is that putting in a scene like that would just make a lie out of everything that happened in Bordentown and lot of what went on afterward. Because that scene I wrote could never have happened. If the beginning of it happened, and if a guy did leave a girl there all unsatisfied, I never would have gone next door. Not the way I felt. If anything I would have just left the motel and gotten back in the car and kept on driving. And if I *tried* to do anything with a girl just then, if somehow I really did make an effort, I'm sure I couldn't have managed to accomplish it.

I didn't leave my heart in San Francisco, but for a while there I guess I left my balls in Bordentown.

FIFTEEN

I GUESS I knew all along I was on my way to Wisconsin. In fact the first night out I tried to figure out just how long it would take me to drive there if I drove sixteen hours a day and slept eight. (If I had tried it, I think I would have killed that Cadillac in a matter of days. It was good for another fifteen years if you didn't push it more than fifty or a hundred miles at a stretch, but it tended to burn oil when it overheated and I would have thrown a rod or burned out a bearing sooner or later.)

But the thing is that I wanted to be going to Wisconsin but I didn't want to get there. I wanted to see Hallie. I always wanted to see Hallie, ever since that one night in September when she came to my room over the barber shop. The next morning she went to Madison to start college, and ever since then I had been not quite going there to see her.

Because if I went there, and if it turned out that there was nothing there for me, then what would I do? I wouldn't have Hallie to send postcards to, or to write letters to and not mail. Or to think about the way knights used to think about the Holy Grail.

Once I was out of Bordentown I really didn't want to see anybody right away, Hallie included. I knew that there had to be some time in between Bordentown and whatever was going to come after it. I don't mean that I spelled all of this out in my mind, but when I think back on it I can see it was something I must have known.

So I took my time, and took down a lot of storm windows and put up a lot of screens, and touched up woodwork and repaired furniture. And before long it was June and the colleges were out for the summer, so there was no point in rushing up there because she would be away on summer vacation.

Of course I knew where she lived, in the same town where I originally met her, a little town on the Hudson between New York and Albany. It stood to reason that she would go home for the summer, and I suppose I could have gone to see her there, but the way I looked at it was that I was already out in the Midwest and it would make more sense to stay there and see her in Wisconsin when the fall term started.

Which meant that all I had to do was kill a couple of months. I didn't even have to pretend I was on the way to Wisconsin. All I had to do was kill time, and I was getting pretty good at that.

I think some of the pressure came off about the time that the school year ended in Wisconsin. I don't know that one thing had much to do with the other. Maybe it did and maybe it didn't, but within a week after the end of the semester, I did something I hadn't done since I left Bordentown.

By this time I was starting to worry about it. Not that I wasn't doing it—because let's face it, I had gone almost eighteen *years* without doing it, so a couple of months off wasn't anything remarkable. But I didn't even *want* to do it. I didn't even particularly *think* about it, for Pete's sake, and it's usually all I *do* think about.

In fact, I wasn't even doing what I had told Lucille it was perfectly normal to do.

I would see a pretty girl on the street, say, and I would tell myself, *There's a pretty girl*. I still had the brains to realize this. But what I wouldn't tell myself was, *Man, would I ever like to ball that chick until her eyes fall out of her head*. And that sort of thing had always been my normal response to a pretty girl, and now it didn't happen, and I was beginning to worry.

For months I had been with Lucille five days a week. The same girl, lunch hour after lunch hour, and I never once got tired of it. I was always ready and willing and able, and it was always good, and I always enjoyed it. And now it began to seem possible to me that (*a*) I was never going to want it again with anybody or (*b*) I was only going to want it with Lucille. And both of these things amounted to the same thing, because I was never going to be able to see Lucille again.

And if (*b*) was true (and it might have been, I couldn't tell, because I wasn't sure I still wanted to make love to Lucille but I couldn't prove that I didn't, either) then it stood to reason that leaving Bordentown had been a mistake. But not one of those mistakes you can do anything about, except maybe cut your throat, which still seemed a little too extreme.

So it reassured me when it finally happened. And it's reassuring me right now, because I can write about it, and if I didn't have some sex in this book pretty soon I suppose Mr. Fultz would give it back to me and tell me to use it to line a birdcage or something. He may anyway.

I hope not.

It was in Iowa. I don't remember the name of the town. (There's another lie for you. I remember it perfectly well, but I'm not putting it in.) The house I was staying at this time was like most of the others, a sprawling old place in

the middle of town with bay windows and gables and
extra rooms that were nicely furnished and everything,
but nothing happened in them and nobody ever went in
there. This house had two widows instead of one. One of
them was about sixty, a plump little old lady with cataracts and hardly any chin, so that her face just curved
back from her mouth to her neck. This took a little getting
used to.

The other widow was her daughter. Her name was Mrs.
Cooper, and her mother's name was Mrs. Wollsacket.
Mrs. Cooper was about thirty-five and she had a perfectly
good chin and no cataracts. She also had a son, who was
about seven years old and retarded. Very retarded. They
had to feed him with a spoon and he would drool most of
it out, and his eyes never seemed to focus on anything.

Between the kid and his grandmother's nonchin, I had
more or less decided not to look for anything that needed
fixing. After breakfast Mrs. Cooper left for work and I
got ready to go, and when I went to pay Mrs. Wollsacket
she started talking about all the things that needed doing,
and how difficult it was to make do without a man around
the place, and how here it was June and the second-floor
storms were still on the windows. (Incidentally, somebody
is missing a good bet; if someone would only sell combination aluminum storm windows to all those lonely old
ladies, half their worries would be over.)

Well, I couldn't just leave. It wouldn't fit the Lone
Ranger image at all to run off yelling "Hi-yo, Silver!"
without changing those storm windows for her. I offered
to do the job for her in exchange for the two-fifty I owed
her and another day's room and board. She said, "Oh, I
wasn't asking *you* to do it, Mr. Harrison," and I started to
say, well, then, I guessed I'd be on my way, and she said,
"but I'm surely glad to take you up on your generous
offer," and I was locked in.

It didn't take long. I took care of the storm windows

and took apart a lamp with a broken switch and put it back together again so that it worked, which completely amazed her. Then I ate a sandwich for lunch and walked around town until I found the library.

The librarian looked vaguely familiar, and when she gave me a tentative smile I realized it was Mrs. Cooper. We had a dumb conversation, and then I looked around until I found a couple of early Nero Wolfe mysteries that I couldn't remember if I had read or not. Mrs. Cooper told me I could take them back to the house even though I didn't have a card. I read them in my room. One of them, anyway; it turned out I had read the other one.

They fed the kid early, thank God. Then the three of us had dinner and I talked about how I was a student at the University of Wisconsin on summer vacation, and trying to see something of the country and possibly earn a little money toward next year's tuition. (I had been saying this since the term ended. Before that I was the same student at Wisconsin but had dropped out in January for lack of funds and hoped to go back in the fall.) I couldn't tell you very much about the dinner conversation because it was basically the same as all my dinner conversations, and I had learned to handle my end of it without paying much attention to anything but the food.

Afterward I took a loose leg off one of the dining room chairs and glued it back on. This went over well. Then I went up to my room and read the other Nero Wolfe, the one I had already read once before. I had forgotten how it came out and was willing to find out all over again.

Around ten there was a timid knock on the door. I opened it, and it was Mrs. Cooper. She was a little bird of a woman, as thin as her mother was fat, with a slightly pinched look around her eyes and nose. She was prettier than that sentence makes her sound, and would have looked very nice, I think, if she had done something, intelligent with her hair. It was the color of a field mouse and she had it pulled back into a bun.

"I couldn't sleep," she said, "and I thought you might like a nice cup of tea, Mr. Harrison."

We had tea in one of the living rooms. Mrs. Cooper talked about how nice it was to work at the library, except that so few people actually read books any more, with so many of them wasting their time in front of television sets. And she talked about how lonely it was in that town, and how she had wanted to leave, but she couldn't leave her mother all alone and besides there was the boy to consider, and she guessed she would just stay there while life passed her by.

"This must be a lonely summer for you, Mr. Harrison," she said.

"It is," I said. "But I do meet a lot of people."

"I'm sure you must."

"Yes, I do." Brilliant, Chip. If you're supposed to be the Lone Ranger, why do you talk like Tonto?

"I suppose you meet a great many lonely women."

"Uh," Tonto said.

She folded her little hands under her little breasts. "You must bring them a great deal of excitement, Mr. Harrison. Excitement that is sorely missing in their wretched and cloistered lives."

Her eyes were shining weirdly, and she moistened her thin lips with her tongue.

I said, "Well, I guess I change a lot of storm windows, if you can call that excitement."

She leaned forward and put her teacup on the coffee table. She did this very deliberately, as if it would slide off the table unless she placed it in just the right spot. I realized suddenly that she was not wearing the same dress she had had on at dinner. And she was wearing lipstick, and hadn't been wearing any at dinner.

She stood up and crossed the room and sat on the

couch beside me. She folded her hands and rested them in her lap.

"My husband died eight years ago," she said.

"I'm very sorry."

"But there is still a fire in me," she said. "My fire has never been quenched."

She put her hand on the front of my pants.

I tried out a lot of lines in my head, like asking her how her husband died, or how long she had been working at the library, or if she thought it would rain tomorrow. Somehow none of them seemed like the right thing to say. I considered telling her that I was a fairy or had been wounded in a campus riot or that I had syphilis. It was like having absolutely no appetite and then having somebody put a plate of boiled turnips in front of you.

"My fire burns for you, Mr. Harrison," she said. She really said that. "Oh, Chip, darling!"

And her hand did things, and of course nothing happened, and I thought, well, maybe I can sort of move the turnips around on my plate. Because while I was sure I would never be able to rise to the occasion, so to speak, I also figured there was more than one way to skin a cat, or quench a fire, and if she had gone eight years without it she could probably get off without too much trouble if I just went through the motions.

So I kissed her.

The way it started out, I was like a Boy Scout helping her across the street. But somewhere alone the way everything changed. It really surprised me. I opened her dress and touched her and kissed her, and in the course of it all I began to groove on her body.

It was a much better body than you would have expected. It didn't look that great—she was much too thin and didn't have much of a waist, so that she was almost a straight line from her shoulders to her feet. Her skin was very soft and smooth, though, and there was no fat on her, and, well, her body just *felt* nice. Some do and some don't, and hers did.

Maybe what I got was a contact arousal from her, because she was certainly excited and she certainly made it obvious. Anyway, I was on the couch with her, just going through the motions, when all of a sudden I realized that I had an erection.

And I thought, Hey, where did *that* come from?

God knows where it came from. But even I knew where it was supposed to go, and it suddenly seemed absolutely essential that I put it there as soon as I possibly could. It didn't seem to matter if she was ready or not, although I guess she must have been ready for the past eight years. All that mattered to me was to get into her, and I shucked my pants and rolled on top of her and jabbed at her with all the subtlety of a tomcat.

It went straight in on the first shot as if she had a magnet in her cervix. She wrapped her arms and legs around me as if she was scared I would take it away. She had nothing to worry about. I kept taking it a little ways away and then putting it back, as fast and as hard and as deep as I could.

Throughout all of this, there was something slightly schizophrenic about the whole thing. Because it was as though there were two Chip Harrisons. One of them was banging away at the poor woman as if he was trying to splinter her pelvic bone, and the other was sitting in a chair on the other side of the room, watching the whole thing and not quite believing what he was seeing.

It went on for a long time, this totally unsubtle relentless sledgehammer screwing, and she came about half a dozen times, and then so did I.

"We'll go to your room now," she said. There was a little puddle on the couch. She put a doily over it, put her dress and my pants over her arm, and took my arm with her free hand. "We'll go to your room," she said, "and do it some more."

"Uh—"

"We'll fuck," she said. "We can try different positions. I would like to try it with me on top, if that's all right with you. That way you can pinch my breasts while we do it. You may pinch them as hard as you like. I won't mind."

"Uh—"

"You may even bite them if you like."

"Your mother," I said.

"She sleeps very soundly."

"Well, uh, I'm not sure I can do it again. It took a lot out of me."

"I know. Most of it is running down my leg."

"Uh."

"You'll be able to," she said confidently, giving my arm a happy little squeeze. "I just know you will."

She was right.

Afterward, it seemed as if there ought to be something to say. I asked her about her husband, and if he died before the kid was born. Seven months before the kid was born, she told me.

And how long had her mother been a widow?

"Eight years also."

"That's really terrible," I said. "You must have lost them both about the same time."

"Exactly the same time."

"Gee," I said. "An automobile accident, I suppose."

"They committed suicide." She was lying on her back. She had taken her hair down and it looked much better. The pinched-in expression was gone from her face. Sex certainly does wonders for a woman's appearance.

"You probably don't want to talk about it."

"Oh, I don't mind," she assured me. "It happened the

very day I told them that I was pregnant. That very day, I told them, my husband and my father, and they went downstairs to the basement and into the tool room, and they got the shotgun, and they put the barrel in their mouth and pulled the trigger and blew off the top of their head."

"Oh."

"I was never married," she said.

"Oh."

"It was my father."

"Oh."

"It started when I was twelve. He came to my room and told me I was a big girl and it was time I learned how to fuck. I hope you don't mind my using that word."

"Not at all."

"And then he fucked me. I didn't like it, but my mother said it was my duty because he was my father. She read from the Bible. About Lot and his daughters. I didn't like it at all for the first few years, but then I got to enjoy it pretty well."

"Oh."

"What I didn't like was he would always pull it out just before the end. And when he couldn't in time I was always lucky, until one time when I was twenty-six years old and I found out I was pregnant and he shot himself." She thought for a moment. "I don't see why he shot himself," she said reasonably. "There was no need."

"Oh."

"I went to Kansas City, and then mother told everyone that I was married, and I had the baby, and then mother told everyone that Mr. Cooper was killed in an airplane crash and I would be coming back to live with her. But I think everybody knows. Wouldn't you think so?"

"Maybe."

"I think they must. Especially with the baby being an idiot and all. I wish they had told me right away he was an idiot. I would have drowned him. But by the time I knew about it I was attached to him and I couldn't do it. That happens, you know. You get attached to them, even if they are."

She went silent then. Thank God. After a while I said, "Uh, I'm kind of exhausted. I have to get to sleep, and you probably ought to go to your own room. I mean, you wouldn't want your mother to find out about this."

"Why not?"

"Well," I said, "I would be embarassed."

"Oh," she said. She thought about it, then nodded. "All right," she said, and off she went, her dress over her arm.

I was just falling asleep when the door opened again. There she was, carrying a cup and saucer. No dress this time. She was still naked.

"I brought you a surprise," she said gaily.

"If that's my tea, I don't really want it."

"It's not," she said.

"I still don't want it."

"Well, it's not for you."

"Huh?"

"Lie down and shut up," she said. "It's for the surprise."

"What surprise?"

"You'll see. You'll like it."

"Look, all I really want is to go to sleep."

"You can go to sleep in a minute. Lie down."

"What's in the cup?"

"Just warm water," she said, and filled her mouth with it, and leaned over me.

Oh, the hell with it. I wasn't going to mention it but it's too perfect, and if it ruins her reputaton that's just the way it goes. I don't think she'll mind, anyway.

It was Waterloo, Iowa. I swear to God.

SIXTEEN

THERE WERE some other girls during the rest of the summer. Some I got to and some I struck out with. None of them were very important.

SEVENTEEN

I DROVE into Madison a couple of weeks after the fall term started. I would have gotten there earlier but I kept putting it off until finally I knew it was time. The old Cadillac got me there in good shape. I started looking around for a tourist home like the ones I had been staying in for the past half a year, and I drove around for a long time without seeing any of the usual signs. Then I remembered that Madison was a university town, and that people with rooms to rent would take in college students by the year.

And I also remembered, just about the same time, that if Hallie was here and stuck in some dormitory it might be pretty stupid to room with some widow. So I got a room at a motel. Sixteen bucks, and payable in advance, and it wasn't even all that much of a room.

I didn't care. I was in pretty good shape financially, with almost two hundred and fifty dollars, which was more than I had had when I left Bordentown. Even with all the gas that the old car burned, I had been earning money faster than I spent it.

I unpacked in my motel room and put my clothes away. I took a shower and shaved, although I had already shaved and showered in the morning. Then I got dressed and noticed I was sweating, and I took another shower and put on a clean shirt and made myself stretch out on the bed and calm down so I would stop sweating.

The campus was huge. It sprawled all over the place. There were a lot of kids sitting in groups under trees and other groups of kids hurrying here and there. I couldn't understand how they could possibly find their way around. It was immense.

I asked a lot of people various dumb questions until someone told me where you could find out where a student was staying, and somebody there told me what dorm she was in, and various other people pointed me toward it.

I went and stood in front of it. I didn't know whether it was all right for me to go in or not. I thought of stopping some girl on the way out and asking her to find Hallie for me, but instead I just waited.

And then two girls came out, and one of them was Hallie.

She looked exactly the way she had looked a year ago. Exactly. She was wearing dungarees and a sweatshirt and sandals, and her granny glasses made her brown eyes look even bigger than they were. Her hair, straight and glossy brown, was a year longer than it had been.

I said, "Hallie?"

She looked at me, and stared, and said, "Chip?"

I nodded, waiting for her to run up and throw herself into my arms. (I had rehearsed this scene a lot.) She didn't exactly do this. What she did was say something to the other girl about seeing her in class, and then she walked slowly toward me, a smile spreading on her lips, and reached out her hands for mine.

Her hands felt small and very soft.

"I can't believe it," she said. "When did you get here?"

"About an hour ago."

"Are you going to be studying here?"

"No."

"Oh."

"I was in the area," I said, "and I thought I would drop in and see you."

"Wow, that's really great. Oh, wow. Like I can't really believe all this."

"Yeah."

"I got your cards. I was going to write to you, but there was never a return address."

"Well, I never stayed in one place very long."

"Oh."

"I wrote you a couple of letters, too."

"I never got them."

"I never mailed them."

"Oh."

"You look fantastic."

"So do you. You filled out a lot, didn't you? You were thinner. You didn't used to be so big in the shoulders, did you?"

"I guess not. Hallie—"

"Could we sort of walk this way, Chip? I have this class."

"Oh, sure."

"I suppose I could cut it."

"You don't have to do that."

"Well, I really shouldn't. They keep a record of cuts. It's pretty idiotic but they do."

"I don't want you to get in trouble."

"It wouldn't be trouble, exactly—"

"I mean, it's not as if I have to be on the road in an hour or anything. I mean, I could meet you after class."

"That would be great."

"What is it, an hour?"

"Uh-huh. If you could meet me out in front? By the step over there?"

"In an hour. Sure."

"Great."

You want to know something? I wasn't going to write all this shit. I had it planned differently. The last chapter, Chapter Sixteen, only has twenty-seven words in it. (In case you forgot: *There were some other girls during the rest of the summer. Some I got to and some I struck out with.* Paragraph. *None of them were very important.*)

Well, it wouldn't have been a hell of a lot of trouble to take those twenty-seven words and make twenty-seven pages out of them. Or even more. Because whether what happened for the rest of the summer was important or not, it might have been mildly interesting. One time I double-dated with this farmhand. We took out two sisters and each screwed one of them and then traded girls and screwed them again. I had never done anything like that before, and it would have been interesting enough to make a scene out of. It would have made a damned good scene, as a matter of fact.

So there would have been plenty to write about, and the book would have been long enough to stop with me just getting to Wisconsin, or just getting ready to drive to Wisconsin. That was the way I originally planned to do it.

Hell.

That would have been cheating. Because the way this book ends, the way I'm ending it now, is sort of the point of it. Or part of the point of it.

But it's a fucking pain in the ass to write it. (They may take that line out. I hope not.)

I went someplace and had a hamburger and a cup of coffee. On one side of me some students were talking about the draft lottery, and on the other side some students were talking about Gay Liberation. They already seemed liberated enough to me.

I was back in front of the building ten minutes before the hour was up. Those ten minutes took another hour. Then some clown rang a bell and a few seconds later people started coming out of the building. Eventually one of them was Hallie, and she came over to me and held out her hands again, and I took them again. I asked her how the class was, and she told me, and we wasted a few words on that kind of garbage.

Then I said, "Is there some place we can talk?"

"My room?"

"I don't know. Am I allowed there?"

"I'll allow you."

"I mean—"

"We have twenty-four hour open halls," she said.

"I thought maybe we could go for a ride."

"Oh, you've got a car?"

"Uh-huh."

"Okay."

When we got to it she said, "Wow, a Cadillac! Look who turned out to be rich."

"It's a '54. I mean it's worth maybe fifty dollars."

"It looks great. When did you buy it?"

"I got it in the spring. Somebody gave it to me."

"Oh."

"It runs pretty good, though."

"I didn't know they made them with standard shift."

"I think this may have been the only one."

"Maybe it's an antique or something."

"I suppose if I keep it long enough."

"Yeah."

There was a lot more brilliant conversation like that. I just drove around forever without paying much attention to where we were, and we kept trying to get conversations going, and they kept being like what I quoted. She told

me what courses she was taking and I told her some of the
places I had been, and I kept getting more uptight about
the whole thing, and I guess she did, too.

At one point I said, "Listen, I have this room. You
know, a motel room. I mean we could talk there."

"Oh."

Eventually there was a red light and I stopped for it. I
turned to her and said, "I don't mean to ball or I would
have said it, but I want to open up and rap with you
because we have to, and I don't want to do it sitting under
a tree or in your dormitory or in this fucking car."

"Okay."

"You don't mind?"

"No, of course not. It's weird, isn't it? A whole year,
and we never really knew each other."

"It'll be all right."

It was still a little awkward at first, partly because the
bed took up about eighty percent of the room, and there
was only one chair. No matter how much you say that you
just want to talk, in a situation like that it's hard to
pretend there isn't a bed in the room. I had her sit on the
chair and I sat on the edge of the bed.

It wasn't really rapping at first, but it got there. I told
her some of the things I had done. I especially told her
about Geraldine and the Sheriff, and how I had sort of
become the child the two of them had never had together.

She told me about her brother, who had been in the
service when we met, just on his way overseas at the time.
They sent him to Vietnam and he was on a patrol and
stepped on a landmine.

"It happened in the middle of December. But they
waited until I came home for Christmas vacation before
they told me about it. We were just starting to get close
that summer. Before then, you know, an older brother and
a younger sister, we never had that much to say to each

other. And now I'll never get to talk to him again. Sometimes I think I'm beginning to get used to it, and then I find out that I'm not."

And later she said, "I never knew you were a writer. *No Score.*"

"Huh?"

"*No Score.*"

"You lost me."

"Your book," she said. "*No Score,* by Chip Harrison. I read it about a week ago."

"It's published?"

"You didn't know? It's all over the stands. All over Madison, anyway."

"That's really weird. I even forgot about it. I mean, I kept looking for it and it never turned up, and I guess I thought they decided not to bother. They didn't pay me very much money and I thought they decided to write it off. What was the title?"

"*No Score.* Don't you even remember the title?"

"I had a different title for it. I guess they decided to change it. It's been about a year since I wrote it." Then something occurred to me. "Oh," I said. "I guess you read it, huh?"

She nodded.

"It wasn't very good, huh?"

"I thought it was good." She had a funny look on her face. "I never expected to be in it, though."

"Oh."

"You didn't even change my name. I thought you could get in trouble that way, not changing names."

"I changed everybody else's name."

"What made me so lucky?"

"I just couldn't think of another name for you," I said. "It was just *Hallie Hallie Hallie* in my mind and I couldn't think of you any other way."

"You put down the things we did and everything. The words we said to each other."

"I didn't think anybody would know who it was."

"Oh, of course not. How could they? Hallie from the Hudson Valley who goes to school in Wisconsin. How could anybody possibly figure out it was me?"

"Oh, wow."

"It's okay, Chip."

"Yeah, it's sensational. I never even thought. I didn't think about anybody reading it that I would actually know. Or that was in it."

"It doesn't matter."

"It doesn't?"

"No. Honest." I looked at her, and she was smiling shyly. "I never guessed it was your first time. With me, I mean."

"Oh. Well, it didn't seem like something I wanted to announce."

"When I first read it I was furious."

"I can imagine."

"What really got me was that I couldn't even write to you and tell you how mad I was. I wrote a letter to your publisher just the other day. If they send it to you, you've got to promise not to read it."

"They wouldn't know where to send it."

"I guess they'll send it back to me then. I'll tear it up." Her face opened. "But after I stopped being mad, I guess it made me proud. Do you know what I mean?"

"I hardly remember what I wrote, Hallie."

"Maybe I can refresh your memory," she said. She stood up and took off her sweatshirt.

I said, "Last time you were wearing a bra."

"I got into Women's Lib a little last spring. I decided they were generally full of shit, but they're right about bras. Do you think I need one?"

"No."

She kicked off her sandals, unfastened her dungarees.
"You've still got all your clothes on," she pointed out.

"Hallie, we don't have to. Honestly."

"Don't you want to?"

"Yeah, but I don't think you do."

"Would I do it if I didn't want to?"

I looked into those big eyes. "You might," I said. "You
might just because you thought you should."

"I really want to, Chip."

"Come here."

I kissed her and felt her breasts against my chest. For
some reason or other I felt like crying. I kissed her again
and let her go, and she took her dungarees off and I
started to get out of my clothes.

We made love.

She had her eyes closed. I put my hand on her stomach. She was shiny with sweat.

After a while I said, "Tell me about it."

"Huh?"

"What went wrong?"

"Huh?" Her eyes opened. "Nothing went wrong. I had
an orgasm."

"I know."

"So?"

"So you weren't really there. You were somewhere else
and it wasn't right."

"Oh, wow."

"Or else I'm a little flaky, which is possible."

"No."

"I'm right, then."

"Yeah. Shit."

"What's the matter?"

She turned away. "I didn't think you would be able to

tell. I guess that was pretty stupid, thinking that. I'm sorry, Chip."

"There's nothing to be sorry about."

"Yes there is. The thing is, oh, I don't know—"

I waited.

"The only way is to say it. I have an old man."

For a minute I thought she meant her father. I had spent the past nine months with people who were several years behind on their slang. Then I realized what she meant and I said, "Oh. A guy."

"Uh-huh."

"Well, I figured you would be seeing guys. And the rest of it, as far as that goes."

(This was a lie. Not that I had ever expected that Hallie would be sitting up in Wisconsin saving herself for me. But I just managed never to think about her with anybody else. I don't much like to think about it now, if you want to know.)

"I'm sort of involved with him."

"In a heavy way?"

"Kind of heavy, yeah."

"Oh."

"Like we're living together."

"Oh." Why did I suddenly feel as though I was dying? "For very long?"

"Well, we were sort of together starting in April, but not actually living together. And he was in New York for the summer, he lives out on the island, and we saw each other a few times during the summer, and when we came back to campus we started, uh, living together."

"In your room?"

"No. He has this apartment off campus. I keep some of my clothes and things at my room because there isn't much space at his place. But I sleep there, and cook meals and like that."

"Oh."

"I don't think it's a forever thing or anything, but, oh, I dig him, you know, and it's very much what I'm into right now."

"Sure."

She turned to me. There were tears running out of her eyes but she wasn't really crying, and the tears never got anywhere near her voice.

She said, "I'm really a bitch. I should have told you out in front and we never should have balled. Maybe all I really am is a cunt."

"Don't talk like that."

"I just don't want you to hate me and you've got every right in the world."

"Why should I hate you? I *love* you, why the hell should I hate you?"

"Oh, *shit*," she said, and this time she let go and cried.

EPILOGUE

October 17, 1970

Miss Geraldine Simms
c/o The Lighthouse
Bordentown, South Carolina

DEAR GERALDINE:

Awhile ago I sent you a copy of a book I wrote called *No Score*. I hope you got it, because otherwise this won't make too much sense. Or maybe it will—it seems to me I told you most of what happened in *No Score* at one time or another.

Anyway, along with this letter I'm sending you the carbon copy of another book I wrote. I just finished it. In fact I haven't finished it yet, I'm finishing it right now.

If you read *No Score*, you may remember that there was an Epilogue at the end that told what happened to me after the actual story of the book ended. I decided the other day that this book ought to have an Epilogue also and I couldn't decide exactly how to do it. While I was trying to work it out in my head I also decided I wanted to write you a letter, and I thought about it some more and decided that, in a sense, this whole book was a letter to you. So I'm killing two stones with one bird.

What I hope you'll do now, Geraldine, is read the carbon of the book all the way through and then come back to the letter.

Did you go back and read the carbon copy? Thanks. And if you didn't, I forgive you. I never heard of a letter with an intermission before.

After Hallie said *Oh, shit* and started crying, that was about it. Of course in books it can just end like that (which is why I ended it like that) and in life it can't, because the two people are stuck there in the room and, unless the boiler blows up and kills them all, they still have certain dumb unimportant things they have to say to each other, like while they're putting on their clothes.

Just as an example:

"You know, Chip, you would really like him. I mean it, you ought to meet him sometime."

"No way."

"No way you could like him or no way you could meet him?"

"Right both times."

"Yeah."

That kind of dialogue, Geraldine. It was tons of fun, believe me. I had a wonderful time.

Then I drove her back to her dormitory, and then she insisted that I wait while she got the copy of my book so I could autograph it for her. I wanted to drive away but I also wanted to see her again.

I won't tell you what I wrote in the book. I wrote something, and closed the book, and told her not to read it until later. She nodded.

"Well," I said.

"Chip."

"What?"

"Write to me."

"Should I?"

"And this time put a return address."

"Really? All right, sure."

"Chip? It was the timing, I think. I mean, oh, you know what I mean."

"Sure."

"I mean, people like us, we'll probably run into each other again."

"We probably will."

There was more but that's enough. I went back to the motel and packed because all I wanted to do was drive away from there, though I was afraid to trust myself on the road. But I couldn't sleep, either.

I thought about getting drunk but if you were between eighteen and twenty-one all they would serve you was beer. I was a couple of days short of nineteen but my ID said I was a couple of days short of eighteen. Maybe they would have served me beer anyway. I didn't really care because I didn't think I could get drunk enough on beer, not the way I felt.

Do you remember the glass of corn whiskey you gave me that last night? That's what I really wanted.

I sat around there for a while feeling numb and empty and lost and alone. I had never felt this alone before because there had always been Hallie somewhere in the distance, and now there wasn't. It didn't feel good.

Then I remembered my book. *No Score*. I had hardly looked at the copy I signed for Hallie. I left the motel and went to drugstores and bookstores looking for it. It was really weird seeing it on the stands. My name all over the place, on the spine and the cover and at the top of every even-numbered page. I wanted to buy all the copies they had, but who was I going to give them to? I bought one copy and took it back to my room and read it.

What a strange feeling. Here was this kid talking, and

he was me, except he wasn't, because when I talk to myself it's something that happens inside of my head, and this kid was talking on a page. Well, quite a few pages, actually.

And he sounded so young. It was just impossible to believe that this punk was me. And just a year ago.

Poor Hallie. It must have been really traumatic to read all that, especially when she had no idea it was coming. I guess on all those postcards I never mentioned anything about writing a book, or that somebody was going to publish it.

I guess the book settled me the way liquor might have. I read it all the way through and then I got undressed again and went right to sleep.

I left Madison early the next morning. I drove east and almost stopped in Chicago but changed my mind at the last moment and took the Belt around the city. I burned a lot of oil but kept stopping for more so that I didn't do any damage to the car. It still runs perfectly, by the way.

I drove all the way to Cleveland. I guess I was ready for a big city again. I put the car in a parking garage and took a hotel room and paid a week in advance. I was in no hurry to go anywhere.

It was easy to find things to do. I would go to a movie and when it ended I would go to another one. I bought paperbacks and read them. Sometimes they seemed to be sending me special messages. I would find great personal meaning in very ordinary things. But I recognized this as just a temporary mild madness and let it pass.

That's the thing. You don't outgrow that kind of garbage, but you learn to see it coming. Maybe growing up is largely a matter of being surprised by fewer things.

Everywhere I went I would see copies of my book. I wanted to tell people I wrote it, but who was I going to tell? I sent you a copy (which I really hope you got) and I sent a copy to the Headmaster of Upper Valley, the asshole who threw me out. I told what a fink he was in the book and I wanted him to read about it.

I couldn't think of anyone else.

Then one day I was looking at ads for jobs, and I could find some things that I probably could do, but I didn't want to do any of them. And I said, Wait a minute, I'm a published author.

I think that's the first time it occurred to me to write another book. I spent a day or two trying to work out a novel but every idea I came up with was corny, and then I thought maybe I could do the same thing I did in *No Score* and just continue that story. I didn't know if the material would be as good, though. It seemed to me when I read it that *No Score* was pretty funny, and my memories of the past year weren't.

I guess that brings it all up to date. I bought a typewriter in a pawn shop and got some paper and started writing. At least this time I knew about keeping a carbon.

The book got written faster than I thought it would.

Well, that's about it. Now I'll drive to New York and let Mr. Fultz look at this. I could sell the car and fly there, I suppose, but I don't like the idea of selling the car. Because you gave it to me.

Geraldine, I read through all of this and it feels very funny. All those changes. There are things I wonder about and can't know, like what happened with Lucille, whether she was really pregnant, whether she had an abortion or had the baby, whether she put it up for adoption or decided to keep it. I have this persistent fantasy in which she keeps the baby as a memento of her dead lover. That would probably be the worst thing for everybody, but evidently my ego gets a boost out of it.

One thing that's bad is that I still can't get away from the idea that sooner or later Hallie and I are going to wind up together. I suppose I'm fooling myself but I can't get it out of my head.

I don't know what comes next, but you never do, do you? Just one damned thing after another. Thanks for suffering through this. It's a pretty funny letter, but then the whole thing adds up to a pretty funny book.

I was just looking at *No Score* to see how I ended it, and it went like this:

I hate it when the author steps in at the end of the book and tells you what it was all about. Either you find it out for yourself or it's not worth knowing about. So I'll just say goodbye and thanks for reading this, and I'm sorry it wasn't better than it was.

That makes a good ending for the book. And for the letter, too.

Love,
Chip

Some Afterthoughts

by Hilton Crofield

I don't know why they asked me to write this. Somebody's original brilliant idea was for me to write an introduction to the new edition of *No Score* and *Chip Harrison
Scores Again,* and I said okay. Don't ask me why. Then
somebody else got the bright idea of calling the double
volume *Introducing Chip Harrison,* which meant that I
would be saddled with the job of introducing *Introducing
Chip Harrison,* and I said that, if you really want to know,
I'd rather go into the bathroom and squeeze a pimple. So
they said okay, we'll make it an afterword, and I said okay
again. Don't ask me why. It's not as if I was getting paid
for this.

Chip Harrison needs no introduction, and I don't suppose he needs an afterword, either, so you can stop reading
right now and tear out these pages if you want. (Don't
wreck the binding while you're at it, though. Take your
time and tear them out neatly and carefully. You might
think about scoring the pages lightly with a pen knife first.
Lightly, for God's sake, or you're going to screw up the
whole operation.)

If you're still with me, I just want to tell you that these
are my kind of book. Chip Harrison is a sort of a lecher
on the wry side. More than that, when you finish the book
you want to call him up and talk about it.

Listen, I've got a tip for you. *Don't do it.* Years ago I
wrote a book and said how sometimes I wanted to call the
author in the middle of the night, and this guy named
Ottinger had his name down as author, and so many weird
kids called him up in the middle of the night that the poor
guy lost it. He went up to Maine or Vermont or somewhere

and quit writing and only leaves his house once a year. He always sees his shadow, and it's always six more weeks of winter.

I wouldn't want that to happen to Chip Harrison. I've already read the books that come after this one, *Make Out With Murder* and *The Topless Tulip Caper,* bound together now as *a/k/a Chip Harrison*. And I know that Chip went to work for Leo Haig and takes care of tropical fish when he's not helping Haig solve crimes. (If you haven't read those books, go out and get them right now. Instead of wasting your time reading this crap I have to write.)

Anyway, I like old Chip. I think Phoebe would like him, too. And I hope you liked him, but if you didn't, well, tough. What do you expect me to do about it, anyway?

Oh, yeah. The business about the name. Lawrence Block is listed now as the author of the Chip Harrison books. They had Chip's name as author originally, but now they're supposed to be by this Lawrence Block. Same as my book is supposed to be by old Ottinger.

Well, I don't have to believe that if I don't want to. And neither do you.